FAKE

A Lark Chadwick Mystery

By

John DeDakis

Published in the United States of America by:

Strategic Media Books, Inc.
782 Wofford St., Rock Hill, SC 29730.
www.strategicmediabooks.com

Manufactured in the United States of America.

Print ISBN
ISBN-10: 1-939521-76-9
ISBN-13: 978-1-939521-76-7

E-Book
ISBN10: 1-939521-77-7
ISBN13: 978-1-939521-77-4

Requests for permission should be directed to:
contact@strategicmediabooks.com

or mailed to:

Permissions
Strategic Media Books, Inc.
782 Wofford St.
Rock Hill, SC 29730

Distributed to the trade by:

Cardinal Publishers Group
2402 North Shadeland Ave., Suite A
Indianapolis, IN 46219

For Cindy
(Again)

Advance Praise for FAKE

"*Fake,* by John DeDakis, is a stunner of a mystery, the kind of book that hooks you at the first page, and then won't let go. DeDakis tells this story of betrayal, tragedy, and political posturing with an insider's view of Washington's underbelly that is so vivid and feels so real that he resets the bar for inside-the-Beltway thrillers."

~John Gilstrap, Author of *Total Mayhem* and the Jonathan Grave thrillers series

"In *Fake,* protagonist Lark Chadwick emerges from a past filled with grief and trauma to gain insight, strength, compassion, and a genuine sense of self. Author John DeDakis writes with the sensitivity that will give you the uncanny feeling that you and Lark are on a parallel journey. Enjoy the ride as *Fake* builds to an intense crescendo."

~Adrienne Kraft, Clinical Social Worker (specializing in loss and trauma)

"In *Fake*, John DeDakis' unique take on the seamy side of newsroom politics makes for a chilling ride along that fine, trembling thread that separates us from the truth."

~Lynne Russell, Former CNN Anchor

Author, *Heels of Fortune*

"I really loved this book. This is John DeDakis at his best as he shows how 'fake news' has become the tail that wags the dog -- especially when it comes to sex. My God, what a world we live in! And DeDakis captures it perfectly. *Fake* is a page-turner. Bravo. Well done.

~Christine Talbott, Psychotherapist

CHAPTER 1

First Lady Rose Gannon, frail and pale, reclined on a divan.

We were in the East Sitting Hall of the private, second-floor residence of the White House.

I sat across from her in an easy chair, our interview about to begin.

Rose was dying of pancreatic cancer. And we both knew it.

A middle-aged butler with salt-and-pepper hair placed two tumblers of ice water on the coffee table between us.

"May I offer you something stronger to drink, Lark?" she asked me. She wore a pale pink silk robe with dark pink fuzzy-puffy cuffs. Her feet were curled beneath her and an afghan covered her legs. Her back was to a gigantic fan window with a view of the Treasury Building.

"No. Thank you," I said. "My stomach's been roiling all day."

"Oh, dear. I hope it's nothing serious."

I shrugged. "It comes and goes."

"Shall I have James bring you some mint tea?" She looked up at the butler now standing expectantly off to my right, then continued her stream-of-consciousness. "Now that I'm on all these ghastly meds, I've found that mint tea settles my stomach. But I don't drink it any more. The mint reminds me of toothpaste, and hot mint is even worse."

I giggled. "You're not making a very convincing case for mint tea," I said, adding, "I'm fine now. But thank you."

She smiled at the butler. "Thank you, James. I think this water will be all we need."

"Yes, ma'am." James bowed slightly and left through the doorway behind me.

Rose picked up her glass of ice water from the coffee table between us and, after taking a sip, turned her full attention to me. "Did I ever tell you about my tea experience with the Russian ambassador?"

"Rudolph Petrovsky? No." I sat forward expectantly and hit *record* on my iPhone for another one of our ongoing interviews.

"It was at the White House Correspondents' Dinner," she began.

"The night you collapsed?"

She nodded.

"You really scared all of us."

That was a month and a half ago. Days later, she'd revealed to me, off the record, that she was dying. The news was still a secret, but I'd been able to negotiate an embargo that would allow me, and the wire service I work for, the Associated Press, to break the story when President Will Gannon and his wife gave the go-ahead. In the meantime, our interviews were for the biography I was planning to write about her, even as she was scrambling to assemble her memoir. We were meeting every day.

She slumped back against the divan's pillows, exhausted, but a bright smile creased her face as she remembered the anecdote. "It was at the beginning of the dinner, right after Will and I arrived. Petro was seated next to me at the head table. He leaned over to me and whispered in my ear conspiratorially in his gruff baritone."

Rose lowered her voice two octaves and did her best to mimic the ambassador's broken English. "'Rose, you should have some exquisite Russian tea. Not this weak, mass-produced poison you see here on table.'"

She was just getting warmed up. I laughed. It was like being an audience-of-one for a "Saturday Night Live" cold open.

Rose continued. "Petro waved a hand dismissively at the teabags packed into a small container in front of us on the head table."

As I listened to her story, I studied the first lady. Rose Gannon was only thirty-five years old, but already the fast-moving cancer had aged her. Her face was drawn. Her hair was graying. She looked ten years older. She'd cut back on her schedule and hadn't been seen in public for a few weeks, but telling the tea story energized her and some color rouged her cheeks.

As she talked, she placed her right hand beneath the folds of the dark green afghan on her lap, then brought the hand back into view, pretending to hold something between her thumb and index finger. "Petro reached into the side pocket of his pinstriped tux and produced a small tea bag. 'May I?' he asked."

Rose continued to pantomime her description. "He then put the teabag into my cup and poured hot water into it, all the while raving about how everything Russian – including tea – is so wonderful." She rolled her eyes.

"And how was the tea?" I asked.

Rose made a face. "Honestly, Lark, it was revolting." She threw her head back and laughed in the brash Lauren-Bacall style I'd come to appreciate.

"Did you finish drinking it?" I asked.

She nodded demurely. "I was . . . diplomatic."

We laughed.

"But my God it was horrible." She looked up and her face brightened even more when she looked behind me. "Hello, darling," she called.

I turned around in my chair and saw the President of the United States leaning jauntily against the doorjamb, dark gray suit coat slung over his shoulder and hooked by an index finger. He wore a white shirt with French cuffs, tie askew. At forty-eight, Gannon still had thick, black, wavy hair graying slightly at the temples.

I shot to my feet, still gripping my phone. "Good evening, Mr. President."

"Hi, Lark." He motioned for me to sit down, but I remained standing.

"Will you be able to join us?" I asked.

He started to answer, but then a look of alarm darkened his face.

"Rose!" he shouted, dropped his suit coat, and dashed past me.

I turned just in time to see the first lady clutch her chest and topple to the floor.

03 ◆ 80

John DeDakis

CHAPTER 2

Rose Gannon rolled off the loveseat and into the coffee table, tipping it over, sending our water glasses flying and a vase of spring flowers spilling onto the room's luxurious wall-to-wall carpeting.

The president rushed past me to get to his wife. I dashed into the hallway where a Secret Service agent was standing guard by the elevator.

"Help!" I shouted to him. "Get a doctor. The first lady's just collapsed."

The agent hustled into the room. I followed, but stayed back a discreet distance at the entryway.

Rose lay face down in a heap on the gold and royal blue carpet.

The president tossed the coffee table out of the way, and kicked the water glasses and vase aside.

"Rose!" Ignoring the puddled water, he knelt next to her and turned her onto her back.

Her face was ashen. Her eyes were closed.

The Secret Service agent quickly assessed the situation and spoke urgently into his sleeve. "Dancer is down! Repeat. Dancer is down. Request immediate assistance in the residence. East Sitting Hall."

Apparently, Rose wasn't breathing because the president began administering CPR. He pressed rhythmically on her chest, then paused to give her mouth-to-mouth.

I stood helplessly off to the side watching, but only for an instant. I was jolted into the realization that I'm still an on-deadline White House Correspondent. I squeezed off a quick picture on my iPhone, then I speed-dialed the desk.

Part of me felt like a vulture, but I pushed back against it. *I'll deal with that later. Now I need to do my job.*

"This is Chadwick at the White House," I said when someone answered on the first ring. "I need to dictate a news alert. You ready?"

"Go ahead, Lark."

"First Lady Rose Gannon has collapsed at the White House. President Gannon is administering CPR."

"How do you know this?" the editor challenged.

"I'm watching it happen right in front of me," I snapped, trying unsuccessfully not to sound defensive. "I just took a picture. I'll text it as soon as I hang up."

"Okay. We'll get this out now."

"Thanks. I'll get back to you when I know more."

By this time more agents had swarmed into the room.

I took a couple more quick still photos, then switched my phone to video mode, but I'd only managed to shoot for ten seconds before a hulking Secret Service agent blocked my view.

"Who are you?" he shouted. He grabbed and glared at my press credential dangling at my chest.

"I'm Lark Chadwick. A.P." I put the phone down to my side, but didn't turn off the video.

"You need to clear the area. Come with me," he said, taking me by the elbow and propelling me away from the scene and toward the elevator.

He had a job to do. It was protecting the first family, not helping me gain access to a breaking story, so I didn't resist.

As he pushed me back, I was able to get one more fleeting look at the tableaux in my wake: President Gannon was continuing his urgent efforts to revive his wife. One Secret Service agent knelt next to the president, another stood over them, looking down at the first lady.

Rose Gannon's face was hidden from view, but her left arm was splayed out to the side, her hand palm up on the carpet. Her legs were extended parallel to the couch. Her feet were bare.

I expected that the agent would merely put me on the elevator and escort me either to the press briefing room, or off the White House grounds – anything to get me out of the way. Instead, he ushered me about thirty yards away from the commotion in the sitting room to the middle of the spacious central hallway, the corridor connecting the east and west ends of the second-floor family quarters.

"What happened?" he demanded.

"We were talking. She collapsed just as the president entered the room."

"State your business here."

"I've been interviewing Mrs. Gannon for a book I'm writing. You know me. You've seen me around."

He nodded, all business. "I need to search you," he said. "Do you have any weapons on you?"

"No. But if you're going to search me, I want a female agent to do it – and a witness." I didn't care if this was an emergency, there was no way I was going to let some entitled former frat boy Secret Service agent feel me up.

His jaw muscles tightened, and he frowned. "Very well." He talked once more into his sleeve. "Send Rodriquez to the Central Hallway of the residence. I have a female witness who needs to be searched, but she insists it's conducted by another female."

We were standing next to a baby grand piano about twenty yards from where Rose Gannon lay. Two EMTs got off the elevator and rolled a gurney into the sitting room.

The agent, whose back was turned to the action, saw me looking beyond him at what was going on. He took me by the shoulders and tried to swivel me so that I wouldn't be able to see.

This time I resisted. "Whoa! Wait!" I slipped out of his grasp. "I'm fine with staying out of the way, but I still need to do my job."

Unfortunately for me, his job comes with a badge, a gun, and plenty of backup. He clamped his strong hands back onto my shoulders and bulldozed me backwards farther down the hallway. His face was flushed and a blue vein in his neck bulged.

At least I could still see what was going on – just not as clearly.

I saw the president stand and step aside when the EMTs got to where Rose lay. If he was saying anything, I was too far away to hear.

A moment later, the EMTs lifted Rose onto the gurney. An oxygen mask covered her face. As they rushed the gurney to the elevator, one of the EMTs continued to press rhythmically, urgently, on her chest.

The official announcement wouldn't be for another two hours at George Washington University Hospital, but I already knew: Rose Gannon was dead.

ↄ ✦ ↄ

CHAPTER 3

"You've experienced a lot of loss in your life, haven't you, Lark?"

The question took me off guard, even though the questioner was Kris, my grief counselor.

I'd been seeing Kris every Tuesday morning for the past month at the Wendt Center for Loss and Healing at the corner of Connecticut and Van Ness in Northwest D.C. This was our fifth session. The first visit was prompted by the recent unexpected and sudden death of my boyfriend, Doug Mitchell, six weeks ago.

"I've certainly experienced 'loss,'" I said, squirming uncomfortably in the sofa, "but everyone does." I fluffed a pillow and positioned it as an armrest for my left elbow. I was now ensconced in a womb-like cocoon of sofa cushions.

I'd liked Kris immediately when we met and I felt comfortable talking to her. I'm twenty-eight. She's at least fifty and widowed, so she has the life experience I lack. Plus she's not emotionally invested in me, so I can tell her anything and not feel judged, even though I can be pretty merciless when it comes to judging myself.

"Yes," Kris said, "everyone experiences loss, but let's review." She began using the fingers on one hand – and then two – to tally all the losses in the pathetic life of Lark Chadwick: "You lost both parents when you were still an infant. You discovered the dead body of the aunt who raised you from infancy. One boyfriend – whose body you also discovered – died in a fall off a cliff. Your latest boyfriend just died of a drug overdose. And that doesn't count all the violent deaths you've personally witnessed."

"Well, yeah. When you put it that way, it sort of does sound like a lot of loss, doesn't it?" I smiled, sheepishly. "I really only came here to talk about Doug. I've dealt with all that other stuff."

Kris returned my smile. "Have you?" Her voice was gentle, almost a whisper.

I pursed my lips.

"And now there's Rose Gannon's death," Kris said.

I nodded and took a tissue from a box Kris always has on hand. I dip into it compulsively during our sessions.

This session had begun with me telling her about Rose's collapse the day before. Once the Secret Service agent was satisfied that I didn't have anything to do with what happened to Rose, he let me go. I caught a cab and filed another few paragraphs on the short drive to George Washington Hospital where Rose was rushed. I also sent the desk the pictures and video from my iPhone that I'd shot of President Gannon trying desperately to revive his dying wife. My first bulletins and the dramatic pictures were retweeted at least hundreds of thousands of times and became part of the saturation news coverage that was still going on worldwide.

When Presidential Press Secretary Ron McClain announced Rose's death later that evening, my editor, Scotty Barrington, and I decided to break the embargo about Rose's pancreatic cancer. We felt that the reason for the embargo – honoring Rose's request to postpone revealing her cancer because it would be a distraction to Will Gannon's presidency – was now rendered moot by his wife's death.

I'd worked the story long into the night, filing updates, doing hourly hits for radio, and appearing on a few prime-time cable news programs. Even though I didn't get home until after two in the morning, I eagerly looked forward to these counseling sessions with Kris, so virtually no sleep? No problem!

"What's been the cumulative effect of all these losses on you, Lark?" Kris asked.

I sighed deeply.

She waited patiently.

"I guess," I began tentatively, "that it all boils down to being able to discern the difference between what's fake and what's real."

Kris leaned forward and cupped her chin in her hand. "What do you mean?"

"Look," I said, groping for words, "I'm a reporter. People lie to me every day. Even before I was a reporter people lied to me: my Aunt Annie lied to me about how my parents died. My English professor lied to me – just before he sexually assaulted me."

Kris raised her eyebrows. "You hadn't told me about that," she said.

10

"Another time," I said. I was on a roll. "The lies intensified after I became a reporter. Even Doug's addiction caused him to lie to me. My point is that if we're going to talk about loss, I think the biggest loss I'm grappling with is the loss of trust. I don't trust men. And, even worse, I don't trust myself to be able to discern the difference between what's fake and what's real."

To my surprise, I was speaking with the kind of passion that comes from the excitement of having a powerful moment of clarity.

Kris looked at her watch. "Let's pick up this thread next time."

ଔ ◆ ଞ

CHAPTER 4

It seems as though I'm always emotionally stirred up after my sessions with Kris. I was coming to realize that might be exactly the reason she sometimes ends my sessions abruptly – just as I'm getting some kind of personal insight. I end up ruminating about our session all week.

I was lost in thought during the entire ten-minute Metro trip back to the White House and the A.P. filing center in the newly-renovated Brady Briefing Room. It's named after the late former White House Press Secretary James Brady who was gravely wounded during an assassination attempt on President Reagan in 1981.

My friend and colleague Paul Stone was just hanging up the phone as I entered our glassed-in cubicle. Even though he's two years older than I am, Paul has that fresh-faced, just-out-of-college look about him.

Paul's had a thing for me since we first met, but the sparks just aren't there. I think I broke his heart when I fell for Doug. But since Doug's death, Paul seems to have magnanimously accepted my relegating him to The Friend Zone. We're now more like brother and sister – a big relief to me because I value Paul as a friend and sounding board, even as I appreciate his journalistic chops and professionalism.

"Rough grief counseling session?" he asked.

I nodded. "How can you tell?"

"You're not your perky self."

I gave him a look over my glasses. "I'm never perky." I studied him more closely. He looked uncharacteristically grim. "You're not so perky yourself, mister. What's going on?"

"I just got off the phone with Dad." Paul's father is Lionel Stone, the legendary Pulitzer-Prize winning former White House Correspondent for the *New York Times* and retired *Times* National Editor. Lionel is also my friend, mentor, and the man who hired me for my first reporting gig at the *Pine Bluff Standard* in Wisconsin.

"What's up with your dad?" I asked.

"He wanted to know more about Rose Gannon, of course, but he really called to tell me that he's selling the paper, selling the house, and he and Mom are moving back to D.C."

"Really?" Lionel, and his wife Muriel, had become like parents to me. "That's awesome!"

Paul merely grunted.

"Or not."

He winced. "It's just so . . . sudden."

"But you get along great with your parents."

"I do. But it's easier when it's at a distance."

"Are you worried that he might become a little too overbearing?" I asked. It was the same problem Lionel had with his daughter Holly. It didn't end well. She died in a fall off the Inca Trail in the Andes Mountains of Peru four years ago – the year before I met Lionel and Muriel.

Paul nodded. "Daily face-to-face contact might be a bit . . . delicate."

"Delicate? I'm not sure I'm following you."

"You and I need to talk."

We agreed to get drinks after the president's press office announced a lid at the end of the day. A "lid" means no more news is expected.

Paul and I spent the rest of the day writing follow-ups on the story of Rose Gannon's sudden death. The White House announced that Rose's funeral service would be held Friday at Washington National Cathedral. In the meantime, a pathologist from the CDC was conducting a routine autopsy on Rose – no results, yet, but the assumption was that she died of a heart attack due to complications from her cancer.

About three in the afternoon, the phone at my desk rang.

"A.P. White House. Lark Chadwick."

"Mizz Chadwick?" The voice was female. Young. Earnest.

"Yes."

"This is Jennifer Schneider at I-N-N. How are you today?"

INN is the Independent News Network, an up-and-coming cable outfit that was quickly gaining on Fox News, CNN, and MSNBC. It had just been taken over by Francine Noyce, a hard-charging entrepreneur shaking up the news biz with kick-ass investigative reporting, but without the political slant. No one could accuse Francine Noyce of being a purveyor of "fake news." She was my hero.

"Hi, Jennifer. I'm good. What can I do for you?"

"The answer is what I can do for you."

"Ohhh-kayyy."

"I'm a booker for INN's 'Early Edition.' We'd like to have you on the show tomorrow morning."

"To talk about Rose Gannon?"

"Yes, ma'am. It's a huge story and you broke it. Are you available tomorrow morning at six?"

I winced. "I can be. Do you administer caffeine via an I.V. drip?"

She laughed. "No, ma'am, but we do have fresh coffee in the green room."

Jennifer told me the network would send a car to pick me up the next morning at five. I gave her my address in Silver Spring, Maryland and we hung up.

The White House press office declared a full lid about six – no pictures or news would be forthcoming the rest of the evening.

I caught up with Paul at Shotzie's Pub, a favorite watering hole of reporters and politicos located a block from the White House at 17th and Connecticut. Paul had left our White House workspace early because he came in before I did to cover the morning briefing for me when I had my grief counseling session.

I found Paul sitting at a corner table across from a dark-haired Adonis. They were both sipping beers from frosted mugs.

"There she is," Paul said when he saw me enter and pause as my eyes got used to the darkened room.

Paul and his friend both stood as I approached.

"Lark, this is my friend, Alex." Paul gestured to Alex who was at least six-three and looking fine in a form-fitting black shirt with French cuffs.

Alex reached out his hand and I shook it. His hand felt smooth and warm, just like his smile.

"Hi, Alex."

We sat.

"Paul can't stop talking about you," Alex said, adding, "I know you two are planning to talk, so I'll get out of your way as soon as I finish my beer."

"Speaking of beer . . . ." A pony-tailed server wearing short shorts stood at my right elbow looking down at me and smiling.

"Perfect timing," I said. "I'll have a Stella."

She withdrew as stealthily as she'd arrived.

"So, how do you two know each other," I asked, looking back and forth between them.

"We're—" Alex started, but Paul interrupted.

"We met at a panel discussion at Brookings about a month ago." Paul seemed suddenly uncomfortable and beads of sweat appeared above his upper lip. "Alex manages other people's money. Harvard MBA."

"Wow. What's it like to be smart?" I asked, turning to Alex.

He chuckled. "I'll tell you when – if – I make my first million."

We laughed. Then the conversation, as they always do in Washington, turned to all things political. Today everyone was talking, of course, about Rose Gannon's sudden death.

Not surprisingly, with the girl who broke the story sitting across the table from him, Alex began pumping me with questions. "How big of a distraction do you think this will be on the president?"

"Too soon to tell," I said honestly. "I can only imagine how massive a psychological blow the death of his wife will be on him. But she was a very strong, upbeat person and a lot of her optimism – even in the face of a terminal illness – rubbed off on Will, um, the president."

"So, now you're on a first-name basis with him?" Alex teased.

I felt myself blush. "Actually, I'm not. But Rose called him Will throughout our long series of in-depth interviews these past couple of months. I think I picked it up from her. But, Rose and I really are –" My voice caught. "Were on a first-name basis. She insisted."

I'm normally uncomfortable in the spotlight – even more so at this moment because I was feeling Rose's death more acutely than I'd expected. I quickly turned the focus onto Alex.

"What do you think, Alex? How do you think this will affect Gannon?"

He thought a moment. "Well, the burdens of being President of the United States go on, no matter what happens in his personal life." He nibbled thoughtfully at the tip of his thumb. "The summit in Beijing with China's new president is coming up. Do you think he'll cancel it?" Alex had deftly, and suddenly, shifted the spotlight back to me.

I deflected. "Good question." I turned to Paul. "Mister Stone? Your thoughts?" I balled up my hand and put it front of Paul's face like a fake microphone.

"My sources tell me it's still a go," Paul said, leaning toward the "mic."

The summit was fewer than ten days away. It had been in the works for a couple weeks following a bloodless coup. Tong Ji Hui, China's Defense Minister – and Will Gannon's good friend from their college days together at Vanderbilt – ousted China's bellicose president who was getting increasingly antagonistic toward the United States. The coup had been a geopolitical bombshell that caused China to swerve away from Russia and into a close friendship with the U.S. The purpose of the upcoming summit with President Tong was to capitalize on the sudden easing of tensions between the two long-time adversaries.

"There's no doubt Gannon still has a full plate," Alex said. "He's barely been in office four months. He has sky-high approvals right now, but the other party controls both the House and Senate and they're mounting a frontal assault to overturn Roe v. Wade."

Paul and I nodded thoughtfully.

Alex finished his beer and stood. "Great to meet you at last, Lark Chadwick." He thrust out his hand.

I gripped it firmly. "I didn't even know about you, Alex, but it's good to meet you, too."

Alex turned to Paul, placed his hand gently on his shoulder and gave it a squeeze, then stunned me when he bent down, kissed Paul on the top of the head – and then he was gone.

I looked at Paul, my mouth agape.

His face was flushed. "That's what I wanted to talk with you about." His eyes made furtive, ashamed glances at mine. "Now you know the real me."

I recovered from my surprise. "And I always thought you had a thing for me," I pretend pouted.

He grimaced. "I did. I'm not gay. I'm bi."

I reached across the table and placed my hand on top of his. "Paul, I support you. It's no big deal."

"Trust me, Lark. It will be to my mom and dad." He made a face and chugged the rest of his beer.

 C3 ◆ ℘

CHAPTER 5

The INN limo picked me up promptly at five o'clock Wednesday morning. By 5:45, I was in the green room of the INN bureau on North Capitol.

I'm no stranger to being booked fairly regularly to appear on morning, evening, or even weekend network news programs – usually cable – but the appearances are mildly annoying because I have to step up my dress-for-success wardrobe.

If it were up to me, I'd wear jeans, sneakers, and either a bulky sweater in winter, or an untucked denim work shirt – or even a t-shirt – in the warmer months. Having the White House gig has forced me to conform to convention, but I still do my best to wear things that don't accentuate my too-ample-for-my-taste chest.

Guys have told me so often I've lost count that I remind them of Lynda Carter, the gorgeous woman who can still be seen in television re-runs as Wonder Woman. I suppose most women would kill to be compared to Lynda Carter, but for me it's a burden because I seem to attract attention from creepy men who want to fuck me, or insecure, jealous women who want to mock me and tear me down.

I try to do my best to downplay my looks. My grief counselor Kris and I talk about this a lot.

On this day, I knew better than to wear a white blouse because producers have told me white washes me out and, if I'm sitting next to an African-American, the bright white blouse will make the other person look even darker – harder for the camera to see their features. Instead, I wore a pale blue blouse with a gray and white striped pencil skirt, sensible two-inch pumps, but no tights or stockings. Even in early April, D.C. can sometimes be humid.

But I keep forgetting that television studios are always frigid – it has something to do with keeping all the electronic gear from overheating. I had goose bumps while sipping coffee in the INN green room waiting to be escorted to the set.

The other thing I keep forgetting is how quiet a live television studio is. While those of us at home are being assaulted by full-volume commercials, the set of a morning news show is often tomb-like during commercial breaks when guests are shuttled on and off the set by young, frazzled floor directors wearing headsets.

The set for INN's "Early Edition" is like a living room with white-upholstered easy chairs and a loveseat, which is where I sat. The anchor team was a typical sexist mismatch: a craggy, sixty-plus man teamed with a blonde, sorority-girl babe. During the course of his thirty-year career, he'd probably been paired with perhaps as many as forty female co-anchors whose shelf life in broadcast journalism expired when they reached puberty.

Yes. I'm being harsh. And maybe I'm exaggerating. A little. Maybe.

I knew the segment would be short – four or five minutes – but I didn't know it would be tough. The young woman co-anchor, Cecilia Rudnick, did the interview. She had straight blonde shoulder-length hair, wore a bright red outfit that barely reached mid-thigh, and four-inch heels. But, by the time Rudnick was finished with me, I realized the depth of my own hypocrisy: I'd judged her on her looks, just as I loathe being judged on mine.

"Joining us now is Lark Chadwick," Rudnick began. "Lark is a White House correspondent for the Associated Press. As we all know by now, Lark was with First Lady Rose Gannon when she died Monday evening. Lark is the one who broke the news to the rest of the world." She swiveled away from looking at the camera and turned her attention to me. "Welcome to 'Early Edition,' Lark."

"Thank you, Cecilia."

"Why were you in the private quarters of the first family?"

"I was conducting one of several interviews with Mrs. Gannon for a biography I'm planning to write about her."

"But that's not the only reason you were there, is that correct?"

"That's right. About a month and a half ago Mrs. Gannon revealed to me that she was dying of pancreatic cancer and that she was interested in doing some writing of her own. She told me our interviews also helped her to clarify her thoughts and feelings for her memoir."

"Why did she tell you about her illness?"

"Excellent question. And it's a question I put to the first lady."

Out of the corner of my eye, I could see the floor monitor, a large TV screen on wheels. As I spoke, viewers at home were watching various beauty shots of Rose and Will Gannon smiling and waving in happier days.

I continued. "She told me she was impressed with me when we first met when Will Gannon was running for president. I was working for a newspaper in Georgia and President Gannon – who was Georgia's governor at the time – held a campaign event in Columbia where I was working. I did a relatively hard-hitting interview with him after the event, and she told me she respected my – as she called it – 'spunk.'"

A red tally light came on one of the cameras and my interviewer's face filled the TV screen as she looked at me.

"So, why didn't you report it when Mrs. Gannon revealed her terminal illness to you?"

"She didn't reveal it until I agreed to go off the record with her," I replied.

"You didn't know what she'd tell you before you agreed to that?"

"That's correct."

"Why'd you agree to go off the record?"

"It wasn't an easy decision."

"Why not?"

"I don't like to keep secrets. I don't like to pretend not to know something, when I know the truth. I'm a reporter. My job is to report the news, not hold it back."

"Yet you agreed to do just that."

"I did."

"Why?"

I smiled, but bared my teeth is more accurate. "Why do I feel like this is an inquisition?"

She laughed, an attempt to be disarming. "Probably because you're being asked questions."

"True. I'm much more comfortable asking them."

"Let's get back to where we were," Rudnick said, glancing at her notes. "Even though you don't like to keep secrets, you kept Rose Gannon's secret. Why?"

"We negotiated the terms under which she would reveal her information."

"What were the terms?"

"We agreed on what's known in journalism as an embargo. Basically, it means the news is to be held for release at a later date."

"But Mrs. Gannon didn't know when she'd die, so how did you two handle the release date?"

"Actually, the president was part of the discussion. He and his wife were in agreement – the news would be released at a point when they felt it was time to tell the general public."

"Why'd they want to wait?"

"They felt that as soon as the news got out, it would divert attention away from President Gannon's policy pursuits. He was still within his first one-hundred days in office, so he wanted to keep the focus there for as long as possible."

"Is it a reporter's job to help the president advance his agenda?"

"Absolutely not. It's our job to report it accurately, explain it clearly, analyze it fairly, and report whatever opposition there might be to it."

"But isn't agreeing to embargo news of the first lady's grave illness in a sense playing ball on the president's team?"

I was beginning to feel defensive. And when I feel defensive, I tend to get snippy. And when I get snippy, my anger intensifies. And when my anger intensifies, I'm at risk of blowing my top. And when that happens, it isn't pretty. I was having a heroic inner struggle with myself at this point to keep my anger in check.

"Have I stopped beating my wife?" I asked.

Rudnick sat up even straighter than she already was. "Excuse me?"

"Look. I know your game. You're trying to back me into a corner."

"No, I'm n—"

"Sure you are. It's good for ratings to generate more heat than light."

She sat back. "Okay. Enlighten me." She cupped her chin in her hand, ballpoint inserted between her fingers like a cigarette.

"Here's why I wasn't, as you say, 'playing ball on the president's team.' One of the terms I negotiated with the Gannons is that if I felt I was about to be scooped by another news organization, I would let the Gannons know and try to get them to let me run with the story."

"Interesting."

"What is?"

"A moment ago you accused me of trying to get ratings."

"Yeah. So?"

"But not wanting to get scooped indicates you're just as concerned about ratings," she said.

"No kidding. Journalism is a business."

"Isn't it supposed to be a public service?" she asked, smiling smugly.

"It's both. It's a public service, but it's also competitive."

"Is that why you decided to take what's now become an iconic picture of President Gannon at the most horrifying moment of his life, desperately trying to keep the love of his life alive?"

"It wasn't so much a decision as it was an instinct."

"So, you're saying you didn't think, you just began shooting?"

"That's pretty much it. There was no time to think."

"Are you saying you were being thoughtless?"

"No. It's not the same thing."

"Isn't it? You just said you weren't thinking."

"I think you're trying to twist my words to fit your own agenda."

"And what's my agenda?"

"You tell me."

"I'm trying to get at the truth."

"And I'm trying to explain that at that moment I was reacting to the situation. I was going on instinct."

"But isn't the truth that at that moment you had the instincts of a vulture?"

I actually reached for the microphone clipped to my blouse and was about to rip the mic off, toss it down, and stomp off the set. But something – a mustard seed's worth of wisdom, perhaps? – kept me from blowing up my career.

Instead, I paused, took a deep breath, leaned in and lasered Rudnick with my eyes.

"Did INN use that picture?" I asked.

She blanched. "Beside the point."

"No. It's not. But I'll be honest with you. Vulture is actually what I thought about myself at that moment. Part of me still feels that way. But journalism is about judgments, some of them split-second ones. At its root, journalism is about truth – what's really going on. Sometimes the truth is raw. Sometimes it's ambiguous or elusive."

By the time I got off the set, I was seething.

By the time I got to the A.P. cubicle at the White House, my words were being taken out of context on social media. A post on Media Bash, a popular website devoted to attacking the "lame stream media," had already amassed three thousand "likes" in the thirty minutes it took for me to get to the office.

"I'm a Vulture," Reporter Confesses

Lark Chadwick, the narcissistic White House Correspondent for the Associated Press, admitted today what the rest of us have known all along: that the media is populated by a bunch of vultures.

Chadwick, appearing on INN's "Early Edition," came clean about her motives for taking the picture of President Gannon desperately trying to save the life of his dying wife.

"I'll be honest with you," Chadwick said. "Vulture is actually what I thought about myself at that moment. Part of me still feels that way."

Chadwick also admitted to being in collusion with President Gannon to cover up the fact that First Lady Rose Gannon was dying of pancreatic cancer.

The piece linked to a heavily-edited video version of the interview in which some of the anchor's hostile questions were left in, and most my responses were left out – only the most damning clip was used, with no effort to give it added context.

But I hadn't yet seen all that when I left the interview set. As the floor director was escorting me to the studio exit, my hero, Francine Noyce, stepped into view from where she'd been standing behind the cameras.

Noyce was stunning in a stark white three-button power suit and jet-black hair that rested on her shoulder blades.

The young woman escorting me stopped and, I swear, literally gasped and nearly genuflected.

"G-good morning, Ms. Noyce," my escort stuttered.

Noyce ignored the nervous underling, focused her hazel eyes directly on me, and held out her hand. "I'm Francine Noyce."

"I-I know," I said shaking her hand so vigorously it rattled her gold bracelet. "I'm a big fan and admirer." I felt like a giddy star-struck middle-schooler.

"You handled yourself well out there."

"Thank you. She's tough."

Noyce nodded. "She is. It's a tough job, but she's one of our best. I've been watching your career, Lark. When I saw you were going to be on the show, I wanted to come down to meet you."

"I'm flattered," I said. "Thank you."

"Are you free for brunch tomorrow about ten?" she asked.

"Not usually. The White House briefing is at eleven."

"Can you get someone to cover for you?"

I hesitated. There are six of us who cover the White House for A.P. Paul fills in for me when I have grief counseling, but he'd just done that, so I didn't feel right asking again.

"I have something very important I'd like to discuss with you," Noyce said. "It can't wait."

"Sure," I heard myself say. "I'll try to swap with someone."

"Let me know by noon today," Noyce said. She then turned to leave without waiting for an answer. "Oh," she said, pausing at the studio door. "Bring your passport." Then she was gone.

I looked at my escort.

"Whoa," she said.

Me: "Whoa, indeed."

03 ♦ 80

CHAPTER 6

I'd barely walked out of the INN studio, heading for Union Station two blocks away, when my cell phone bleeped. I pulled it out of my messenger bag and saw *Lionel Stone* on the screen, along with a picture of him scowling at the camera (his version of a smile), his rugged face and lined eyes wreathed in snow white hair and an alabaster beard to match.

"Hey," I said. "It's kind of early out there in Wisconsin. What are you doing up at this hour?"

"Am I speaking to Narcissistic White House Correspondent Lark Chadwick?"

"Excuse me?"

"You probably haven't seen it yet, have you?"

"Seen what?"

So, my friend, mentor, and former boss was the first to inform me of the awful piece about me currently making the rounds on the internet.

After he finished reading it to me, I said, "I'm so angry, Lionel. They totally took me out of context."

"I know."

"You do? How?"

"I saw the interview live."

"It was painful."

"Yeah. But you pushed back. I'm proud of you."

I grunted.

"You don't believe me?"

"Not really. I think, to be honest, she probably has a point. I did feel like a vulture. And still do."

"It comes with the territory."

"How did you handle it back in the day?"

"Well, times and technology were a lot different back then, but you're right: it's all about going on instinct."

"Did you ever make the wrong decision?"

"Nope. Never." His answer was immediate and decisive.

"C'mon, Lionel. We all make mistakes."

"Yeah. Probably. But if I ever did, I've forgotten them and moved on. You should, too."

"Easier said than done."

"True."

"Hey, Paul tells me you and Muriel are planning to move back to D.C."

"Yep."

"That's awesome."

"Paul didn't sound so thrilled."

"Kids these days."

"Any idea why he was so nonplussed?"

"Oh, Lionel. Don't triangulate."

"Whuh?"

"Don't sound so clueless. You're one of the smartest, savviest people I know. Don't try to use me to find out what's going on with your own son. I won't play."

"Really?"

"Really. But nice try."

"Shit."

"I have some news and could use your take," I said, changing the subject.

"What's up?"

"Francine Noyce."

"Smart lady. What about her?"

"She came down to the set and introduced herself to me after the interview. Had nice things to say about me."

"That's not hard to believe. I've always been impressed with you, but I'm hopelessly biased."

"She invited me to brunch tomorrow."

"Cool. She's a mover and shaker. Really shaking up the news biz – and in a good way. I never thought I'd say this, but I think it's long overdue for a woman to be in her position in television news. Kay Graham broke the mold at the *Post*. But Noyce is just what the business needs."

"Why do you think so?"

"Twenty years ago, I was her editor at the *Times*. She's tough. She's no bullshit. Good journalistic instincts. Fierce independence. She's not gonna be in any guy's shadow. Think of her as a younger female version of, well, me."

"Um, Lionel, didn't you used to be the world's biggest chauvinist?"

"That was then, this is now."

"What changed?"

He laughed. "I met you."

"Very funny. Is Muriel there?"

"Yeah. She's firing up the coffee pot. Just a minute, I'll get her." His voice pulled away from the phone and I heard him call, "Hey, Muriel. It's Lark. She wants to say hi."

There was a moment's delay followed by a rustle and clunk, then Muriel's soothing Wisconsin accent came on the line.

"Hello, dear."

"Hi, Muriel. I hear you guys are moving back to D.C."

"Yes."

"When?"

"Things are moving very fast, Lark. We already have an offer on the newspaper – and the house – so we could be there in, well, no time." I loved the way she drew out and flattened the O sound in "no."

"Are you excited?" I asked.

"I always loved Washington, so yes. But it won't be the same without . . . ." Her voice caught, then she regained her composure quickly, ". . . without Holly, but with both you and Paul there, it'll be like having both our children together again."

Muriel's sudden emotion threw me for a moment. I hadn't expected it and had to steady myself emotionally. I'd never met Holly, but my path crossed with Lionel and Muriel Stone when they were in the midst of their own grief over losing their daughter. Since then, we'd been through so much that they both felt like the parents I never knew.

By this time, the subway train was swooshing along the platform of the Union Station Metro stop.

"Muriel, my train's here and I'm going to lose my signal in minute, so I need to hang up. Give Lionel my love. I'm really pumped you're coming to live in D.C."

As she said goodbye and hung up, it sounded as though she was stifling a sob, but it could also be that I mistook the swish of the doors opening for her snuffles.

I had to stand in the stuffed subway car during the ten-minute rush-hour ride to Metro Center, but I was so lost in thought that I missed my stop and got out, instead, at Farragut North.

No one talks on the subway during the morning rush, so it was easy for me to concentrate on what Lionel had said about Francine Noyce.

I'd long been watching Noyce's career from afar. After leaving the *Times*, she made her millions as an exec at various Silicon Valley tech companies, yet seemed unsullied by the chauvinistic frat-boy culture. Stylish and beautiful, she'd never married, but dated a lot. Usually the men by her side were easily twenty years older than her forty-five years.

Long before I became a journalist, I studied her life for clues on how to live my own. *The Atlantic* did a profile of her that really impressed me. There were two take-aways for me from the article: 1. She believed strongly in mentoring, especially helping young women advance in a man's world, and, 2. She seemed to have been able to strike just the right balance between career and romance. "I'm not anti-male," she said, "I just haven't found the right one for me. But," she added, "I'm not looking for Mr. Right."

I made a mental note to put this on the agenda for my next grief counseling session with Kris. I found myself looking forward with great intrigue and anticipation to spending some quality time with Francine Noyce the next day.

When I got to street level, I saw a text waiting for me from Scotty Barrington. He's my boss, the D.C. Bureau Chief at the Associated Press.

Lark, please stop by the bureau on your way to the White House. We need to talk, Scotty wrote.

Shit. This can't be good, I said to myself.

The bureau is at 13th and L. It was a nice day, I wasn't in a hurry, plus right after my interview at INN I'd changed from pumps to sneakers so I wouldn't have to suffer while walking to and from the Metro. The pumps were tucked in my messenger bag with my laptop.

The ten-minute walk to the bureau gave me time to give myself a stern lecture. It went something like this:

Okay, Lark. Scotty's probably pissed. He's seen the "vulture" piece and is going to drill you a new asshole. He might even fire you. Nah. Probably not. But maybe. Or maybe he'll just piss and moan. Whatever. Under NO circumstances should you stoop to his level. Do NOT pout. Do NOT cry. Do NOT be petulant.

By the time I arrived at the bureau, I was ready to hand in my resignation.

Scotty didn't keep me waiting. He saw me immediately.

"Have a seat, Chadwick," he said, rising from behind his massive, cluttered desk.

I was about to sit in one of the two chairs in front of his desk, but he came around the side, picked up a sheet of paper and waved it toward a more informal seating area in the corner.

"Let's sit over there," he said.

I sat at the end of a leather couch. He took the chair to my right. We were on the same level with no Power Object between us. I relaxed a little, but was still wary.

"To what do I owe the honor?" I asked, trying mightily to make my tone sound jauntier than I felt. I had a good rapport with Scotty. He'd hired me nearly a year earlier and had been my champion when others at the bureau wished me ill.

Scotty smiled ruefully. "The honor is all mine," he said.

"That's encouraging."

"Actually," he said. "I think I owe you an apology."

"Ah . . . how come?"

"I saw your INN interview this morning."

I made a face.

"You did fine. Well, mostly fine. You got a little defensive."

"I know and I'm sorr--"

He waved a hand. "No need to apologize. I get it. You're used to asking the questions."

"That's for sure."

"Your vulture comment got me thinking."

"Uh oh."

"No. Really. Journalism has been under attack ever since the Trump presidency. And with some justification."

"It even goes farther back than Trump," I said.

"Absolutely. I'm sure Lionel Stone could tell you stories of what it was like to cover Nixon during Watergate and Vietnam."

"Oh, he has. He was actually on Nixon's 'Enemies List.'"

"But your vulture comment got me thinking that we need to do more to explain our craft to the general public."

"I agree. I think that's a good idea."

"I don't want you twisting slowly in the wind on this vulture thing," he said.

"Ah. A Watergate reference. Nicely done."

He laughed. "I thought you'd appreciate that."

The reference was a comment President Nixon's domestic policy advisor, John Erhlichman, made about L. Patrick Gray, the president's FBI nominee. Gray had suggested during his nomination hearing that the White House was covering up Watergate. Erhlichman's famous quote in response to Gray's comment was to let Gray "twist slowly, slowly in the wind" – a grim reference to a public hanging.

Gray's nomination was eventually withdrawn, but the damage had already been done. Mark Felt, the number two at the FBI, was pissed that he wasn't nominated by Nixon to head the FBI. Felt is better known as Deep Throat, the guy whose leaks to Bob Woodward of the *Washington Post* eventually helped to topple Nixon.

Lionel had headed the Watergate investigation for the *New York Times* and had written a best-selling book about it. But privately, Lionel told me, "Every morning I'd wake up with a pit in my stomach, worrying about how Woodward and Bernstein would kick our ass yet again."

"So, what do you plan to do to keep me from twisting in the wind?" I asked Scotty.

He handed me the sheet of paper he'd been holding. "This press release is going out as we speak."

FOR IMMEDIATE RELEASE:

Scotty Barrington, Washington Bureau Chief for the Associated Press, said today that he takes full responsibility for the A.P.'s decision to publish the controversial picture of President Gannon's desperate attempt to revive his wife Monday evening.

First Lady Rose Gannon was pronounced dead at George Washington University Hospital moments after the picture was taken.

The photo was snapped on a cell phone by A.P. White House Correspondent Lark Chadwick who was interviewing Ms. Gannon when the first lady collapsed.

"Lark went with her gut and did the right thing," Barrington said. "But it was my decision – and my decision alone – to publish the photo."

Barrington said, "At its most basic, journalism is show and tell. We at the Associated Press write what is essentially the first draft of history. History is made up of unexpected dramatic events that change the course of human lives as well as nations. One of those events is the sudden death of a president's wife. Reasonable people can and will disagree about what constitutes 'tasteful' versus 'intrusive' coverage, but I stand by Lark's split-second decision to chronicle the event, and my decision to publish it," Barrington said.

When I handed the press release back to Scotty, there were tears in my eyes.

CB ◆ ℬ

CHAPTER 7

It was still early – barely eight a.m. – when I left Scotty's office in the bureau. Paul and I had already been in touch by text and he said he'd be at the morning gaggle in press secretary Ron McClain's office, so I had time to dawdle on my way to the White House.

I stopped at a Starbucks and got coffee and a blueberry scone. As I was disguising my coffee with skim milk and Splenda, a woman brushed against me.

"Were they out of vulture today?" she snapped, looking disdainfully at my scone.

I looked up at her, surprised, but all I saw was her back as she shot for the door. She had mousy brown-gray hair braided into a ponytail that hit at the center of her back. By the time I got outside, she was gone.

I nibbled on the scone as I strolled to the White House, my annoyance slowly intensifying about the blow-back from my INN appearance and subsequent public shaming by the Media Bash website. Scotty Barrington's unexpected, but much appreciated, kindness was the only thing helping me to hold my emotions in check. He had my back, and that meant everything.

The half-mile walk to the White House took me through Franklin Square, so I sat on a bench there and finished my scone and sipped coffee. A few pigeons gathered at my feet, competing for the crumbs I accidentally-on-purpose dropped.

One of D.C.'s ubiquitous homeless people shuffled up to me. He had scraggly gray hair, baggy clothing too hot for the weather, and a blank expression on his face.

"Can you spare some change, ma'am?" His voice was so soft I could barely hear it.

I fumbled for my wallet in my messenger bag as the old man waited patiently, his hand still out.

I found what I was looking for.

"Do you know where McDonald's is?" I asked.

"Oh, yes." He gestured over my shoulder. "There's one that way. 'Bout a block."

I handed him what looked like a credit card. "There's five dollars on here that's good at any McDonald's."

His eyes brightened. "Thank you, ma'am. God bless you."

"And you, too." I smiled.

Street people always make me uncomfortable. All too often, I avert my eyes and either pretend I don't see them, or mumble an apology which I also know is a lie because I have plenty of money on me.

I justified my hard-heartedness any number of ways: they'll just use cash to buy drugs, or alcohol; if I give something to him, I've got to give to everyone else and pretty soon I really will be broke; or they're just scamming me – the guy probably hauls in more in a day than I do and has a comfy place in the 'burbs.

But a couple months after moving to D.C., I was liking myself less and less after ignoring or turning down yet another beggar. So, I decided to stock up regularly on McDonald's gift cards. Every week I stop at the McD's in Union Station and spend twenty bucks on four $5.00 cards. I still feel guilty, but I've now assuaged my guilt at least a little by providing something tangible that meets a real hunger need, but isn't cash that might merely enable an addiction.

After finishing my scone, I resumed my leisurely trek to the White House, grateful for the extra time. As I walked, I realized that one of the reasons for my slowpoke pace was that I was still recovering from losing Doug exactly forty-three days earlier (but who's counting?). The person ultimately responsible for his death died in a shootout right in front of me – a shooting I captured on video and broadcast to the world, once again earning me unwanted attention and even a little fame.

My slower pace these days was a realization that grief is exhausting, plus taking time to stop and smell the flowers is a wise thing to do, especially when so much of my day as a journalist is a mad-dash scramble. I was learning to recognize the difference between what's important, and what's not.

I realized that for the first time since the traumatic events surrounding Doug's death, I was beginning to experience, well, peace.

Speaking of smell, I passed a hotdog vendor setting up his sidewalk stand at the curb near Fifteenth and I Streets.

Who eats hotdogs for breakfast, especially hotdogs that smell like kielbasa rotting in a landfill? I nearly hurled my scone.

At Fifteenth and Pennsylvania, traffic evaporates – the final leg of my walk to work was on the pedestrian mall along Pennsylvania Avenue that's been closed to traffic ever since the threat of terrorism became a daily worry.

To my left, I passed the Treasury Department, an imposing statue of Alexander Hamilton standing in front of it, the Riggs Bank across the street.

A bit farther west, Lafayette Square on my right looked inviting, the tall trees beginning to bud.

On the left, the White House came into view. Every day I pinched myself that I was able to gain easy access to the Holy of Holies of American politics. An imposing black-barred fence separated the president's residence and office from everyone else, yet the alabaster executive mansion had stood there for more than two hundred years.

I stopped for a moment and looked at the oceans of flowers and candles strewn along the sidewalk, a make-shift shrine. Tears suddenly came to my eyes as I remembered my talks with Rose Gannon. She was such a lively person, bursting with enthusiasm and curiosity. In journalism, even though there's a natural and necessary arm's-length emotional distance between reporter and reportee, I'd found myself getting closer and closer to Rose as she opened up so generously about her life. We both knew she was dying, but I never expected she'd be snatched away so suddenly, with no opportunity to say goodbye.

My thoughts turned to President Gannon. He, too, had become not a friend, exactly, but someone familiar, accessible, and human. On several occasions, he had sat in on my conversations with Rose in the upper rooms of the White House where the first family lives. I've never been married, but I, too, have suddenly lost men I'd been close to. I could only begin to imagine how bereft Will Gannon must feel. Back when I was negotiating with Rose about the terms of our news embargo, I'd also gotten the president to agree to an on-the-record conversation after Rose died about lessons he was learning from grief. I made a mental note to look for a time when I could reach out to him through his press office.

Tourists clustered at various points along the White House fence taking selfies or group pictures with the White House as an imposing backdrop. The mood seemed somber. Uniformed members of the Secret Service strolled among the tourists, keeping an eye out for anything suspicious.

I showed my press pass at the Northwest gate and was buzzed into the guard shack. I put my messenger bag on a conveyor belt that went through a metal detector and flashed my credential into a scanner on the left, then walked through a metal detector and picked up my bag on the other side.

I then strolled up the driveway toward the low-slung West Wing where the briefing room is located and, behind it, the A.P. cubicle. On my right was "Pebble Beach" where the various television networks have their cameras pre-set for reporter live shots with the North portico of the White House in the background.

As I walked along the sidewalk that approached the double doors to the briefing room, I remembered the first day I'd been here – Valentine's Day, nearly two months ago. Doug was taking a barrage of pictures of me, chronicling my first day on the job. I remember I'd been annoyed at him for giving me the silent treatment all weekend. But my heart mellowed barely an hour later when we were caught up in a breaking story. Now all I had of him to remember the day were some of the pictures he'd taken of me.

I entered the briefing room through the side doors and made a left toward the A.P. cubicle. The briefing room is always a swirl of activity. It's above what used to be a swimming pool, built in the 1930s for President Roosevelt who found relief there for his polio-crippled legs.

There's only enough seating room for forty-eight people. A few reporters sat on blue leather upholstered seats reading newspapers or their tablets, while other reporters stood in small groups of two or three talking quietly.

On my way to the A.P. workspace I passed the back of the room where a row of television cameras lined the back wall and a cluster of mostly male photographers sat shooting the breeze. Many of them had been Doug's friends and several said hello to me as I went by.

Paul was eating a bagel and scowling at his laptop when I entered our cozy workspace.

"Have you seen—?"

I cut him off. "Yes. I've seen. Thank you very much."

"It's only been up for a couple hours and it's already gotten nearly a hundred thousand hits."

"Did you see the press release Scotty put out?" I asked.

"I did. But it doesn't seem to make a difference to Media Bash. They're ignoring it."

I scowled. "Life goes on."

Paul grunted.

I set down my messenger bag and fired up my computer. "Anything special at the gaggle?"

The gaggle is a small, informal gathering of reporters in Ron McClain's office at seven to get an early jump on the day.

"He says he'll be making a major announcement at the eleven o'clock briefing."

"About what?"

"Dunno. We tried everything to get him to tip his hand, but no dice."

"Thanks for going."

"Sure. No problem."

"I'll do the front-row this morning, but can you take it tomorrow? I've got an, um, a meeting." I wasn't sure I should say too much about my brunch with Francine Noyce because I didn't want to prompt speculation, gossip, or questions I can't answer.

"Okay," Paul said.

"Thank you. I definitely owe you."

"I'll probably be collecting when Mom and Dad move here. I'll need you to run interference."

"I got a preview this morning."

"Oh?"

"Yeah. Your dad senses you're not thrilled that they're moving here. He tried to pump me for information."

Paul looked up, worried. "What'd you tell him?"

"I told him you're a one-man gay pride parade."

"What?!"

"Nothing." I pantomimed zipping my lips. "I told him nothing. Come on, dude."

"Fuck you very much," he sighed.

I spent the next few hours reading in, getting caught up on all the overnight news.

By the time the press office announced the two-minute warning for Ron McClain's briefing, I saw that the vulture story on the Media Bash site was up to a million views – a rate of about fifty a second.

I got to my front-row center seat right in front of the lectern at 10:55 – the same seat the legendary Helen Thomas occupied for most of her fifty-plus years as a White House correspondent for UPI. Reporters for ABC and CBS sat to my immediate right and left but, by tradition, the first set of questions would go to me because the wire service I work for reaches literally half the world, and most major news organizations are subscribers.

A little after eleven, Ron McClain entered the briefing room via a pocket doorway behind and to the left of the podium where his office – and the Oval Office – is located.

He was followed by a few senior administration staffers who sat along the side wall. Ron wore a dark suit, button-down blue Oxford shirt and red tie – which seems to be government-issue because the ensemble is virtually everywhere in Washington.

"Hi, Lark," Ron smiled at me. "I see you're famous again."

"Yeah. But not in a good way," I frowned.

"Welcome to the club," he laughed.

Press secretaries are never ultra-popular, but Ron is one of the best of the best. It helped that the president he served was in the middle of the traditional honeymoon period, a honeymoon that was probably about to be extended as the country sympathized with the fact that he was now suddenly a widower.

One late-night comic was already taking flak for a tasteless joke meant to capitalize on Will Gannon's Justin Trudeau good looks: "Does this mean Gannon's dating again?"

The audience groaned.

"Too soon?" the guy asked.

"Yes," the audience answered in chorus.

Ratings for the show were already plummeting. Which probably helped explain the popularity of the piece taking me to task for not respecting the president's privacy.

Ron waited a few minutes for stragglers to take their assigned seats before beginning.

"A couple of housekeeping issues. First," he said fiddling with the pages of his briefing book splayed out in front of him on the podium. "There will not be a briefing on Friday because of the first lady's funeral at National Cathedral. The travel pool will assemble here at ten-fifteen."

He nodded his head toward the side doors to the Rose Garden behind and to my left.

"After the funeral, the president will leave immediately for Camp David where he'll spend the weekend."

McClain shuffled the papers on the lectern, then looked up at the TV cameras in the back of the room.

"President Gannon will be traveling to Beijing, China next Wednesday, April 10th for a summit meeting with China's new president Tong Ji Hui."

It was obvious that Ron was reading from a prepared press release because he was making eye contact with the cameras, not us, and looking down frequently to read from the prepared text.

"As you know," McClain continued, "President Gannon and President Tong are long-time friends, a friendship that began when they were students at Vanderbilt University, and was renewed when President Tong came to power two months ago. In his formal invitation to President Gannon, President Tong said he hopes the two leaders can strengthen and stabilize the relationship between their two countries."

When McClain had finished reading his statement, I raised my hand.

"Lark?"

"Has the President shown reluctance to hold this summit, given the sudden death of the first lady? Did President Tong offer to delay it?"

"It's been in the works for some time," McClain replied. "The actual invitation was extended before Monday's unfortunate event. But the president told me he doesn't want to wallow and is eager to stay busy."

"Is 'wallow' the word he used?" I asked.

"Yes. That's a quote."

"How is the president?" I asked.

"He's sad."

"Can you be more specific?"

"I'd rather not."

Other reporters asked about what issues would be discussed at the summit. Still others had nutsy-boltsy questions about Friday's funeral. The briefing, which is often a rambling, confrontational, free-for-all, petered out after only about half an hour.

As I made my way back to the A.P. cubicle to write up and file the news from Ron McClain's briefing, I found myself wondering even more about what effect Rose's death was having on Will Gannon, the man. And what effect that would have on the nation and the rest of the world.

⚜

CHAPTER 8

After filing the "China Summit" story, I wandered through the briefing room and into the lower press office through the sliding pocket door to the side rear of the podium. A uniformed Secret Service agent sitting at a desk smiled and nodded me past when he saw my press pass.

Ron McClain's office is down a narrow hallway on the north side of the West Wing. He has an open-door policy for members of the accredited press corps and I was glad to see the door open and Ron alone behind his massive semi-circular desk. He was on the phone, but when he saw me in the doorway, he waved me in.

I sat in the chair in front of the desk as he finished up the phone call and turned his attention to me.

"What's up?" he asked.

"As you know, I was meeting regularly with Rose Gannon before she died."

He scowled. "I'm aware. Now."

"As you may also know, the conversations were at Rose's initiative with the knowledge and approval of the president."

"But not the knowledge and approval of this press office."

"Whose knowledge and approval I didn't need. First Family trumps press secretary."

"Touché. Your point?"

"As you may not know, at the beginning of my talks with Mrs. Gannon, the president agreed that he would do a one-on-one sit-down interview with me after Rose died to talk about the grief process."

"You're right. I didn't know. So now, lemme guess, you want to get him to cash in on that promise, right?" He didn't wait for me to respond. "Lark, he's kind of b—"

"I know. He's kind of busy right now. I'm not asking him to do the interview right away."

"Then what are you asking?"

"I'm merely asking you to remind the president of our agreement and let him know I'm ready to sit and talk whenever he's ready. No hurry. No pressure."

McClain's face relaxed. "Sure. I'll let him know."

"That's all I ask. Thank you, Ron." I stood and headed for the door.

"Hey, Lark," he called.

I turned and looked at him.

He was smiling. "Be careful out there."

"I will. Thanks."

When I got back to the A.P. cubicle, the Media Bash vulture story on me was closing in on two million hits – about a hundred a second.

I made the mistake of reading some of the comments. One person suggested that I should be pecked to death.

∝ ♦ ∝

CHAPTER 9

I covered for Paul at the seven-a.m. gaggle in Ron McClain's office on Thursday, then headed to Francine Noyce's office at INN for "brunch." As soon as I arrived in her office at ten, she led me back to the street where a limo was waiting for us on North Capitol. The limo whisked us across the Potomac to a private jet waiting for us at Reagan National Airport.

"Where are we going?" I asked as Francine climbed the stairway to the jet.

At the top of the stairs she turned and looked down on me, smiling enigmatically, and looking elegant in a gray-blue wool suit with dark blue velvet trim. "Brunch," she said, then turned, ducked her head, and entered the jet.

I decided to keep my mouth shut, not ask any more questions about our destination, and roll with it. I'm used to flying steerage, so Francine Noyce's jet was, shall we say, a new experience for me. The spacious interior was all white, with various groupings of chairs and tables.

She sat in a chair facing me and crossed her legs, showing off her knee-high black suede boots.

As soon as we buckled in, we were cleared for takeoff, hurtled north down a runway that paralleled the Potomac River, and were airborne by 10:30. The sun was still relatively low in the sky out my right window as I marveled at the Capitol dome, Washington Monument, and Lincoln Memorial all laid out in a straight line along the green National Mall. The White House was almost an afterthought, nearly hidden in a grove of trees north of the Mall.

When we were above the clouds, a flight attendant delivered two flutes containing a yellow liquid.

"Your mimosas, Ms. Noyce," he said.

"Thank you, Cedric," she said and he withdrew. "To your health." She held her glass out to mine. "And to a productive brunch."

"Cheers," I clicked the rim of my flute against hers.

The mimosa was strong – more like champagne with a splash of vitamin C.

"Dear me," Noyce said. "I forgot to ask. You do drink, don't you, Lark?"

"Yes, but not usually this early in the morning." I wished I'd had something more substantive for breakfast to soak up the alcohol. I wanted to stay clear-headed and sharp.

"You'll get used to it." She took another sip.

I sipped, too. And waited for her to reveal her agenda.

"Tell me a little bit about yourself, Lark."

"First, a question to you: why am I here?"

"Ah. Just like a journalist to turn the tables and get right to the point. I like that."

She didn't say more. Neither did I.

Finally, she spoke: "I want to get to know the real Lark Chadwick better. I already know the public one: orphaned as an infant, mentored by none other than the legendary Lionel Stone, solver of crimes in dramatic and public ways, strong, fearless. You're a modern-day Wonder Woman in a pencil skirt."

I cringed inwardly at the all-too-familiar comparison.

"But who are you really?"

I shifted in my seat uncomfortably and took another sip of my mimosa to stall for time. "I'm probably not nearly as strong or fearless as I might appear on the outside, but thank you for the compliment. In many ways, I'm still trying to figure out what I should be doing with my life."

"You mean you don't know?"

"I only seem to have enough light for the next step."

"What do you see when you look back at the path you've taken?"

"That's a very good question. It would seem that the path has been a straight one once Lionel got me into journalism."

"You mean it wasn't straight before then?"

"Not really. I suppose for some people it is, but I think there are a lot of people like me who feel a little wobbly about their future while they're in college."

Francine looked out the window, a distant look on her face. "Yes. I suppose that's true."

"Were you a little wobbly when you were in school?" I asked.

She waved away my question as if it were a pesky fly. "Not really. But back to you. I'm intrigued by your use of the word 'wobbly.' What caused you to feel that way and – more important – were you able to obtain stability? And if so, how?"

In the few seconds I had to weigh how I would answer, I took quick stock of what might be the best path. I still didn't know why I was here or how much personal stuff I should reveal.

The truth is I didn't have good role models growing up. After my parents died, my nut-case libertine Aunt Annie raised me. I grew up fast because I had to be her mother. Then, being sexually assaulted by my English professor was so traumatic that I'd dropped out of college just before graduation. I was still reeling from that when I came home from my waitressing job to find Annie dead on the floor, the victim of carbon monoxide poisoning.

That's the truth behind the wobbliness.

This is what I decided to tell Francine Noyce:

"If you know my bio, then you know the aunt who raised me died about three years ago."

"Yes." She nodded. "Tragic."

"It was when I was investigating her death that I met Lionel and his wife Muriel. I credit them with helping bring about whatever stability I have. They're like the parents I never had."

"Does he guide your career?"

"As much as I let him," I smiled. "But he speaks highly of you."

She smiled. "He was a great boss. I learned a lot from him. Too bad he's married."

I chuckled knowingly. Lionel told me he'd sowed many a wild oat before he met Muriel while he was on tour promoting a book he wrote about the Vietnam War that won a Pulitzer. When they met, he was fifty; Muriel was twenty-two.

Noyce went on. "But enough about Lionel. This is about you."

"But why is it about me?"

"There you go again, Lark Chadwick," she smiled. "Always turning the tables. In due time. I'll tell you what this is about in due time."

"Can you give me a hint?"

"No. But thanks for asking."

"Well, let me at least say that I've admired you from afar. And I'm definitely grateful for the opportunity to spend some time with you. But I do hope I, too, will get a chance to ask you all the questions I have."

She smiled. "You're very kind. The question I'm asked most is enough to make me want to puke." She made a face and, in a mocking tone, mimicked the vapid voice of an imaginary questioner: "'How are you able to balance work and romance?'"

I smiled, relieved that wasn't my question. I wanted to ask her how she was able find success in a man's world. "Why is that question so sickening?" I asked.

"Successful men never get asked how they balance work with romance. Plus, the question presumes there can even be a balance. Probably the secret to my success is that business is pleasure. I'm literally in love with what I do – and, by extension, I'm in love with the people I interact with. There need not be an artificial dichotomy between work and romance."

"Interesting."

"But do you agree?"

"Not sure. I'll have to think about it."

I looked out the window. As near as I could tell, we were flying north, but beyond that, I was still in the dark. About two hours after we took off from D.C., the plane banked and began approaching the airport of a large city on a river.

"Do recognize where we are?" Noyce asked.

I shook my head, smiled, and continued to look out the window in wonder.

"That's the St. Lawrence River," Noyce said, pointing.

"Are we in Canada?"

She nodded.

"Montreal?" I asked.

She beamed. "Very good. Have you ever been?"

"No. First time." If she only knew, I thought to myself. I've hardly been anywhere.

Noyce became my tour guide in the sky, pointing out various landmarks.

"That's the Olympic Stadium for the 1976 summer games."

"It looks like a big O," I said.

"Interesting you should say that," she laughed.

"Why?"

"The locals call it 'The Big O,' but they spell it o-w-e – the Big Owe because of its exorbitant cost."

"How much did it cost to build?"

"More than a billion bucks. Billion with a B."

I whistled.

"It took thirty years and a tobacco tax to pay it off."

"Wow."

"And there's Mount Royal," she said, pointing out the window at a hill immediately west of downtown. "Mount Royal is where Montreal gets its name."

"Interesting."

"It was probably a volcano 125-million years ago. Now it's a cool park, designed in 1876 by Frederick Law Olmsted, the same guy who designed New York City's Central Park, D.C.'s National Zoo, and the landscaping around the U.S. Capitol."

Once we were on the ground, we breezed through customs and immigration in less than ten minutes, then a waiting limo whisked us to a restaurant where the view of the river was spectacular. The day was sunny, breezy, and cool – barely forty degrees – so we sat inside by a huge window.

Francine ordered a Bloody Mary. I had an Arnold Palmer. Her meal was a salad and a fish dish. I had a Caesar salad and chicken noodle soup.

"Come here often?" I teased.

"Fairly." She wasn't kidding. "Okay, Lark. Let's get down to business. I like you as a person. And I've always been impressed with you as a reporter. Your reputation preceded you to Washington. I was already aware of you when I still lived in California. So, I jumped at the chance to meet you when I learned you'd be on our air."

"Thank you."

"I'll get right to the point: I want you to be INN's White House Correspondent. It's a three-year contract, starting at 750-thousand dollars, and escalating 250-thousand every year. I'll do the math for you. If all goes well, after three years, you'll be hauling in one-million, 250-thousand dollars. I'm willing to bet that's a helluva lot more than what they pay you at the Associated Press."

I nearly choked. "That's a very good bet. And a very generous offer. I'm flattered. Thank you."

"Do you accept?"

"Do you have it in writing?"

She opened her Gucci tote bag and handed me a sealed business envelope with the INN logo in the upper left-hand corner. "Here. Look it over while we're on the plane."

"Okay."

"But I'll need your response by the time we land. This is a one-day only offer."

I was so stunned, I didn't know what to say, so I gulped and kept my mouth shut until I'd had a chance to ruminate a bit more about her unorthodox methods.

The waiter delivered our food and we ate in silence. My mind was a swirl of questions. Finally, I settled on one. "Is there an escape clause?"

She laughed. "Interesting first question. Yes. There's an escape clause, but it's only for INN. It's rather boilerplate – we can fire you for any reason, or no reason. You're bound by the contract for the full three years, but a window opens for you a month before the end of the contract allowing you to negotiate with other prospective employers – but INN reserves the right to match or exceed an offer from a rival network. There's also a non-compete clause. If you go to a rival network, you won't be allowed to work on air for a year after your tenure at INN comes to a close."

"Okay. Thanks. I need to do more thinking."

"I understand."

More silence. Some eating.

"Dessert?" she asked.

"No. Thank you."

"Really? The sorbet here is amazing."

We had raspberry sorbet for dessert. She washed hers down with a flute of champagne. I stuck with water.

As we were finishing the meal and she was signing the check, I asked, "I don't understand why you need an answer today. I'd like to run it past a lawyer."

"I have my reasons, Lark. In the end, it's all about trust."

"But—"

"We need to go."

When we got back to the plane, she said, "I'm going to my private cabin to take a nap. Study the contract. We can talk about any other questions you might have before we land. But I'll need your answer by the time we get back to Washington."

"I'd at least like to talk about this with Lionel."

"I'm sorry. There's no cell service while we're in the air."

03 ◆ 80

CHAPTER 10

The flight back to Washington was agony. I was alone in the cabin except for Cedric the steward, who asked if I wanted something to drink. I decided on coffee, feeling I needed to be as clear-headed as possible as I weighed the pros and cons of Francine Noyce's offer.

Cedric brought me the coffee in a fine porcelain cup with a brown sugar cube on the saucer. The coffee was dark and velvety, but not too acidic. The cup was warm and comforting in my hands. It was divine.

Snap out of it, Lark. Focus. You have a big decision to make.

I read through the contract slowly several times, each time noting in my reporter's notebook questions or concerns I had. I then began a ledger list of reasons for and against accepting her soon-to-expire offer.

The first thing I wrote in the con column: *Manipulating me to make a quick decision without being able to seek outside guidance.*

But, the more I thought about that, the more I was able to see how that was, at least from Noyce's point of view, a positive. On the pro side of the ledger I wrote: *She expects me to be able to keep my own counsel so I can make split-second (but wise) decisions in the spur of the moment.*

I put the pen to my lip and gazed out the window. The countryside far below reminded me of the farmland of Wisconsin where I was born and grew up, a place that felt as tranquil as Washington, D.C. was fraught.

Another notation on the pro side: *$750,000!!!!!* I underlined it five times, then amended it with a hyphen and appended it to read, *$1.25 MILLION!!!!!!!* I reasoned I'd be a fool not to consider the money. But how much of a consideration should money be? I know a lot of people who would jump at the money. But I'm not a lot of people.

My first experience in television news at WMTV, the NBC affiliate, channel 15, in Madison, Wisconsin was a disaster. I felt awkward and unnatural on camera, plus I felt uncomfortable being that recognizable. Having a byline and writing important news stories is one thing; being an easily recognizable "star" is something else. Whatever fame I have has been mostly unsought by me. All too often, events beyond my control have thrust me into the public eye. If anything, I've been pondering for quite some time the thought of leaving journalism and pursuing a career in psychology.

On the con side of the ledger, I wrote, *Money shouldn't be the sole reason.*

I continued to ponder.

What would Lionel say? What would Muriel say? What would Paul say? What would Kris say?

I knew them well enough to know that none of them would tell me what to do. All of them would say that I should go with my gut. And Kris would put that into a question for me to answer: "What does your gut say?"

My gut was still in not-sure mode.

On the pro side, I wrote, *A chance to work with and learn from Francine Noyce.* That was actually the easiest of all of the things to write, so far.

I realized that she was wooing me big time. She was making it clear that she really wanted me on board. But, did she care about me as a person, or was she more interested in what I could do for her bottom line?

Yes, she was personally curious and flattering. But she deals with millions of dollars every day. To me, a million dollars is more money than I've ever had. To her, it's chump change. The cost of "brunch" in Montreal alone is probably costing her (actually INN) close to a hundred thousand dollars – private jet included.

And, I thought to myself, who am I kidding? Once she lands me, I'm not going to be her best buddy. Yes, I'll probably talk with her from time to time, but most of my learning will be from afar and by reading between the lines. It's also possible that the closer I get to my hero, the more I'll see and be disillusioned by her inevitable feet of clay.

On the con side, I wrote: *Might be disillusioned by my "hero."*

I was still in Ponder Mode when the steward interrupted my reverie. "Ms. Noyce would like to see you in her cabin," he said.

I unbuckled my seatbelt, took the contract with me on my walk to the back of the plane, and knocked on the door to her cabin.

"Come in," she said.

I opened the door and walked inside. The room was cramped, but opulent. There was just enough room for a bed, a desk, and an easy chair. She was sitting on the edge of the bed wearing a luxurious white robe. She stood when I entered.

"Close the door," she said.

I closed it.

"We'll be landing shortly. Have you made your decision?" She was smiling warmly.

"It's a very generous offer, Ms. Noyce."

"Francine. I want you to call me Francine. Or Fran, if you wish." She took a step closer. "You're worth every penny I'm willing to pay you, Lark. Maybe even more. I'm excited about being able to work with you."

"And I'm very flattered, Ms., um, Francine, but I feel I need more time to think about it."

Until that moment, she seemed almost in a daze, as if my agreeing to join INN was a foregone conclusion. But suddenly her expression hardened.

"Really? More time? Lark, I'm offering you more than a million fucking dollars. And you want more time to think about it?"

"As I said, it's a very generous offer, but—"

Francine took another step forward. She snatched the contract from my hand, tossed it onto the bed, then grasped me firmly by both shoulders and pushed me against the door.

"I want you, Lark. It's that simple."

She then kissed me roughly on the lips and even tried to force her tongue into my mouth.

I didn't think. I reacted. Even though I was pinned against the closed door to her cabin, I still had use of my arms. I placed my hands on her shoulders and shoved her hard away from me.

Her face was frenzied, delirious.

I then did what I've never done to anyone else before in my entire life. I raised my right hand and slapped Francine Noyce hard across the face.

The slap stung my hand.

Her head snapped all the way to her right as a resounding *smack* echoed in the small cabin.

I then clawed at the door, opened it, and dashed from the cabin.

છ ♦ ૪

CHAPTER 11

As I escaped Francine Noyce's cabin, I bumped into Cedric, the steward. He'd been right outside the door.

"Is everything alright, ma'am?" he asked.

"N-no." I pushed past him, then, on instinct I turned to face him. A look of confusion and concern was on his face. "Would you come with me, please," I said to him, trying my best to maintain my composure.

"Of course."

I went back to my seat, strapped in, and rummaged in my messenger bag. When I retrieved what I was looking for, Cedric was standing next to my seat.

"What's wrong?" he asked.

"Your name is Cedric, is that correct?"

"Yes, ma'am."

I handed him my business card. "Cedric, I'm Lark Chadwick with the Associated Press."

He took my card and examined it.

"Cedric, something just happened between me and your boss which is extremely upsetting to me."

I looked at his face and tried to gauge his expression. It seemed concerned but otherwise impassive.

"Uh huh," is all he said.

"I may need your help."

"In what way?"

"I honestly don't know. In fact, it's possible I won't, but, for now, would you mind letting me have your contact information?"

"Sure. I suppose."

I looked anxiously at the door to Noyce's cabin, but it remained closed. I opened my reporter's notebook to a blank page, handed it to him along with a pen. "Here," I said, thrusting them into his hand. "Please write down your name, email, and cell phone number."

"Of course," he said. It only took a moment for him to write down his information and give it back to me.

I gave it a quick look to make sure he wrote legibly. His penmanship is way better than mine. He printed so clearly he could have been an artist.

"Is everything alright?" he asked again. "What just happened?"

"Your boss just physically assaulted me, so I . . . well . . . I-I slapped her."

All color drained from his face.

"Hard."

"Is she alright?"

"She'll be fine. She might have a black eye, or a welt on her face, but she's fine."

"I see."

He didn't. I could tell by his furrowed brow and blank look.

"Does she bring other people onto this jet and whisk them to Canada for brunch?" I asked.

"Sure. Sometimes."

"Has anything like this ever happened before?"

"Not when I've been on board."

"Have you heard any talk among your colleagues?"

He shrugged, but said nothing.

"Well, Cedric. She's a very powerful person. And I'm guessing she's used to getting her way. But she didn't get her way with me."

"Uh huh."

"And now it's my word against hers." To myself, I thought: I've never even heard of a woman sexually assaulting another woman. I can barely believe it, yet I just experienced it. Why should I expect anyone to believe me?

"Are you going to sue?" he asked.

"I'm more concerned that she might. I hit her pretty hard."

"With your fist?"

"No. I slapped her, actually. But hard."

He nodded.

"You heard it, didn't you?"

He nodded again.

"Look, Cedric. Maybe nothing will come of this. I know she's your boss. And I don't want to get you in trouble. But just knowing . . . ." I didn't know what else to say, but he filled the silence.

"I understand," he said. "I'll try to help, if I can."

"Thank you."

"Of course."

Noyce remained in her cabin in the rear of the plane for the duration of the flight. When we landed back in D.C., she emerged wearing a scarf and sunglasses.

As soon as Cedric opened the plane's front door, I bolted from my seat and scurried ahead of Noyce and down the stairway that had been rolled to the plane.

A limo was parked at the bottom of the stairs. The driver stood holding open one of the back doors for me but, to his surprise, I charged past him and walked briskly into the terminal.

I'd never been in this part of the airport before, but just looked for the nearest exit sign, put my head down and barreled toward it. I didn't look back to see if Noyce was coming after me.

My heart was galloping and my breaths were short and rapid. I was still making it up as I went. I hailed a cab and asked the cabbie to take me to the A.P. bureau.

As he drove, I stewed.

It was about four in the afternoon and D.C.'s formidable rush hour had already begun. What should have been a ten-minute drive to the bureau was stretching out longer and longer, so I pulled my laptop out of my messenger bag and began banging the keys. Hard.

The words flowed easily:

To: Scotty Barrington
From: Lark Chadwick
Re: Sexual Assault

Scotty – I'm writing this to you in the immediate aftermath of an extremely distressing situation. After my interview on INN yesterday morning, the network's new president, Francine Noyce, came to the anchor set, introduced herself to me, and invited me to brunch this morning. Brunch turned into an unexpected whirlwind trip to Montreal in Canada where she treated me to a meal, and offered me a three-year, $1.25-million contract.

Her offer was unexpected and flattering. I asked for time to at least study the contract before responding. She let me go over the contract during the flight back to Washington, but indicated I needed to give her my decision by the time the plane landed. I was still weighing my options when Cedric Boyd, the steward on the INN jet, summoned me to Noyce's private cabin.

When I told her I needed more time to weigh her offer, she became enraged. She pushed me against the closed door of her private cabin, pinned me against it, and tried to kiss me.

I pushed her away, slapped her hard across the face, and escaped.

Before the plane landed, Cedric, who said he was an ear witness to my slap, gave me his contact information. I'm writing this to you now to merely inform you of the events because, all-too-often in a he-said, she-said (or in this case, she-said, she-said) situation, it's one person's word against another's without any contemporaneous notes or conversations to corroborate the version of events.

What, if anything, will result from my encounter with Francine Noyce is unknown, but I want you to know the facts in case she files charges.

I have not yet consulted with an attorney. I feel that you, as my immediate supervisor, should be the first to know what has just transpired.

Thank you for your support and encouragement in the past. Here's hoping nothing more will come of this.

Sincerely,
Lark Chadwick
Thursday, April 4
4:43 p.m.

I hit *send* then gave Scotty a call on my cell. I got his voice mail, so I left a message: "Scotty, it's Lark Chadwick. It's 4:45 Thursday afternoon. I've just sent you an extremely important email. Let me know if you have any questions or need to talk about it with me. Thanks."

Copies of the email went to Lionel, Muriel, and my friend Paul Stone.

In my cover email to them I wrote: "Hi, guys..... I was extremely agitated when I wrote this, but felt, even though the contents are embarrassing and troubling, that I needed to go on the record to let people close to me know about this. I don't know what, if anything, will come of it, but I now feel a little better knowing that I've done what I can to keep myself from wallowing in painful and corrosive isolation."

When I hit *send*, it finally felt as though I could exhale.

CB ♦ EO

CHAPTER 12

The next morning I was at Washington National Cathedral for Rose Gannon's funeral. National Cathedral has the familiar and comforting feel of St. Stephen's Episcopal Church in Madison, Wisconsin where I was spiritually nurtured as a youngster – with one exception: "Saint Sven's" is cozy, whereas "Saint Nats" is inspiring magnificence on steroids.

As part of the travel pool for the White House press corps, I was among the few reporters with a front-row seat to keep an eye on the president. Not to be too morbid about it, but we call the assignment "the body watch" because whenever the president travels, a small cadre of print, broadcast, and wire service reporters – plus a camera crew that rotates among the television networks – tags along to keep an eye on the prez in case something horrible happens like, God forbid, an assassination attempt.

We were ushered to our seats in the south transept just moments ahead of Will Gannon's arrival. From our vantage point near the pulpit, we could clearly see the president. A man in a purple robe escorted Gannon from the back of the church to the seat at the end of the front row on the left side of the center aisle.

The organist played something soothing and pastoral. I glanced at my bulletin to note the organist's name – Benjamin Straley. He was playing "Prelude on Rhosymedre" by Ralph Vaughan Williams. I didn't recognize the tune, yet it felt familiar, nostalgic. I found myself instantly having to fight to keep my own emotions in check.

God and I aren't always on speaking terms. It's a love-hate thing. I've talked about this a lot with Kris, my grief counselor. I began to seriously question the faith of my youth when I was sexually assaulted in college and found myself lurching toward atheism, yet I didn't lose my faith completely. Yes, there's plenty of evidence God doesn't exist. So many assholes live long and easy lives, while good people like Rose die young.

Francine Noyce's attack on me the day before was at least an example of God's aloofness. So far, there'd been no blow back from Noyce after I slapped her. Nor had I heard anything at all from Scotty Barrington after I'd sent him my email alerting him to the attack. Lionel had called that evening. I thanked him, but said I didn't want to discuss it. At our cubicle at the White House this morning, Paul merely smiled at me tightly and said, "Hang in there."

The soothing organ prelude gave me some time to relax and ruminate.

I wondered – yet again – about God. As I've thought about the vastness of the cosmos and the complexity of even the tiniest forms of life, I've recognized an amazing symmetry that suggests to me the existence of an intelligent designer behind the universe's intricate design.

But that's not proof God exists. It's only evidence. The rest is faith.

My faith amounts to one mustard seed. Maybe two. But not three. That's because of the events of the past few years – not to mention the past twenty-four hours.

To be honest, my faith is tested the most by the sanctimonious intolerant certainties of the doctrinaire extremists who use God as a cudgel. Yes, I'm talking to you, Osama bin Laden. But I'm also talking to you, Westboro Baptist Church and your "God Hates Fags" gay bashing.

When being brutally honest with Kris – and myself – I realize that most of the times that I pray, I'm in some kind of a jam. But lately, I'm seeing a certain gratitude emerging. I can now argue, with a smidge of confidence, that God not only exists, but has probably gotten me out of a lot of tight situations.

Or, as Lionel often tells me, "You're smart and courageous."

Or, as I often reply, "I'm very lucky."

All those thoughts and biases were a-swirl in me as I settled in for the funeral service for Rose Gannon, First Lady of the United States of America.

An air of expectation descended on the cathedral as the president took his seat in the front row next to his eight-year-old daughter Grace. Next to Grace sat a handsome couple in their seventies – Rose's parents. Notably absent: the Gannon's four-year-old son Thomas. I assumed he was with a nanny, but made a quick note to confirm that with Ron McClain.

Sitting in the rows behind the president, members of his cabinet. Behind them sat various representatives of the diplomatic corps, including Russian Ambassador Rudolph Petrovsky.

I smiled to myself as I remembered the amusing story Rose was telling me about "Petro" just before she collapsed and died. He wore a snazzy black pinstripe suit, dark tie, and crisp white shirt. As I watched, he removed his gold-rimmed spectacles and wiped his face and his high forehead with a handkerchief.

Quickly, I switched my attention back to President Gannon. It was the first time anyone had seen him in public since Rose died four days ago. His face was grim and lined and he gripped a white hanky tightly in both hands.

The vice president, sitting behind the president, leaned in and briefly whispered something to the president. I'm a terrible lip reader, but it was probably something comforting because the president nodded, smiled, and mouthed a thank you.

In the days leading up to the funeral, I researched and filed a report on presidents who have been widowed while in office.

President John Tyler's wife Letitia, who was already in ill health when Tyler took office, died of a stroke in 1842. Fewer than two years later, while still president, the fifty-year-old Tyler married twenty-four-year-old Julia Gardiner.

President Benjamin Harrison's wife Caroline died of tuberculosis in 1892. Harrison's oldest daughter Mary Scott Harrison McKee hosted White House social functions for the remainder of Harrison's term. He remarried in 1896 after leaving office.

To me, the most intriguing story of presidential widowing surrounds the life of Woodrow Wilson, the third president whose wife died while he was the nation's chief executive. Wilson's wife Ellen died of kidney disease in 1914.

Seven months later Wilson met, fell in love with, and proposed to Edith Bolling Galt, the widow of a wealthy D.C. jeweler. That led to nasty, but unsubstantiated, rumors that Wilson had cheated on his wife and then murdered her so that he could be with Edith Galt.

For the sake of appearances, Wilson and Galt decided to delay their wedding until after the customary one-year mourning period. They were married at the end of 1915, a year and a half after Ellen Wilson's death.

Scholars and historians have had a field day studying the relationship between Woodrow and Edith Galt Wilson. In 1919, Woodrow Wilson suffered a debilitating stroke. By this time, Edith was his most trusted companion, so she essentially ran the country while Wilson, himself, was mostly out of public view.

Ironically, Wilson's final resting place is about thirty yards from where I was sitting.

As I sat in National Cathedral, watching the nation's fourth grieving widower president, I wondered how – or if – Woodrow Wilson's presidency could have weathered the current deadline-a-second news cycle in which anyone with a cell phone and a Twitter account is a "journalist."

Will Gannon was now the world's most eligible bachelor. Already tacky, click-bait stories about that were surfacing on the internet – even before Rose had been laid to rest.

I could only imagine how hideous it must be for the president not only to have to contemplate a future without Rose's companionship, but to have to wonder constantly about the motives of all the beautiful women he regularly encounters throughout the course of even a single day. I made a mental note to ask him about that, if I got my chance at a one-on-one with him. Will he deal with his grief by putting on blinders to block out all potential romantic distractions, and dive into the crushing responsibilities of the presidency by giving the job his undivided attention? Will he become a playboy president, making up for time lost while married?

My presidential reverie was broken by a disembodied female voice coming from the back of the cathedral: "I am Resurrection and I am Life, says the Lord."

Rose Gannon's funeral service was beginning.

೦೩ ◆ ೮೦

CHAPTER 13

Everyone stood, their rustling echoed throughout the vast chamber.

"Whoever has faith in me shall have life, even though he dies," The Voice continued.

I looked to my left toward the rear of the cathedral where the verger – the guy who ushered the president to his seat – walked slowly down the center aisle carrying Rose Gannon's ashes in a container covered by a bright, white pall.

The bishop, a woman, followed the robed verger, reading the words of scripture from the Episcopal Book of Common Prayer that she held in front of her. She wore white vestments and a high pointed cap called a mitre – (a useless piece of trivia I still remembered from my kid years in Sunday school).

The two-person procession reached the foot of the steps to the altar and paused as the verger placed Rose's ashes atop a marble pedestal that stood in the center aisle, almost within reach of the president. He reddened noticeably when the covered urn came into view, his jaw muscles tensing.

The verger and bishop then walked up the steps as the bishop kept reading: "Happy from now on are those who die in the Lord! So it is, says the Spirit, for they rest from their labors."

The organ surged and the capacity congregation of nearly three thousand, singing as one voice, joined the purple and white robed choir in singing the hymn. The choir also included nearly two dozen girl and boy choristers.

Tears suddenly welled in my eyes because the hymn was the same one sung at Annie's funeral three years earlier at Saint Sven's in Madison. It's an Easter hymn: "Jesus Christ is Risen Today."

I instinctively picked up a hymnal and was about to join the singing when I realized I was there as a professional – a detached observer, not a congregant. But I studied the words and wished I could ask Rose for her opinion.

Sadly, she and I had never gotten far enough along in our conversations to explore religion. But the grounded sense of certainty and somber triumph of the music, coupled with the confident hope expressed in the text ("... who did once upon the cross ... suffer to redeem our loss . . . but the pains which he endured ... our salvation have procured . . . .") seemed to reflect the hopeful spirit of the Rose Gannon I'd been getting to know.

In spite of my wavering agnosticism, the music embraced and comforted me. I attributed the feeling more to the familiarity of my upbringing than with any kind of spiritual certainty.

Glancing ahead in my order-of-service program, I saw that this would be a succinct and efficient service. Rose would have approved.

To my surprise, I also noticed that President Gannon would be giving "brief remarks."

When the hymn ended, the bishop faced the congregation and said, "The Lord be with you."

The congregation responded, "And also with you." There was so much power in the responding voices that it seemed as though the place was standing room only.

"Let us pray," the bishop said. After a moment of silence, she continued. "O God of grace and glory, we remember before you this day our sister Rose. We thank you for giving her to us, her family and friends, to know and to love as a companion on our earthly pilgrimage. In your boundless compassion, console us who mourn. Give us faith to see in death the gate of eternal life, so that in quiet confidence we may continue our course on earth, until, by your call, we are reunited with those who have gone before; through Jesus Christ our Lord. Amen."

My job wasn't to close my eyes and pray; it was to keep my eye on the president, which I did. During the prayer, his head was bowed, and his eyes were closed.

In my reporter's notebook, I scrawled, *Face flushed, but seems composed.*

At the end of the prayer, President Gannon's lips mouthed "Amen." He opened his eyes, lifted his head and turned it slightly to his right and looked in my direction.

I was sitting barely fifty feet from him.

When the president saw me looking at him, he nodded slightly to me, then turned his attention to the elevated stone lectern at the front where the vice president's wife was about to read from the Old Testament – a passage from Isaiah in which God promises to comfort those who mourn.

After the reading, the choir stood to sing an anthem written by Herbert Howells based on Psalm 42:1-3 The words were printed in the bulletin:

Like as the hart desireth the waterbrooks,
So longeth my soul after thee, O God.

My soul is athirst for God, yea, even for the living God.
When shall I come and appear before the Presence of God?

My tears have been my meat day and night, while they
continually say unto me, Where is now thy God?

Earlier in the week, I'd filed a look-ahead piece on the funeral and learned that Howells, a Brit, wrote the anthem in the early 1940s when England was enduring Hitler's blitz. The music has a surprisingly bluesy feel, melancholy with only glimmers of comfort. The innocently clear voices of the Cathedral choristers added a pristine purity to the sound.

There's something about music – especially when it's sung angelically. It's able to evade my intellectual defenses and touch me in an emotional place so deep that it's hard for me to explain – and I'm a person who makes her living writing.

In spite of my best efforts to remain cool and objective, this service was stirring me up inside.

I'd only known Rose Gannon for a handful of months. She'd reached out to me in kindness when Doug died and my grief was at its gut-wrenching worst. Now, as the choir sang movingly, I remembered my frequent conversations with Rose. Even though we were supposed to be discussing her life, her interest in me was so strong that I had to keep reminding her "this is about you, not me."

She knew she was dying, yet she was so full of life. "I'm a realist," she often told me.

As I sat surrounded and dwarfed by the grandeur of National Cathedral – stained-glass sunshine splashing bright blue, yellow, and red on its Indiana limestone walls – I realized that Rose Gannon was like the flashy-impressive big sister I never had.

I bit my lip. Hard. I had to keep fighting against the overpowering emotions that threatened to blur my judgment and prevent me from doing my job as a skilled professional.

The anthem ended and the vice president read a passage from the New Testament. This verse from the book of Revelation jumped out at me: "God will wipe away every tear."

Dude, I said to the Almighty, *wiping away my tears will be Your full-time job.*

The choir stood and as it sang a setting of the Twenty-third Psalm, I had to choke back outright sobs. I tried to keep my emotions hidden, but the Reuters correspondent sitting next to me must have noticed my shoulders heaving. She reached out her hand and gave mine a quick squeeze.

It helped. A little.

The hymn tune ("Brother James Air," according to the bulletin), was the same one sung at the funeral of my boyfriend Jason who died in a fall from Granddad's Bluff back in Wisconsin a few years earlier. He and I had worked together briefly at a television station in Madison. I found his broken body at the foot of Table Rock.

Grief, as I was coming to realize, is always lurking. Just about the time I think I have a handle on it, something triggers a memory and I'm right back in that moment of anguish.

The God-as-shepherd motif continued with the bishop reading the words of Jesus from the Gospel of John: "I am the good shepherd. I lay down my life for the sheep."

The vague beginning of a possible lead line for my story formed in my head. In my reporter's notebook, I wrote, *Words of comfort and hope* – a scrap of an idea I might be able to use later.

I wondered how much of a say Will Gannon had in the planning of the service – the choice of hymns and scripture – and made a note to ask him if that one-on-one interview about grief ever came to pass.

It was now time for Will Gannon's "brief remarks."

I leaned forward, expectantly.

President Gannon stood and moved to the center aisle. He paused for a long moment and rested his hand lightly on the white pall that covered Rose's cremains. The president bowed his head, pursed his lips, and took a deep breath.

As crass as it sounds, Gannon gazing sadly at the white pall draping the urn containing all that remained of his wife was "the money shot," the picture that would dominate social media, the front pages of newspapers around the world, and on television where it would be replayed repeatedly, then archived on history's highlight reel.

The president's hand trembled as he lifted it from the white pall covering Rose. He walked slowly toward the stone lectern. Trudged is probably a more apt word. His shoulders were hunched and it looked as though he'd aged in the few days since I'd last seen him.

I wondered – and worried – if the president would even be able to get through his remarks.

As Gannon got to the top of the stairway that leads to the elevated lectern, I readied my iPhone to record his remarks so that my notes would be accurate.

"Good morning," the president began, his voice sounding husky as it reverberated and echoed off the chancel's glass and stone.

He spoke slowly, deliberately, with more force than I expected, and with just a hint of his Southern drawl.

"First, I want to thank those of you from all over the world who have sent me messages of sympathy, support, and encouragement at this difficult time. Your prayers and thoughtful concern have been comforting beyond words."

His voice broke. He paused and swallowed hard.

"Your first lady – my wife – was a woman of quality and courage. A few years ago, Rose and I visited the Brandywine River Museum in Chadds Ford, Pennsylvania near Philadelphia where we walked through an incredible exhibit of the paintings created by the artist Andrew Wyeth.

"For those of you not familiar with him, Wyeth divided his time between rural Pennsylvania and Maine. Throughout his seventy-year career, he painted mostly winter landscapes and scenes containing some of the people who were fixtures in his life. His paintings are notable for their intricacy – their attention to detail.

"As Rose and I strolled through the art exhibit, the thing that struck me is that Wyeth repeatedly painted places and people who were familiar to him throughout his life. He said that the more time he spent studying and exploring the same places and people, the more details he saw. And, with each fresh discovery, he said his appreciation for his surroundings deepened.

"Being married to Rose was like being immersed in Andrew Wyeth's world. The more time I spent with her, the more deeply I loved and appreciated her. She and I would only have a dozen years together, but they mark a turning point for me. A turning away from loneliness to discover companionship. A turning away from superficiality to discover the depths and joys of intimacy. A deepening. A maturing. I'm a better man because Rose was in my life."

Here the president paused. He was fighting his emotions. When he spoke again, his voice quavered precariously. "Rose was never boring. Always interesting. Insatiably curious about everything – and everyone – she encountered.

"We met at a party in Nashville. She was a ballroom dancing instructor and had just opened her own studio. I was teaching constitutional law at Vanderbilt, was thinking about getting into politics . . . and had two left feet."

He paused and the congregation murmured its mirth.

"When I saw her dancing, I was mesmerized by her gracefulness as she glided effortlessly across the dance floor. I had to meet her. So I did.

"I got her to teach me how to dance. And she tried. But I still have those two left feet." Will Gannon smiled impishly and the congregation chuckled softly.

"Eventually, we did more talking than dancing. I quickly discovered she was unlike any woman I'd ever met before – or since. She was smart, sassy, confident, courageous, kind, inquisitive, caring, funny."

I noticed immediately that the president didn't describe Rose as beautiful. Why not? I scribbled *beautiful*??? in my notebook and underlined it three times. Rose Gannon was one of the prettiest women in the world. Was Will Gannon's omission an oversight – or deliberate? I had my own suspicions, but wanted to give him a chance to explain first.

He smiled broadly, but his eyes were wet. "God, she was funny. For example: We were together when the news broke that Playboy founder Hugh Hefner died. Without missing a beat, Rose leaned over to me and said, 'The playing field's wide open for you now, Will.'"

The congregation laughed. A full-throated guffaw. That's because a major part of Gannon's popularity is his sex appeal. That, and the added heft of his smarts. When Will Gannon was elected, it was as if Justin Trudeau had just become President of the United States.

The president, still smiling, waited for the wave of laughter to pass through the vast and vaulted limestone and marble space. Then, he turned serious. "I still have two left feet, but I don't have Rose any more. And neither do you.

"We have lost a national treasure."

As soon as Gannon spoke those words, I knew I had my lead and jotted down the phrase in my notebook.

"But we still have Rose's memory to cherish," the president said. "May those memories be vivid – and eternal. Amen."

"Amen," the congregation – including me – responded.

He'd spoken for fewer than four minutes. As he made his way sadly back to his pew, the cell phone in my hand vibrated.

I looked. A bulletin from the Associated Press Moscow bureau:

> *Russian President Dimitry Yazkov today said he is unilaterally scrapping all nuclear arms reduction and proliferation treaties with the U.S. and announced his intent to provide nuclear weapons to Iran.*

Stunned, I shot a look toward where Russian Ambassador Rudolph Petrovsky was sitting to see if I could read anything in his expression, but I couldn't. Petro's seat was vacant. He was gone.

CB ◆ EO

CHAPTER 14

The rest of Rose Gannon's funeral service went by quickly. Her ashes were placed in a vault in St. Joseph's Chapel, the basement crypt of Washington National Cathedral. That portion of the service was private and closed to cameras.

The stunning news out of Moscow caused a stir among us in the press pool – and I even saw many of the Very Important People in the congregation sneaking peeks at their smart phones as the news rippled through the chancel. Some people actually got up and left. I presumed they were needed immediately at the Pentagon, State Department, and even the White House.

I kept my eye on Gannon. He seemed oblivious to what was transpiring around him and in cyberspace, but I noticed him glancing our way from time to time, a slightly quizzical expression on his face as he observed most of us in the press corps distracted by our phones.

The president must have been briefed during the short motorcade ride back to the White House right after Rose was laid to rest because, instead of helicoptering to Camp David for the weekend, the president delayed his departure to meet with his national security team in the Situation Room.

When I got back to the White House, I went immediately to the Associated Press cubicle. I filed my story on Rose's funeral and then worked the phones with Paul to get a better handle on the meaning, nuances, and public policy implications of the breaking story out of Russia.

Late in the afternoon, we were herded to the South Lawn where we'd be able to view the president boarding Marine One, the helicopter that would take him to Camp David. Just as we were assembling in the briefing room to be escorted out the side doors, a young woman's voice came through the overhead speakers:

"Before departing for Camp David, the president will be making brief remarks on the south lawn about the situation with Russia. He will not be taking questions. The president will be at the podium on the south lawn in two minutes."

The announcement immediately electrified us. Almost simultaneously everyone was on their cell phones alerting the desks at their respective news organizations. The television photogs were especially energized – and impatient to get into position so they could set up their gear. Most of them carried short, lightweight aluminum stepladders so they could stand behind and above the rest of us to get a clear view of the president.

Much of statecraft is stagecraft, so I watched with interest to see how the White House would set up the president's announcement. There are any number of ways and backdrops a president can use to frame his message. Usually, when presidents go away for the weekend, they emerge from the main residence by the rounded Truman Balcony and stroll to the chopper waiting on the south lawn. They wave at the cameras and to a throng of White House staffers and their friends and family members who have been granted special access for the day so they can be seen in the background waving enthusiastically at the prez.

On this day, President Gannon emerged from the Oval Office still dressed in the dark suit he'd worn to his wife's funeral just hours earlier. He looked . . . well . . . presidential.

As Gannon walked along the sidewalk that sloped from his office down to a small podium on the White House driveway, the only sounds I could hear were some birds chirping and the shutter clicks of the still photogs as they snapped shot after shot of the president making his way toward us.

The thirty seconds it took for him to walk from the Oval to the podium would provide TV reporters with what they call "B-roll" – video they can "voice over" to set up the president's key sound bite.

The expression on President Gannon's face was serious-grim, befitting the grave crisis he faced, yet the impromptu nature of the setting fell far short of elevating his remarks to the important level of a formal Oval Office address to the nation that President Kennedy's speech did at the height of the Cuban Missile Crisis in 1962.

The visual message Gannon was sending to the world: *Yes. This is serious, but I've got it under control, folks.*

When he got to the makeshift podium, Gannon ignored those of us closest to him and eyed the television cameras behind us.

"Today's sudden and stunning announcement from Russia is disturbing. I call upon President Yazkov to consider the potentially grave consequences his decision has set in motion. I urge him, in the strongest terms possible, to reconsider his decision. It's not too late."

Gannon glanced quickly at the notes on the lectern, then spoke again to the cameras.

"President Yazkov needs to know that the United States of America is ready, willing, able, committed, and determined to defend our NATO allies against any Russian challenge to their sovereignty or against any physical attack from Iran or any other Russian ally."

Here, the president's tone shifted from stern to soothing, and he spoke directly to Russia's president.

"Dimitry. Our two great countries have come a long way since the days of the Cold War. We have learned to put down our weapons of mass destruction. We have partnered in the exploration of space. We have been adversaries, but we need not become enemies. I urge you to reconsider your decision. It's not too late. Let's talk."

Gannon stopped talking, but maintained steely eye contact with the cameras behind me in the half-circle scrum by the portable podium. The president then turned to his right and stalked toward Marine One where it waited on the South Lawn.

Yes. We were told the president wouldn't be answering any questions, but that didn't prevent us from asking. We shouted a cascade of them at him. Most were drowned out as the huge rotors of the chopper began to spin, but he heard mine:

"Are you still going to China for the summit?"

Gannon turned toward us, gave two thumbs up and said, "Full speed ahead."

Then, on cue, and probably to underscore his humanness and the high stakes of the crisis, the president's two young children, Thomas and Grace, scampered across the lawn toward him from the south entrance beneath the Truman Balcony.

The president got down on one knee and both children zoomed into his open arms so hard that their momentum nearly knocked him over.

They were all obviously delighted to be with each other, and the warm family tableau brought a lump to my throat. The children wore brightly-colored windbreakers and jeans.

When the president stood, he kept four-year-old Thomas perched on his left forearm, the boy's right arm draped around the back of his dad's neck, while the president and eight-year-old Grace held hands. The wind from the chopper blades tousled their hair and threw the president's tie over his shoulder.

Just as they got to the foot of the stairway to the chopper, while the president dropped Grace's hand to salute the Marine guard, Thomas, looking back toward the White House from the safe perch on his dad's arm, waved impishly at the press corps – another money shot.

Jesus, I thought to myself, *is that family photogenic, or what?*

The herd of reporters and photographers gathered on the South Lawn to gawk at the departing helicopter stayed there until it flew over the White House and out of sight. We were then ushered by the press office underlings back to the briefing room where most of us dashed to our cubicles to file our stories about the president's direct personal appeal to Russian President Dimitry Yazkov to knock it off, and Gannon's firm resolve to defend our NATO allies if push comes to shove.

The press office declared a "full lid" about six o'clock, meaning no news or photo ops were expected for the remainder of the day.

"Got plans for tonight?" Paul asked.

When I was dating Doug, that kind of open-ended question would cause me to flinch. I knew Paul had had a crush on me. But that was then. Now I knew that I was off the hook and could relax, knowing that Paul's affections had lurched in a new direction.

"Depends," I said. "What's up?"

"I just got a text from Dad. He and Mom are in town for the weekend to close on their new house. We're having dinner at their hotel – and you're invited."

"Geez. Things are moving faster than I even expected."

"I know. They did their house-hunting on the sly. Dad said he wanted the move to be a surprise."

"And it is."

"So, you'll join us for dinner?"

"Absolutely!"

"Whew."

"Excuse me?"

"I really need you to be there."

"Why?"

"Speaking of surprises, I've invited Alex. It's time Mom and Dad know the real me."

Paul Stone, the most upbeat person I've ever known, looked like the evening ahead was not going to be a festive dinner with his parents, but an appointment with a firing squad.

CB ◆ ED

CHAPTER 15

It's always good to see Lionel and Muriel, so I was looking forward to being with them as much as Paul was dreading it. We met in the lobby of the George Hotel where they were staying near the Capitol.

"There she is!" Lionel hollered when I came through the door, along with Paul and Alex.

Lionel seemed almost giddy and gave me his biggest bear hug ever. He's a big man; I couldn't get my arms all the way around him. He kissed me on the top of my head as I pressed my right ear against his chest.

Muriel, typically the more reserved of the two, was beaming, nonetheless. "I hope you and I get some time to talk," she whispered in my ear as we hugged.

Lionel and Paul shook hands heartily, then Paul took a step back. "Mom. Dad. This is my friend Alex."

Alex, who'd been standing off to the side, stepped forward. He wore a snazzy double-breasted suit, with a muted brown tie and matching handkerchief pocket square. He kissed Muriel's hand and shook Lionel's, adding, "Mr. Stone, I've been a fan of yours for many years. It's an honor, sir."

"Any friend of Paul's, is a friend of ours. Delighted to meet you, Alex," Lionel said.

As we migrated to the hotel's restaurant, I fell in step with Muriel. "Poor Alex," I said to her. "Little does he know that he's about to get a grilling from Lionel."

She laughed. And sighed.

Lionel and Muriel sat at opposite ends of the table. I had a side of the table all to myself with Lionel to my right and Muriel to my left. Alex and Paul sat directly across from me.

During the first round of drinks and appetizers, Lionel did what Lionel does best: he got to know Alex. To some people, it's intimidating to be on the receiving end of Lionel Stone's relentless curiosity. Alex was not only a good sport, he seemed to appreciate Lionel's attention.

"So, tell us about yourself, Alex. Where are you from and what brings you to D.C.?"

"I'm from New York City, sir. Got an MBA from Harvard. Now I'm a money manager."

"What do you make of the latest dust-up with Russia?" Lionel asked.

"I'm definitely keeping an eye on it right now."

"What are you advising your clients?"

"It depends on their individual situations, but generally my advice is to sit tight and not panic."

"Got a girlfriend?"

"Lionel!" Muriel said, shooting Alex an embarrassed look.

"I can ask," Lionel said peevishly. "He doesn't have to answer."

"I'm dating someone," Alex answered diplomatically.

"That's not a surprise. Handsome guy like you. You should have invited her, too."

I glanced at Paul. He seemed particularly interested in the guacamole dip.

"And Lark." Lionel turned his attention to me. "You had quite an experience with Francine Noyce."

I blushed. "I did. But maybe now's not the best time to explore that," I said, repeatedly glancing at the stranger in our midst and hoping Lionel would get the message.

He did. "Oh. Right. Maybe later."

Alex turned to Paul with a curious expression that looked like he hoped Paul would bring him up to speed about Noyce.

I changed the subject and brought Muriel into the discussion. "What kind of a place did you two find?" I asked her.

That subject took us to a place where Paul and I could both sit back and relax a bit as Muriel told us about the home they found and how they found it.

"I would have liked a retirement community," she said.

"But I think a retirement community is for old fuddy-duddies," Lionel said. "That I'm not!" he scowled.

"You only talk like one," I teased. "I haven't heard the word fuddy-duddy since nigh unto a coon's age."

Everyone laughed, even Lionel, but I think Muriel laughed the loudest and longest.

By the time we finished the second bottle of wine, the meal had turned festive as the conversation ricocheted from topic to topic. For the most part, Alex remained on the fringes of our banter, but now and then he chimed in.

"What do you think of the situation with Russia, Mr. Stone?" Alex asked as the waiter cleared the table of our meal's detritus.

"It reminds me of a joke I first heard during the Cold War when it was fairly common to refer to the Communists as "reds" after the color of the Soviet flag. Now that Rudolph Petrovsky, the Russian ambassador, is in the news lately, I remembered the joke."

"Here we go," Muriel said. Obviously, she'd heard the joke before, probably several times.

"Now don't give away the punch line, dear," Lionel scolded his wife.

"I wouldn't dream of it," she smiled. "In order for me to do that, the joke would have to be funny."

Alex and I laughed.

"Anyway," Lionel began. "A man and his wife were on a guided tour of Red Square near the Kremlin. Their tour guide was a local guy named Rudolph." Lionel started to chuckle in anticipation of the belly laughs to follow. "During the tour, the weather suddenly turned bad. Was it rain, or was it snow? They couldn't be sure. The husband insisted it was snowing, but their tour guide disagreed and said it was raining. Here's how the wife settled the dispute: she gave her husband a stern stare and said, 'Rudolph the Red knows rain, dear.'"

Muriel rolled her eyes.

Alex and I laughed.

Lionel laughed loudest of all.

Paul seemed preoccupied.

Alex said, "All joking aside, though, I'm interested in hearing your analysis of the current crisis with Russia, Mr. Stone."

"You're right. It is very serious," Lionel said.

"Why do you suppose Yazkov is being so provocative?" Alex asked.

"I think there are a couple of reasons," Lionel began. "First, you have to understand the psychology of the situation. I think the coup in China upset the world balance of power."

"How?" Alex asked.

"The U.S. and China are now closer than they've ever been in history. There is a real chance that China will become a full-fledged representative Democracy with all the freedoms that come with it, including economic freedom."

"And that's a threat to Russia?"

"It needn't be, but that's where psychology comes in. In many ways, Yaz is an insecure bully who demands loyalty and loves to be the center of attention. But now the spotlight has shifted to the China-U.S. relationship and Yaz can't stand it."

"So, he needs to do something audacious to reclaim the spotlight?" Alex asked.

Lionel nodded. "Exactly. And what better time to do it than when the U.S. president is crippled by the grief of having just lost the love of his life."

"Do you think he's bluffing?" Alex asked.

Lionel considered this. "Yes. Maybe. But maybe not. It all depends on if Yazkov actually makes good on his announcement and allows Iran to get its hands on nuclear weapons. If that happens, it's a whole new ballgame."

Before Lionel could pontificate any longer about the Russia crisis, Muriel intervened and shifted the spotlight to Alex. "How did you and Paul meet?" she asked.

"Paul was on a panel discussion at Brookings that I attended," Alex said. "We got to talking afterward – and we haven't stopped talking since." He reached over and patted the top of Paul's hand.

Paul coughed uncomfortably and said. "Now's probably as good a time as any."

Lionel and Muriel both looked at their son, confused.

Alex sat stoically, playing with a crumb on the white linen tablecloth.

I held my breath.

"Dad. When Alex told you he's dating someone, there's actually more to that story."

"Oh?" Lionel asked, still confused.

"Uh huh," Paul replied. "The person he's dating is . . . me." He took Alex's hand.

"Oh my!" Muriel said, involuntarily putting her hand over her mouth.

Lionel reddened, but said nothing.

ᴄ⅗ ◆ ℬↃ

CHAPTER 16

The next morning, Saturday, I met Muriel for a walk along the old Chesapeake & Ohio Canal in Georgetown.

The C&O, otherwise known as "The Grand Old Ditch," ferried coal from the Allegheny Mountains to D.C. in mule-drawn boats from 1831 to 1924. Now the 185-mile stretch between D.C. and Cumberland, Maryland is a National Park. The towpath where the mules walked passes the ruins of about 70 locks that helped the boats gradually descend more than 600 feet as they came south. Little known fact: the infamous Watergate complex got its name because it's located by milepost one of the C&O.

The musty-fertile smell of spring was in the air as Muriel and I walked. Early-morning joggers rushed past us.

"You said last night that you wanted to talk?" I asked.

"I do. Now more than ever."

"How are you doing after Paul's bombshell?"

"Better than Lionel."

"How's he doing?"

"He was pretty shocked."

"I know. I could tell."

Dinner had turned icy after Paul's announcement. Lionel ate his dessert cup of ice cream in silence, his slow burn seeming to melt the single scoop of vanilla faster than he could eat it. Muriel did her best to remain cheery, but it was an uncomfortable struggle for her, too. "That's nice," was about all she could muster.

"It certainly was a shock," I said.

"Yes."

"Are you okay with it?"

"Oh, Lark, I always knew Paul was gay."

I turned to look at her, stunned. "Really? How?"

"Mothers just know. But I always hoped he'd marry a girl and I'd have grandchildren." Her voice trailed off and she sighed deeply.

"You still could. There's always adoption."

She nodded and smiled bravely. "True. Alex seems like a fine young man."

"What about Lionel? How's he doing?"

"Oh, he'll be alright." She chuckled. "He's such a bundle of contradictions."

"How so?"

"He sees himself as a virile man's man, but he also prides himself on being open-minded. I think his feelings and his thoughts are fighting with each other right now."

"What are they?"

"He's never been anti-gay or homophobic, but—"

"But it's different when an abstraction becomes real and hits home?"

"Precisely."

"Has he said this in so many words?"

"Oh my, no. He's still processing it."

"How do you know?"

"I've known him for at least twenty-five years. He'll come around. It'll just take him some time."

"If you don't mind my asking, how are you two doing?"

Muriel and Lionel had had a nasty blow-up a couple years ago when I was staying with them briefly while going through a hard time of my own. Strife prompted them to get marriage counseling.

"We're doing much better. Thanks."

"Are you still seeing a marriage counselor?"

"No. Counseling seemed to do the trick. Lionel's still Lionel, but I don't feel as invisible to him as I used to."

"I notice you're still quiet around him."

"That's just my nature. It's a classic case of opposites attract. But I'm bolder now about speaking my mind rather than letting my feelings fester. Marriage counseling helped a lot. I found my voice and Lionel learned to listen to it."

"May I ask one more none-of-my-business questions?"

She laughed. "This is why I love talking with you, Lark. Go ahead and ask."

"How do you feel about the move back to D.C.? Was this foisted on you, or is it a joint decision?"

"It's both."

"How so?"

"It was his idea, but I think it's the right one."

"Why?"

"We get to be closer to you and Paul. But I think it was long overdue for Lionel to give up the newspaper."

"Was that hard for him?"

She shook her head. "Not as hard as I thought it would be. Every time he'd complain about something, I'd gently plant one more seed suggesting that just maybe running the paper wasn't fun for him anymore. He would have dug in his heels if I'd said he was getting too old. But fun? He gets that."

"He thinks selling the paper was his idea?"

"Yup." She smiled triumphantly.

We walked in silence for a few moments. A kayaker floated by and we exchanged waves with him.

"How's your health? And Lionel's? Is everything okay?" I asked.

She nodded. "Thankfully, yes. Lionel's been taking better care of himself since his last heart attack. I think selling the paper has done much to reduce his stress level."

"What does he plan to do here?"

"He's going to be an adjunct at the University of Maryland journalism school, plus he'll have more time to work on his memoir."

"He'll always need to have a major project going, won't he?"

"Yes."

"Well, I for one am delighted that you'll both be close by. I've missed you."

She put her arm around my shoulder and gave me a strong squeeze.

"How are you doing, Lark?"

I shrugged. "Okay, I guess."

"You're a very strong person."

"I wish I felt that way."

"You've been through so much, yet you not only bounce back, but I feel your resilience makes you even stronger."

"That incident with Francine Noyce really threw me."

"I can only imagine. Do you feel like talking about it?"

"I don't even know where to begin."

"Begin with your feelings. What are they?"

"Anger. Fear. Confusion."

"Have you been able to talk about it with anyone?"

"You're the first. I meet with my grief counselor on Tuesday."

"How can I help?"

"You already are."

"I am?"

"You're here. That's a lot."

"Anger I get. What is it you're afraid of?" Muriel asked.

"Noyce is a very powerful person. I really clobbered her. That's assault."

"Has she filed charges, or taken any action against you?"

I shook my head. "That's why it's so insidious. It's like waiting for a shoe to drop."

"Have you considered that she, too, might be afraid?"

"Of what?"

"Of you and what you might do."

I laughed. "I can't imagine anyone being afraid of me."

"Oh, don't be too sure. You're a very formidable young lady, Lark Chadwick."

"So you say."

"I do say."

"You might be right, though, Muriel. Noyce and I both have something on each other. It's like the threat of mutually assured destruction holds each of us in check."

"Yes. But I think you were very wise to chronicle the event as soon as it happened, and to let your boss know about it."

"But it's been crickets from him ever since."

"That's okay. You're on record. That's important."

"Yeah. I guess."

"And confusion?" she probed.

"Uh huh."

"What are you confused about?"

"Not sure what else I should do about it."

"Want my advice?"

"Absolutely."

"You've already done what you can. Now forget about it and move on."

I snapped my fingers. "Just like that?"

"Just like that."

I gave her a doubtful look.

"The more you stew about it, the more inner confusion you'll create," she said.

Just then my phone rang. I dug it out of my jeans and looked at the display. *White House.*

"I should take this," I said to Muriel.

"Go ahead."

I put the phone to my ear. "This is Lark."

A woman's voice said, "This is the White House operator calling for Lark Chadwick."

"Speaking."

"Please stand by for President Gannon."

I looked at Muriel wide-eyed and mouthed, "It's the president."

"Oh dear," she said.

03 ◆ 80

John DeDakis

CHAPTER 17

By four o'clock that afternoon, I was sitting in front of the President of the United States. A fire in the hearth at Camp David's Birch Cabin took away the early spring chill.

"Lark," he'd said when I took his call, "It's Will Gannon."

"Hello, Mr. President."

"Ron McClain told me of your request to do that grief interview. I'm ready to do it."

"That's wonderful, sir. When's good?"

"Today. Now. Or as soon as you can get to Camp David."

"Um—"

"I can send a car to pick you up."

And so it was set. A sedan from the White House motor pool picked me up on Wisconsin Avenue in Georgetown by the C&O Canal. I'd Metroed into D.C. from where I live in Silver Spring to meet with Muriel, plus I always carry a notebook and my White House press credentials with me, so I had all I'd need.

The president made it clear that the atmosphere at Camp David is "come-as-you-are casual."

"But I'm wearing jeans," I said.

"So am I," he replied.

I had time to think through my questions during the hour and fifteen-minute drive north to Catoctin Mountain Park in north-central Maryland, just south of the Pennsylvania state line.

The secluded presidential retreat was built in the 1930s during the Depression by President Roosevelt's Works Projects Administration

(WPA). FDR called it Shangri-La, but Eisenhower changed the name to Camp David after his grandson.

I was impressed and surprised by how sprawling the place is. Even though it's technically a military installation, it's more like a five-star resort complete with tennis courts, swimming pool, hiking trails, and plenty of private cabins. The place is rich with history. Summits have been held here. Jimmy Carter brokered peace between Israel and Egypt here.

But today it was just me, a grieving president, plus a White House stenographer, and an official White House photographer.

It helped that the president and I had developed a personal rapport over the past year – first when I interviewed him after a campaign event in Columbia, Georgia when he was running for president. And then we met several times during the course of my extensive interviews with Rose before her sudden death.

Will Gannon is an intoxicatingly genial person. He's comfortable in his skin, and because he's personable, he's good at making even the most self-consciously nervous person, like me, feel at ease.

True to his word, Gannon wore faded jeans, a navy-blue pull-over fleece and moccasins. We sat in over-stuffed easy chairs on a throw rug in front of the fireplace. A White House stenographer sat off to the side holding a tape recorder. She held a long omni-directional shotgun microphone to transcribe the conversation that would be posted later on the White House website.

I, too, was recording the conversation on my iPhone and had my reporter's notebook open to the list of questions I'd prepared on the 66-mile drive from Georgetown.

"Ready, sir?" I asked the president.

"Fire away." he said jauntily.

"So, how are you doing?

It was an open-ended softball question, but he weighed his words interminably as if I'd just asked him to defend his PhD thesis. Finally, he spoke.

"It's hard, Lark. Rose was such a big personality. The White House is so empty without her. So is Camp David."

"How are you coping?"

"Coping is probably the best way to describe it," he said. "Fortunately, the presidency is a huge job. And certainly that keeps my mind occupied."

"Speaking of the presidency," I said, "before we dive back into the subject at hand, I'd be remiss not to bring up the action by Russia."

He nodded.

"What more can you add to your comments yesterday?"

"Nothing."

"Have you and President Yazkov been able to talk?"

"As you can imagine, it's an extremely delicate time, so I don't want to say any more. It's safe to assume that there are what I'd call quiet attempts behind the scenes on many different levels to defuse the situation."

"Diplomatic efforts?"

"Yes."

"Care to elaborate?"

He smiled impishly. "No."

"Are you optimistic?"

"Actually, I am. But, just as Rose was a realist, so am I. I'm optimistic, but not overconfident."

Satisfied that I'd gotten the president to make a little breaking news, I moved back to his grief about Rose.

"This may sound like a cynical question, sir, but you know better than anyone that stagecraft is a big part of statecraft. Why are you choosing this particular moment – an international crisis and days before leaving for an important summit in China – to talk about something as personal as your grief?"

"I don't consider the question cynical at all, Lark. The point is that there's nothing more human than an excruciating loss. Everyone has experienced it. Pain is a universal experience. Probably the biggest lesson I'm learning from Rose's death is that pain and loss are central to the human experience and can be a catalyst for healing and connection."

"Connection?"

"Sure. If we, as citizens of the world, can recognize our common experiences, we're less likely to be intolerant of our differences."

"Some would say that's naïve."

He flinched, almost imperceptibly, but recovered quickly. "Yes. To the cynic, hope is naïve. And there's plenty going on in the world that can justify cynicism, but I'm a hopeful, realistic, optimist. I just am."

"Where does that hopefulness come from?"

"A lot of it comes from Rose."

This guy's good, I thought to myself. *He knows how to pivot back to The Talking Point.*

"And where do you suppose Rose got her hopefulness?"

He shrugged. "From her faith, I think."

"I grew up in the Episcopal Church, as she did," I said. "That's probably one of the few Christian denominations that's not doctrinaire or dogmatic. Cynics would call it 'the church of anything goes.'"

"Yes. Cynics would say that. But Rose wasn't a cynic."

"What role did you have in planning her funeral service?"

"None. It was all Rose."

"Scripture? Music?"

He nodded vigorously. "All Rose. She knew she was dying. 'Funerals aren't for the dead,' she told me once. 'They're for those of us who are left behind.'"

"So, in a sense, her funeral was the gift she left for us? For you?"

He nodded and I saw his lower lip tremble.

"I've been meaning to ask you about your eulogy."

"Uh huh."

"You listed so many of her attributes, but I noticed you left out one conspicuous one."

"Her beauty?"

"Yes! Why did you do that? I have a hunch, but I'd like to hear from you first."

"No. You go."

"No. This is about you, Mr. President." There was no way he was going to manipulate me into hand-delivering his answer. "You already know why you left it out so, you first with no prompting from me." I smiled.

He shifted in his chair and gave me a look I interpreted as *I'm glowering at you, but I don't really mean it.*

"Very well," he said simply. "There is no doubt that Rose was a gorgeous woman. But she didn't want to be defined by her looks. If there's anything I learned from her it's that women of substance, like Rose, despise being put on a pedestal. They want to be appreciated for their brains and their character."

I was nodding vigorously, and beaming.

"That's what you thought, right?" he asked.

"Yes. Thank you for clarifying that."

I glanced at the word prompts written in my reporter's notebook – I don't like to get bogged down reading my questions off the page like a script. I'd written *Lessons*.

"I know it's still early in the process, but what lessons have you learned so far from grief?"

He sighed heavily and studied the wood-beamed ceiling before answering. "First, grief is exhausting. And it's lonely. I keep coming back to how empty it is without Rose filling these rooms."

He paused, but I could tell he was looking for the right word, so I held back and waited for him to fill the silence.

Finally, he went on. "Probably the biggest lesson I'm learning is that grief really is – as you call it – a process. And that process is probably going to take a long time. The road ahead without Rose looks long, empty, and arduous. But I'm realizing that if I try to look too far into the distance, I'll get discouraged. It's like trying to climb a mountain. It's better to focus on the next step rather than on the countless ones it'll take to get to the top."

"How will you know when you've gotten to the top?"

"Good question. I don't like psychobabble words like closure. I think a better word is healing."

An important lesson I learned from Lionel about interviewing is to listen to what the person says and not be so hung up with asking all the questions on your list that you don't follow up on points the person makes that you didn't anticipate. This was one of those moments.

"Why don't you like the word closure and how do you define healing?" I asked.

"To me, closure sounds too neat and tidy. Grief, I'm finding, is messier than that. I don't think I ever want closure because it feels too much like I'm buttoning up my feelings for Rose and putting them away in a box. Grief is messy. And so is healing."

All of a sudden, I felt myself beginning to tear up. He was describing my own grief experience precisely. When he looked away briefly, I swiped away a tear that was about to cascade down my cheek.

Gannon continued to speak. "I haven't thought enough about the word healing in this context to give you a well thought out answer, but right now, I'd describe healing as having the emotional strength to move forward."

"If that's your definition, then it sounds like you're already healing."

"Yes. I guess you're right. But healing is a process. I'm not as strong now as I hope to be, but I can see that I'm stronger than I thought I'd be. And healing doesn't mean there won't be emotional scars."

"What do you miss most about her?"

Gannon immediately got a faraway look, tears welled in his eyes, and the shadow of a smile curled his upper lip. When he spoke, it was barely a whisper. "Her. I just miss her."

He started to say more, but stopped. Suddenly, Will Gannon, the President of the United States, the most powerful man in the world, buried his face in both hands and sobbed.

CB ◆ 80

CHAPTER 18

I sat stunned, frozen, unsure what to do. The stenographer looked shocked, too. We exchanged panicked glances, but she otherwise remained stoic and continued to hold the mic toward Gannon.

The president's entire body was heaving, but his sobs were silent. He hid his face behind his huge hands, the firelight reflecting off his wedding ring.

The White House photog behind me had been steadily shooting pictures as the president and I spoke, but right after the president put his hands to his face, I only heard one more shutter click – then silence.

As a reporter, I've been in plenty of situations where people cry, but this was a first. Not only had my interviewee broken down completely, but this was the Fricking President.

I'm a human being first and a reporter second so, as Will Gannon continued to weep, my own grief over Doug, and Jason, and Annie surged to the surface. In spite of my best efforts to remain stoic, the lump in my throat gagged me and tears spurted into my eyes. If you'd put a gun to my head, I wouldn't have been able to talk without weeping.

Finally, even before I regained my own composure, I reached out and gently touched Will Gannon on the arm.

I withdrew my hand as soon as I had established what I intended to be a comforting physical connection, but Gannon's silent sobs went on for at least another fifteen seconds. Eventually they slowed, he took several deep breaths, and finally removed his hands from his face.

His cheeks were red and wet with tears.

So were mine.

"Whew," he said. "That sure happened fast." He looked at me sheepishly. "I'm sorry, Lark."

"That's okay, sir," I said sniffing and swiping away my own tears. "I can relate."

Gannon looked at the photog and stenographer and then at me. "So, are we done here?"

I had a few more questions, but enough material to craft into a story.

"Of course. Thank you for your time, Mr. President."

The stenographer and photog left the room, but the president remained seated. A Secret Service agent stood silently at the door.

Gannon fished a handkerchief from the back pocket of his jeans and gave it to me. "Do you have dinner plans, Lark?"

I blew my nose – discreetly. "I haven't thought that far ahead. I still have to file my story." I handed him the hanky, but he waved me off.

"Keep it. A souvenir," he smiled. "Can you stick around?"

"Well, I—"

"Nothing fancy, just me and the kids."

"I have to file."

"And I need to spend some Dad Time with Grace and Thomas. Will two hours be enough time for you to file?"

"Sure."

"Good. You can work here." He gave me the password for the Wi-Fi, then added, "I'll send someone over to fetch you in a couple hours. It would be good to spend some time with you, plus I have some questions of my own for you about grief."

"I know you're a busy man, Mr. President. I don't want to intrude or waste your time."

"Nonsense. I'll be busy enough in the next few days getting ready for the summit – not to mention dealing with Dimitry. Presidents get to relax, too, don't they?"

I smiled. "I would hope so. I'd be honored to join you for dinner. Thank you, sir."

We stood, shook hands and then he and the Secret Service agent were gone.

I immediately banged out and filed an update on the Russia story – just a few lines:

President Gannon said today he is "optimistic, but not overconfident" that tensions can be eased with Russia.

In a brief, exclusive interview with the Associated Press at the presidential retreat at Camp David, Gannon described the situation with Russia as "delicate."

The president would not say if he has spoken directly to Russian President Dimitry Yazkov, but hinted that "quiet" diplomacy is going on "behind the scenes on many different levels to defuse the situation."

President Gannon is resting at Camp David following yesterday's funeral for his wife Rose at Washington National Cathedral. The first lady died suddenly Monday after a brief battle with pancreatic cancer.

Next week President Gannon leaves for Beijing where he'll meet with China's new President Tong Ji Hui.

The grief interview was more problematic. Gannon and I had only spoken for fewer than ten minutes before he broke down, so I played back the audio recording I made of the conversation and transcribed it. I also put a stopwatch on his sobbing. It took thirty-two seconds for him to regain his composure.

It took me more than an hour to write and file the grief story. I also filed the audio of my interview so the radio guys could chop it up and use sound bites for their hourly newscasts.

The one thing I like about working for a wire service is that the emphasis is on being factual, not fancy. Consequently, the story I wrote was a straightforward summary of Gannon's comments. The trick and the challenge is to come up with the lede (or lead) – the opening line of the story. Once I have that, everything else usually falls into place.

As a journalist, I've always been amused to see how many different ways various reporters begin their stories after having witnessed the same event. Their ledes depend on a lot of things: the editorial emphasis of the news organization, but also who the reporter is as a person – their values, experiences and, yes, even their biases.

I heard someone joke once that if a reporter had been present when Moses came down from Mt. Sinai, the lede would be, "God revealed Ten Commandments today, the most important of which is ..."

I toyed with several ways to lead the Gannon Grief story:

A day after burying his wife, President Will Gannon talked about his grief.

Nope. Too tepid.

I tried again.

President Gannon said today he's "coping" a day after burying his wife.

Nope. Too dispassionate.

I tried again. This time I considered a feminist angle:

President Gannon today explained why he didn't use the word "beautiful" when he eulogized his wife Rose at her funeral yesterday.

Nope. Too clunky. Plus, this isn't about me and my "issues."

Back to the drawing board.

As I pondered, I realized that on a subconscious level I felt myself wanting to protect the president and avoid calling attention to the moment when he lost his composure. Yet, the more I thought about it, that was the news.

President Will Gannon wept today as he described the loneliness he feels following the death of his wife Rose.

After I wrote that, the rest of the story flowed through my fingers. I wrote the 400-word piece in a fast thirty minutes, proofed it, then filed. Ten minutes later, a guy from AP Radio called and recorded a short interview with me to get my first-hand, personal observations.

After I hung up, I checked the WhiteHouse.gov website. A couple photos from our interview had just been posted – a wide two-shot taken from behind me showing Gannon and me sitting in front of the fire – him talking, me listening, plus a tight shot of the president's serious, earnest face, but nothing that showed his breakdown.

A recording of the interview and its transcript were also posted on the Briefing Room page after my story cleared the wire. I noticed that the clip didn't contain the lengthy dead air when he was crying. It simply ended with his last words: "Her. I just miss her."

I forwarded the photos to the AP National Desk in New York, making sure they credited the photo to the White House because the interview came about so suddenly, I wasn't able to get an AP photog to shoot the session.

I missed Doug a lot at that moment. He probably would be with me right now had he not . . . well . . . you know . . . .

My reverie about Doug was broken when one of the president's aides knocked on the cabin door. He was a young guy, maybe even a college intern, a hunch confirmed as I made chitchat with him on the short walk to Aspen Lodge, the private residence of the president when he's at Camp David.

The aide, Toby, whisked me past a stern Secret Service agent standing guard outside the front door of Aspen Lodge, and dropped me off at the kitchen where President Gannon and his two children were gathering.

"Hi, Lark," the president greeted me jovially. "We're just getting started."

The kitchen was bright, spacious, and modern. The president took a seat at the head of the table, flanked by Grace on his left and Thomas on his right sitting in a booster seat. A matronly Asian woman brought serving dishes from the stove and placed them on heating pads at the center of the table.

Gannon gestured for me to take a seat at the end of the table opposite him.

"Thank you, Olivia," the president said to the woman who I presumed was the cook. "We're dining in style tonight, Lark. Macaroni and cheese, plus—" he took the cover off one of the serving dishes with the flourish of a magician pulling a rabbit out of a hat – "HOTDOGS!"

"Yaaaaaay," Thomas and Grace shouted and clapped.

"Guys," the president said to his children, "this is my friend Lark Chadwick. She's going to hang out with us for a little bit."

"I want a popsicle," Thomas said.

"Maybe later for dessert," Gannon smiled. "Can you say hello to Lark?"

"Hel-lo," Thomas said. I could tell he liked me because his smile was coy and he kept sneaking glances at me, but he was too shy to maintain eye contact for more than a nanosecond at a time.

"And this is Grace," Gannon said, nodding toward his daughter who sat demurely, her face buried in a book.

"Hello, Grace," I said, extending my hand to her.

She smiled demurely and gave my hand a polite squeeze. "Hi." She then retreated back to her book.

I asked Grace, "What are you read—"

"I'm Thomas!" the boy interrupted. "I'm four years old!" He thrust out his hand. "Pleased to meet me."

I laughed and gave his hand an exaggerated shake. "Pleased to meet me, too, young sir."

"Put your book down now, Grace," Gannon said grasping both his children by the hand. "Let's pray, okay?"

Instinctively each child reached for my hand. I grasped theirs, completing the prayer circle around the table.

"God is great, God is good," the president began and his children fell into step and recited along with him. "And we thank Him for our food. By His hand we all are fed. Thank you, God, for daily bread."

"Amen," Grace said with her father.

"A-HEM!" Thomas added for emphasis. He gave me a sly glance to see if I was amused (I was) then he quickly looked away.

The table grace took me by surprise. It wasn't a habit in the home where I grew up back in Wisconsin. I was touched and felt honored to be part of this family tableau. I had to keep reminding myself that this was The First Family because they seemed so . . . well . . . normal.

In my typical reporter-as-barn-owl fashion, I did my best to sit back and watch the proceedings. Gannon bantered easily with both children. I could tell that they adored him.

In spite of my best effort at being aloof and unobtrusive, Grace and little Thomas lured me into their circle and made me feel at home.

Grace reminded me a lot of Rose, especially when the little girl turned to me and asked, "What do you do for a living, Miss Lark?"

"I'm a reporter. Do you know what a reporter is?"

She nodded. "They say bad things about my daddy."

I glanced at Gannon. He smiled impishly, but held his tongue. He seemed to be enjoying this and wanted to see how it turned out.

"Yes. I suppose some reporters do," I said, "But mostly we just tell people about the job your dad's doing."

That seemed to satisfy her and she shoveled another spoonful of mac and cheese into her mouth.

"What's the book you're reading? I asked her.

She swallowed. "This one," she stabbed a forefinger onto the front cover. "It's *Little House on the Prairie*."

"I read that," I said. "Do you like it?"

"Yes. I like Laura. She's a lot like me." Grace paused. "My mommy got me that book," she said softly. Suddenly, her face turned red, her lower lip quivered, and tears trickled down her cheeks.

Instinctively, I reached for her hand.

She took mine and gripped it, trying hard to be brave.

"I never knew my mommy," I said, tears welling in my eyes.

"Really?" she looked at me, surprised. "Why not? What happened?"

I glanced at the president. He, too, was struggling with his emotions.

"My mommy died in an accident when I was a little baby," I said, not sure if the concept of death would compute with an eight-year-old girl. "I miss your mommy, too," I added. "I liked her a lot."

"Who wants another hotdog?" Gannon asked, moving the conversation back to the emotional safety of the mundane.

"I do!" Thomas yelled.

"So," I asked the president, "who was keeping an eye on, ah, your youngest," I nodded discreetly toward Thomas, "during the, um, during the—" I paused, not wanting to say "funeral service."

Gannon rescued me. "During the event?" he asked.

"Yes. Thank you."

"Olivia's sister Octavia is their nanny," Gannon said. "They've both been a huge help."

Thomas, who'd been boisterous during the meal, was now getting fidgety. "I want to play with my trucks!"

Gannon looked at the boy's plate. "You didn't finish your applesauce."

"I don't like apsaw," Thomas announced.

"Okay. Eat one more spoonful of applesauce. Then you can go play. Who knows? Maybe this time you'll like it," Gannon said.

Thomas looked dubious, but scooped a tinsy bit onto a spoon, into his mouth, and swallowed.

"Nope." He made a face and put down the spoon. "I still don't like it." With that, Thomas slid out of his booster chair and scampered from the room.

"May I be excused?" Grace asked her dad. "I want to finish my book. It's right at the good part."

He checked her plate. Satisfied, he said, "Sure, sweetheart."

"It was a pleasure to meet you, Miss Lark," Grace said to me. She had regained her composure and was now a poised version of her mother. "Will you come back again? I'd love to talk about books with you sometime."

"That would be wonderful," I said. "We'll see."

She stood and stepped to a spot next to Gannon's chair.

"See you later, sweetie," Gannon said as he reached for her.

She held her arms out to him. He scooped her onto his lap and kissed her on top of her head.

Seconds later, both her arms were hugging him tightly around the neck. "I love you, Daddy."

"I love you, too, honey." He was crying.

So was I.

After a moment, Grace slid from his lap, grabbed her book from the table, and left the kitchen.

Gannon wiped away his tears, stood and began shuttling plates and glasses to the sink. I got up and helped. Olivia then loaded the dishwasher.

"They're adorable," I managed to whisper.

He smiled and nodded. "Were you able to file your story alright?"

"Yes. Everything went fine. Thank you again for making the time to talk about something so deeply personal and painful."

"Glad to do it," he said. "I think it was therapeutic."

I nodded.

Gannon said, "I know you have a life and probably need to get back to town soon, but do you have time to go for a short walk? It's beautiful up here at sunset, plus I'd like your advice."

If he only knew, I said to myself. Since Doug died, I not only don't have a life, but I feel myself drifting – maybe floundering is a better word. The idea of getting a degree in psychology was continuing to nag at me, but I didn't have a clear vision yet about how I'd use the degree. Plus the emptiness Gannon described during the interview felt all too familiar.

I liked this man. I liked being with him.

"Sure," I said. "Let's walk, but I have to say, offering advice to the president seems pretty daunting."

At the closet by the front door, he got out a windbreaker and put it on. I was wearing a fleece pullover and jeans. He'd already changed out of his moccasins and into hiking boots. I was still wearing my hiking boots from my morning walk with Muriel, so I was ready.

It was about 7:00. The sun would be setting in about a half hour. The shadows were lengthening and there was a chill in the air, but no breeze.

As we descended the stone steps of Aspen Lodge, the agent who'd been guarding the door walked behind us at a discreet distance. Gannon directed us toward a trail that led away from Aspen Lodge and into the woods.

"You were wonderful with Grace," Gannon said. "Thank you for that."

"She definitely took me by surprise." I shook my head. "I can only imagine how challenging it must be for you now – being president and a single dad."

"Yes. He said. "I'm just taking it one step at a time."

We walked a few more feet in silence, then he said, "Here's my question for you, Lark. The cliché is that time heals. I know you've already had more than your share of grief. Does time really heal?"

"Clichés got to be clichés because there's an element of truth to them," I said. "Yes. Time does heal, but the personal loss of a wife, or a lover, or a close family member changes you forever."

"If you don't mind my asking, how have those losses changed you?"

I didn't answer right away. We walked deeper into the forest in silence. The place was raucous with wildlife – birds, squirrels, gophers, even deer.

I thought back to when I found Annie's body. And Jason's. And Doug's.

"How have I changed?" I said, finally. "I'm still figuring that out, but I think I'm stronger now."

"In what way?"

"I'm less afraid of things. I've already experienced some of the worst life can dish out, yet I'm still standing, so I think I've learned to better discern between what's important and what's not. Little things are less likely to piss me off. I save my anger for the big stuff."

"Anger?"

"You've heard of the stages of grief?"

"Pioneered by Elizabeth Kübler-Ross? Of course. Isn't anger the first stage?"

"There aren't stages, per se, like there's some script that you must follow. Instead, anger is just one of the ways grief might manifest itself. "

"So, anger is sort of an offshoot of grief, or an aftershock?"

"Right. I think I was more prone to anger issues before and right after Annie died than I am now."

"Annie?"

"She's the aunt who raised me after my parents were killed in a car accident when I was a baby. Annie died of carbon monoxide poisoning. I found her body."

He touched my arm. "I'm sorry," he said.

"Thank you."

We walked in silence again. Soon we came to an outcropping of rocks that overlooked a spectacular valley. We stopped to look. The sun was nearing the horizon and as it sank lower, the light reflecting off the cottony clouds deepened the colors. It was like watching a painting that kept changing, getting more and more beautiful every minute.

The word "normal" kept ricocheting through my mind. Walking in the woods with a handsome man was a balm for me. I kept having to remind myself that this situation was anything but normal.

Yes, he had a delightful family. Yes, he was easy to talk with.

But, my head kept screaming at me, *This is so not normal. This guy is the President of the United States. We're not just walking in any old woods. This is Camp fucking David. And we're certainly not alone. We're being chaperoned by a heavily armed Secret Service agent.*

Not. Normal.

So, I asked myself, *why do I feel so comfortable?*

"Rose liked you a lot, Lark," Gannon said, breaking the silence and into my thoughts.

"It was mutual."

"I think that's why I enjoy talking with you. It's like you're a connection to her."

I nodded, but didn't know what to say.

We stood next to each other a few moments longer, then he said, "Okay. You say time does, indeed, heal. That's encouraging. And you say you're stronger. Good to know. How else has grief changed you?"

"I cry more easily now."

"Yeah. I get that," he said.

"For me, crying is like an emotional safety valve. It releases the pressure before the pain has a chance to build up and fester and corrode."

"Your loss is still pretty fresh, too, isn't it?"

I nodded. "Yes. Very."

"How are you doing?"

I shrugged. "Good days and bad. But there's one thing you said earlier that still hasn't changed for me."

"What's that?"

I turned to face him. "Lonely. Empty. I still feel that way, sir."

"It's Will," he said. "When we're alone, call me Will."

ೞ ◆ ೫

CHAPTER 19

It was Tuesday, my regular weekly counseling session with Kris. So much had happened during the past week that I spent a lot of time just bringing her up to date. Francine Noyce's assault seemed like ancient history.

I'd tried to move up my appointment to Monday, but Kris didn't have an opening in her schedule, so I had to wait until our regularly scheduled time on Tuesday morning. In the meantime, I tried to keep from navel gazing and stewing. I spent part of Sunday with Lionel and Muriel. I was excited about their move back to D.C., so hanging with them took my mind off myself.

Monday was quiet, but busy. The president planned to stay at Camp David until Wednesday when he'd be leaving for China. No public events were on his schedule, but Ron McClain told us Gannon would be meeting with his various advisors monitoring the crisis with Russia, and planning for the summit.

"Do you remember how we ended our session last week?" Kris asked.

I didn't, and gave her a confused look.

"We were talking about trust," she prompted.

"Trying to discern the difference between fake and real?"

"Right."

She waited.

I pondered. My gaze drifted to the small aquarium that stood next to the wall on my right. A few goldfish glided gracefully back and forth.

Kris waited some more.

Finally, I spoke. "Francine Noyce sure threw me for a loop. Didn't see that one coming at all. But the president took me by surprise, too."

"Oh? How?"

"In a lot of ways." I began ticking off examples on my fingers. "I was surprised he was willing to do the interview so soon after Rose's death, and in the middle of an international crisis. I was surprised that he seemed to have his grief so well in hand. I was surprised that he invited me to have dinner with him and his kids, then go for a walk." I paused. "And . . . ."

"And what?" she asked when my voice trailed off.

"And I was surprised he didn't make a move on me. Based on my experience, most guys would have."

"How do you feel about the fact that he didn't?"

"I'm relieved he didn't try anything," I said, decisively.

"Why?"

I reached into the box on the arm of the sofa and pulled out a handful of tissues, trying to buy some time as I groped for an answer and dabbed at my watering eyes.

"He knows I'm still emotionally fragile after Doug's death, yet he didn't try to take advantage of me. It tells me that even though he misses his wife, he isn't trying to anesthetize his emotional pain by having a fling with me."

"How do you feel about that?"

"I like him." My answer was immediate. And firm.

She nodded and cupped her chin in her hand, forefinger on her lower lip. "Go on." Her voice was soft and soothing.

"That sunset moment with him at Camp David was electric, Kris. There were definitely sparks between us. He'd allowed himself to be extremely vulnerable with me during the interview, so I think he, too, felt a connection to me."

"Did he say anything?"

"He said – and this is a quote – 'We should be getting back.' And then the moment was gone."

"Looking back on that moment, what new insights – if any – do you have about trust?"

"That's an interesting question." I took a moment to refluff the sofa cushions I'd been using as armrests. "It confirms to me that he's trustworthy."

"What do you mean?"

"He could have made a move, but chose not to. I, on the other hand, was in that situation despite my better judgment."

"What do you mean by 'better judgment.'"

She was making me think. That's why I liked her. All weekend and into Monday, I'd been avoiding just this question, consequently the answer remained lurking in my subconscious, waiting to be plumbed.

"My better judgment would have been to decline his invitation to dinner."

"Why?"

"Because by doing so I allowed myself to be lured into his family. His children are adorable. He loves them, he misses his wife, and he's a good dad."

"Why is it against your so-called 'better judgment' to let him – as you say – 'lure' you into the middle of his family circle?"

"Because that led to me accepting his invitation to go for a walk."

"Why did you agree to that, and, more importantly, why do you think it was unwise of you to walk with him?"

"I went on the walk because he said he wanted my advice about grief."

"And helping a grieving president is unwise because . . .?"

"Because I'm a reporter and he's my beat."

"So?"

I started to cry.

"Why are you crying?" she asked gently.

"Because I feel so confused."

"About what?"

"I'm a journalist, but I'm losing my emotional detachment."

"Is it only that?"

I bit my lip. "And I feel guilty."

"Why?"

"Because . . . Because . . . . "

"Because why?"

"Because he loves and misses Rose. And I miss Doug."

"But why does that make you feel guilty?"

"Because . . ." my lower lip was quivering spasmodically. I whispered, "Because I think I'm falling for him." I buried my face in my hands and sobbed.

Kris sat back and waited patiently for me to regain my emotional footing. It took me another five minutes – and then our session ran out of time.

CB ◆ EO

CHAPTER 20

By the time I left my counseling session with Kris, I'd pretty much pulled myself together. I had a doctor's appointment up the street in Kensington, so I'd driven into D.C. from Silver Spring in the morning rather than take the Metro.

As is my habit when I drive, I talk to my car. I've named her Pearlie because she's a yellow V.W. Beetle, and yellow reminded me of a pearl. It made sense at the time.

"Kris really makes me think, Pearl."

Pearlie never answers, but she's a good listener – a lot like Kris.

"Yes. It's true. I think I've fallen for Will. But nothing's happened, so I think if I lean back, I'll be fine. I know I'm being delusional. Sure, we have sparks, but he's still in love with Rose. Plus – he's the fricking president. Half the women in the world are in love with him."

I got a text from Paul while I was in the waiting room: *Hey! I need to talk later. When u free?*

I have a doctor's appointment. I'll give u a shout when I'm done, I replied.

I was going to be on the president's trip to China, so I was glad to be getting my counseling session and physical out of the way before leaving tomorrow.

I like my doctor. She's a woman. Call me sexist, but whenever I can, I always choose women – especially if I'm inviting them to inspect my privates.

Dr. Nadira Ashkani and I bantered during my routine exam. She's Pakistani. She was excited to hear about the upcoming presidential trip I'd be on to China, but as the exam went on, she became increasingly quiet – even concerned. Her forehead furrowed as she typed her notes into the HMO's computer system.

"How are things looking?" I finally asked.

She set aside the keyboard and scooted her rolling stool so that she faced me as I sat at the end of the examining table, my bare feet dangling and swinging slightly.

"You're going to have a baby," she said simply.

My feet stopped swinging.

଼ ◆ ଼

CHAPTER 21

"I can tell by your reaction that this news is unexpected." Dr. Ashkani scooted her stool closer to me. "Are you alright?"

I sat at the end of the examining table, still in the hospital gown, my mouth agape. "I-I don't know."

She rolled herself a few feet away and selected several pamphlets from a rack mounted on the wall, then she rolled back to me.

"Here," she said, handing them to me. "You might find these very helpful. There are some big changes ahead for you – and some big decisions."

I shuffled through the pamphlets, but I couldn't focus on them. "How can this be?" I finally managed to whisper.

"Do you know who the father is?" she asked.

I nodded dumbly. "I do, but he's dead."

"Oh, dear. I'm so sorry."

"I-I don't know what to do."

"These pamphlets might help," she said again. "Have you been experiencing morning sickness?"

I shook my head. "No, but come to think of it, my stomach's been churning more than usual. I was just attributing it to getting a whiff of something that smelled bad, like the kielbasa stench that comes from those sidewalk vendors."

She nodded. "Yes. Smell can trigger morning sickness."

"Is there medicine I should take?"

"Not unless your nausea gets really bad." She grabbed another pamphlet and handed it to me. "My advice? Saltine crackers."

"Really?"

"Yep. That's what got me through my pregnancy two years ago." She pointed to the pamphlet. "There's a lot of practical stuff in there that'll help."

"Thanks."

"Do you have any other questions for me?"

"When? When's the baby due?"

"You're about six weeks along, so probably in November."

My mind was racing, spinning – too fast for me to focus.

Dr. A rolled herself back to the computer and typed some more. "I'm referring you to gynecology. They'll be able to answer all your questions, once you've had time to let the news sink in."

She printed out a few pages, stood, and handed them to me.

"Thank you," I said, automatically.

"This can be extremely overwhelming, I know," she said gently, "but we can help you."

"Okay. Thank you." I felt like an empty-headed moron.

She left and I was alone. I don't even remember getting dressed.

ℭ ◆ ℬ

CHAPTER 22

The next thing I remember is when my phone went off signaling a text from Paul. I'd been sitting, numb, in Pearlie in the HMO parking garage, still trying to absorb the news. Was it good news? I wasn't sure.

Hey, you done at the doc's yet? Paul texted.

Yeah. Got some bombshell news. We need to talk, I replied.

More and more, Paul was feeling like the brother I'd never had. He'd already confided some pretty heavy stuff, so I felt I could use him as a sounding board, as well.

I didn't want to talk with him in our cramped cubicle at the White House, or in a crowded place like a pub or restaurant, so we agreed that I'd pick him up at 17th and Pennsylvania and then we'd walk the National Mall.

"So, how was your time with the doc?" he asked when he got into the car.

I turned to him, tears streaming down my face, and gave him a look.

"Oh. Okay," he said. "We'll talk."

He was quiet for the drive to Ohio Street near the Lincoln Memorial where I was able to find a place to park along the Potomac.

"Let's go sit by the water," he suggested.

Reluctantly, I dragged myself from behind the wheel. My feet felt like they were stuck in sandbags.

The day was beautiful. We found a place to sit in the grass and looked west across the river. The late afternoon sun felt good.

"You needed to talk?" I asked.

"I do, but you go first. Seems like your news is more important."

"I'm pregnant, Paul."

"Oh my God." He touched me lightly on the arm.

"Yeah."

"It's Doug's, right?"

"There are no other candidates."

"How do you feel about it?"

"Numb, I guess. I have no feelings."

"A minute ago you were crying."

As if on cue, I began crying again. "I don't know. Maybe I've got too many feelings to sort out."

Paul waited until I caught my breath. "Try one. What was your reaction when you heard the news?"

"Stunned. Surprised."

"You had no inkling?"

"None. My stomach had been a little woozy, but I never made the connection."

"Missed period?"

"Late. But I've always been erratic." I laughed wryly.

Paul looked confused.

"Erratic," I said. "Story of my life – a sick metaphor, obviously."

Paul was quiet, letting the news sink in and, because his mind works like mine, I assumed he was trying to figure out his next question.

We watched a kayak glide downstream.

Finally, he spoke: "How do you feel about the idea of being a single mom?"

He was being diplomatic. I probably would have been more blunt and asked "Are you planning to keep it?"

"That's what's throwing me. It's so overwhelming – and so unplanned. I've literally never given any thought to being a parent, let alone a single one."

He touched my hand. "I'm so sorry, Lark. I want to be helpful, but this is way out of my league. Have you thought about talking with my mom?"

"I haven't even thought that far ahead, but yes, talking with Muriel makes total sense. Thank you."

Paul had been more helpful than he realized. He asked just the right questions, in just the right way. It must have required a lot of wisdom and inner strength to resist a reporter's tendency to probe relentlessly. He'd helped me identify and articulate my first reactions. Muriel, I decided, would be the person to help me think through the next steps.

I felt myself relax – at least a little, enough to turn my attention to Paul and away from myself.

"Now you," I said. "What did you want to talk about?"

He stood suddenly. "Let's walk."

I didn't feel quite so weighted down, so I was game. I got up and we walked north along the riverbank, crossed Independence and walked along 23rd, the short street that leads to the Lincoln Memorial, now looming in front of us.

Once we'd successfully dodged traffic, it was my turn to get Paul talking. "What did you want to talk about?"

"My folks."

We walked to the steps on the east side of the Lincoln where Martin Luther King, Junior delivered his "I Have a Dream" speech in 1963. There's now a small, circular, bronze marker embedded into the marble marking the place where he stood as he looked out at the Washington Monument and U.S. Capitol in the distance.

There are a lot of steps – and a lot of tourists on them – so we didn't speak again until we got to the top.

Instead of ducking into the Greek-style temple to pay homage to the iconic sculpture of Abraham Lincoln, Paul led us around to the backside colonnade that faced the Potomac River and Virginia.

There were fewer tourists over here. He sat next to one of the huge Doric columns. I joined him and we dangled our legs over the side, swinging them as we watched the beginning of the rush-hour exodus cross Memorial Bridge. The gleaming white Kennedy Center was to our right.

"I thought your parents took the news about you and Alex relatively well," I said.

He turned to look at me, unconvinced.

"Didn't you?" I asked.

"It could've been worse, that's true," he said. "Dad's still not talking to me."

"He'll come around," I said, channeling Muriel.

Paul shrugged. "Yeah. Maybe. But Friday night was only my opening gambit."

"You mean there's more?"

He nodded.

"Are you and Alex getting married?"

"Maybe," he said. "It all depends."

"On what?"

"On how Alex feels about me being a woman trapped in a man's body."

"I'm not following you."

Paul turned to look at me. "I'm actually trans, Lark. I'm not really Paul, I'm Paula."

"Whoa!"

"Yeah."

That was a shocker, so I sat silently with the news a moment before I asked, "You are trans, or you think you are?"

He answered immediately. "Oh, I are."

"How do you know?"

"I started cross dressing at a very young age. I kept it secret, of course, but I was always more interested romantically in boys than girls."

"What about the crush you had on me?"

"I think that for a long time I've been confused about my sexual identity."

"So, Alex doesn't know?"

He shook his head. "I plan to tell him tonight. I can tell him anything. But I wanted to tell you first."

"Thank you, but why?"

"You may not believe this, especially now, but I feel that you're not only strong, but you're wise and you're honest."

I scowled. "You're right: I don't believe it. But I'll take the compliment. Thank you."

"So, what do you think?" he asked.

"I think you need to take your time with this and really think it through before you do anything drastic. It's one thing to be gay, or bisexual. It's quite another to physically change your gender. That's a huge step."

"I know."

"What's your plan?"

"Step one was to tell you. Step two: tell Alex." He paused, thinking. He looked unsure.

"Step three?"

"That's where I get stuck."

"Do you want my unsolicited opinion?"

"Absolutely! Yes!!"

"Go slow. Tell Alex, but hold off on telling your mom and dad. You've already given them plenty to absorb. In the meantime, I strongly urge you to talk with a counselor."

"A shrink?" He frowned. "I'm not crazy, Lark."

"I didn't say you are. And I don't believe you are. A psychologist – especially someone who specializes in this subject – will be able to help you think things through."

He thought about it. "Yeah. Maybe you're right. It makes sense. Thanks."

As we got up and returned to Pearlie, I wished I could see my way forward as clearly as I was able to advise Paul.

೫ ♦ ৶

CHAPTER 23

Air Force One is frickin' huge. It's amazing to me how this thing even gets off the ground, let alone stays in the air.

And it literally gleams. I saw a documentary on it and learned that they don't wash it down because it would leave water spots, so it's polished by hand. The job requires more than 200 rags and all of them have to be accounted for before the plane is allowed to take off.

It was six a.m. Wednesday. The sun wasn't even up yet. I stood at the foot of the stairs craning my neck to look up at the gigantic presidential aircraft. It's as tall as a six-story building.

I was part of the travel pool, so I'd be riding in the press section in the rear of the plane for the 14-hour flight to Beijing, punctuated with stops in Georgia, California, and Hawaii where President Gannon would give pep talks to U.S. troops.

President Gannon had just arrived and bounded up the steps near the front. He paused at the top, turned to give a jaunty wave for the cameras, then ducked into the cavernous plane.

The rest of us mere mortals were herded up the rear stairs. This was my first flight aboard the flying White House. A steward handed me a certificate with my name on it noting the "first."

On the Fancy Scale, the press section is a notch down from First Class, but decidedly more comfortable than Economy. Two tan leather bucket seats are on each side of the aisle. The seats don't recline and there are no individual television screens, but we get complimentary packets of red, white, and blue M&Ms embossed with the presidential seal.

I was just settling into my seat when I got an email notification from Media Bash:

BREAKING NEWS:

ROSE GANNON POISONED!!

My jaw dropped. I don't consider Media Bash a reliable source for anything, yet I felt it was my duty to keep up with it, not only because they'd begun trolling me, but because the website had about twenty million followers – it was incredibly influential.

"Holy shit!" someone sitting behind me exclaimed, as the news began spreading through the press pool.

I read quickly, my emotions jangling.

> A reliable source tells Media Bash that an unspecified poison was found in the system of first lady Rose Gannon when she was autopsied last week. Gannon died suddenly ten days ago of what was said to be pancreatic cancer.

> Lark Chadwick of the Associated Press was with Gannon when she collapsed and died at the White House. Chadwick had been keeping secret the news Gannon was dying of pancreatic cancer.

> It will now be interesting to see if Chadwick's reporting continues to protect our hunky president by hiding the news that his beloved wife was murdered.

Obviously, whoever wrote the Media Bash piece doesn't even have a nodding acquaintance with what objective – not to mention accurate – reporting really is (Rose died at GW Hospital, not at the White House), but ever since Donald Trump's presidency, the reliability of journalism and journalists has been undermined so much that more trust is put into narratives that reinforce the "fake news" bias.

The Media Bash piece was irresponsible on so many levels: they based their reporting on only one unnamed source, but it amounted to a gratuitous ad hominem attack on me.

Even so, the news was so explosive, all of us in the press pool felt the need to at least try to match or advance the story.

Several of us bolted from our seats and scrambled forward to the section of the plane carrying the White House staff. We clamored for a statement from Ron McClain, but he was behind closed doors and unavailable.

I sent Ron a desperation text, hoping I could get something on the record so I could at least file something before we took off – but got nada – then sent Scotty Barrington a quick email:

> Tried to confirm the Media Bash story alleging that Rose Gannon was poisoned. Ron McClain mum.

Recommend we keep digging, but hold off on going with anything until we can confirm (but you already know that).

Scotty replied with a terse, "Agreed."

And then Air Force One began taxiing down the runway of Andrews Air Force Base. The ride is so smooth that had I not been looking out the window, I wouldn't even have been aware that we'd taken off.

The sun was just coming up as we went wheels up. There's something restful about being able to look down on Washington, D.C. It felt like I was leaving all of life's turmoil behind in the rapidly receding distance.

But it only felt that way for a moment. Once we got above the clouds, I was alone with my thoughts – and my music.

My music is an eclectic mix of classic jazz from the sixties, rock, R&B, some hip-hop, and even pop. Most of my playlist has an emphasis on what I call my "Power Girl Music" from artists like Dorothy, Selena Gomez, Beyoncé, and Grace Potter.

I put in my ear buds and settled in with something by Norah Jones called "Man of the Hour" – an amusing ode to a dog.

My thoughts were a jumble of personal concerns and professional responsibilities. I was finding it hard to focus.

So far, only Paul knew I was pregnant. Talking with him had been extremely comforting – but it was only a start. I'd have to wait until next week to talk to Muriel – and Kris. In the meantime, all I could do was sit and stew.

Every time I tried to think rationally about being pregnant, it was like trying to open a balky program on my laptop – it would open for a nanosecond and then default to a blank screen. I finally came to the realization that whatever was going on inside me was being processed somewhere in my subconscious, out of view and out of reach of my rational mind. Whatever.

Since talking with Kris about my feelings about Will (yes, in my mind, I was calling him by his first name), I found myself thinking about him a lot. But every time I did, I scolded myself for being such a child. Yet, I couldn't deny the connection I'd felt – and strongly sensed that he did, too.

Before we parted at Camp David, he'd given me his personal cell number, but I was determined not to take advantage of the special access I now had. I still needed to think through where my professional responsibilities as a reporter ended, and my personal feelings could begin. At this point, I felt they must stay separate, but I was feeling myself slipping. I realized I also needed to talk with Lionel to get a strong and bracing reality check.

Blurring those feelings was the bombshell about Rose. Was it possible that she'd been poisoned? If so, how, and by whom?

Our next chance to see the president – and shout questions at him – would be in two hours at Fort Benning, Georgia.

CB ◆ BO

CHAPTER 24

We were only on the ground at Fort Benning for less than an hour as the president made brief remarks to the troops in a noisy and cavernous hangar. The traveling press pool (me and a handful of my print and broadcast colleagues) were kept far enough away from the prez so that we couldn't shout embarrassing *"was-Rose-poisoned?"* questions at him.

Not that we would have.

Or would we?

Yeah. We probably would.

While Gannon was glad-handing, I cornered Gannon's press secretary Ron McClain.

"C'mon, Ron. What gives about the Media Bash story that says Rose was poisoned?"

"Sorry, Lark, I've got nothing for you on that." He turned away, but I tugged at the sleeve of his sport coat.

"Have you seen the autopsy report?" I asked.

"No."

"Let me back up. When did the CDC do the autopsy?"

"I don't know for sure."

"Can you find out?"

"Sure."

"Will you find out?"

He gave me an annoyed look.

After I filed my piece about the president's Fort Benning remarks, but before we were wheels up, I called the bureau to give Scotty Barrington a heads up.

"Hey, Lark. What's up?"

"I'm with the president in Georgia."

"I know. I just okayed your piece for the wire."

"They wouldn't let us get close to the prez, so we weren't able to ask about the Media Bash story."

He grunted. "I don't know if screaming questions about a sketchy and explosive story is such a great idea anyway."

"Yeah. You're probably right. I was thinking of phrasing my question innocuously."

"Like how?"

"Do you have a comment on the Media Bash story about Rose?"

"Yeah. That might work. Once he comments, that legitimizes the story and we can run with it."

"Exactly."

"Which is why he won't comment. He's too smart for that."

"Sometimes I miss Trump. Sometimes."

"What's McClain saying?" Scotty asked.

"He was unavailable during the flight here, but I got him alone for a minute while Gannon was on the ground."

"And?"

"He said, and this is a quote: 'I've got nothing for you.'"

"Yeah. That figures."

"He said he didn't read the autopsy report and doesn't even know when the CDC did it."

"We checked," Scotty said. "She was autopsied the morning after she died."

"What's the report say?"

"Dunno. It's sealed."

"Sealed?" I asked, surprised.

"Right."

"Who ordered it sealed?"

"The family, according to the CDC."

"'The family.' That would be President Will Gannon, right?"

"Uh huh."

"Smells," I said.

"It does."

"McClain told me he'd check into it."

"He's stalling."

"Yup. So now what?"

"We've filed a FOIA"

Scotty pronounced it FOY-ah. It's a routine request for government documents under the Freedom of Information Act.

"That's probably our only hope. Think it'll do any good?" I asked.

"It's worth a try."

"The government will stonewall."

"They always do."

"Will you go to court when they do?"

"Yeah. I think so," he said. "It's not my call, but I'll argue forcefully that we do. If it's true that she was poisoned, it's a huge story."

"Has anyone else picked it up yet?"

"Nope. Just Media Bash and some fringe anti-media groups, but nothing mainstream."

"There's a lot of interest here in the pool."

"Keep digging."

"We're wheels up to California next. I'll do my best to see if I can get any more during the flight. I'll call you again from Cali."

"Okay, Lark. Safe travels."

"Thanks, Scotty."

When I got back to my seat on Air Force One, I took out my phone and gave it a good, long look. Gannon had given me his personal phone number when we were at Camp David. My heart began beating faster as I considered my options.

At times like these, there are two Lark Chadwicks inside me, both arguing for the upper hand in my decision making:

RESPONSIBLE LARK: Don't text him.

SELFISH LARK: Why not?

RESPONSIBLE LARK: Because he probably gave you his cell number as a personal gesture.

SELFISH LARK: So?

RESPONSIBLE LARK: So, it means he'd get pissed if you took advantage of his personal gesture to crassly work a story.

SELFISH LARK: But if it's a "personal" gesture, then he wants me to get personal with him.

RESPONSIBLE LARK: Yeah. Maybe. But that's the problem.

SELFISH LARK: What's the problem? He's a hunk and he's into me.

RESPONSIBLE LARK: Yeah. And that's the problem.

SELFISH LARK: No. It's not.

RESPONSIBLE LARK: Yes. It is.

SELFISH LARK: Why?

RESPONSIBLE LARK: Because if you text him about a story you're working, then you're taking advantage of his generosity. You're being selfish.

SELFISH LARK: But if you text him and say, "Hey, you little stud muffin. Let's hang," that's not you being selfish?

RESPONSIBLE LARK: I would never do that because I'm too—

SELFISH LARK: ...boring.

RESPONSIBLE LARK: I was going to say "responsible."

SELFISH LARK: Still boring.

RESPONSIBLE LARK: [Silent. Sulking.] Besides, who says "stud muffin"?

SELFISH LARK: [Smelling blood and moving in for the kill]: So, let me see if I understand this. Because you're so responsible—

RESPONSIBLE LARK: I hear that cynical tone.

SELFISH LARK: Don't interrupt.

RESPONSIBLE LARK [petulantly]: But you did!

SELFISH LARK: Yes, but I was being selfish. It's my nature.

RESPONSIBLE LARK [sighing]: Go on.

SELFISH LARK: As I was saying – Explain to me how you're being a responsible journalist if you decide not to use the special access you have with the president to check out the bombshell story that his wife was murdered.

RESPONSIBLE LARK: Um . . . .

SELFISH LARK: Right. Just as I thought. Try using the I-was-just-being-responsible argument on Scotty Barrington when you get scooped by Reuters.

My thumbs were trembling as I typed this text to Will Gannon:

It's Lark. I need to talk with you. Alone. It's urgent.

I took a deep breath to keep from hyperventilating, then hit *send.*

SELFISH LARK [smugly]: Nicely done, Lark. But you're so selfish.

CS ◆ ⵉⵎ

CHAPTER 25

I was still jittery after sending the text to the prez. I checked my phone every few minutes before we took off to see if he'd responded, but got crickets. I tried to read, but my mind kept wandering. Finally, I tried to sleep.

Have you ever tried to sleep? Dozed was about as good as I could do. But it must've worked because I jolted to alertness when Air Force One touched down at Los Angeles Air Force Base in El Segundo, California near LAX.

The base is the headquarters of the Air Force's Space and Missile Command (SMC). Until this trip, I'd never heard of it but, according to a handout from the White House press office, it's been around in various configurations since 1954 when the Cold War was hot.

Right now SMC specializes in, among other things, Global Positioning Systems and something called the Remote Sensing Systems Directorate whose mission is to "develop, deploy, and sustain surveillance capabilities in support of missile warning and missile defense."

That got those of us in the press pool wondering if this stop had anything to do with the current crisis with Russia.

As usual, the traveling press pool was herded off the plane and positioned at the foot of the stairs to chronicle Gannon's arrival. California is bright in the middle of the afternoon. Even brighter if you forget to bring your sunglasses – which I did. Actually, I didn't forget them because I don't own a pair. I think it has something to do with my prejudice against "Hollywood types" (my term) who hide their eyes behind shades of aloofness. Geez. I can be so judgmental sometimes. I don't like that about myself.

It seemed like we were standing around on one foot for hours, but Gannon finally appeared at the top of the stairs and waved at the large crowd that had turned out to catch a glimpse of their commander-in-chief. A roar of warmth and excitement erupted from the crowd when they saw Gannon. He paused at the top of the stairs and seemed to bask in the adulation of the crowd, which included spouses and children of all ages.

Gannon bounded down the stairs to greet the governor and other dignitaries. Once again, the whine of the engines made it impossible for us to shout questions at the prez, so we stood mute as the pool photogs got their pictures.

Just as he did in Georgia, Gannon made brief remarks to pump up the morale of the troops and their families, then he did what he does best: came out from behind the blue podium with the presidential seal and immersed himself into the throng of people who heartily shook his hand and posed for selfies with him. I'd just seen his deep agony over Rose's death, so it amazed me to see him so upbeat.

Either this guy fakes it really well, or the crowds energize him, I thought to myself. *Or both.*

Once again, Gannon didn't, as we in the pool liked to say, "commit news," but the pictures of him surrounded by an adoring crowd were a press agent's wet dream.

Less than an hour after arriving in California, the president was gliding up the stairs to Air Force One where he gave a parting salute at the top before ducking back inside the magnificent blue, white, and gold flying White House. When I got back to my seat, I filed a quick four-paragraph piece chronicling the president's appearance, then called Scotty Barrington.

"I see the president managed to avoid the limelight while basking in it," Scotty observed.

"Yep. No news is good news for him. I've still got nuthin' on the poisoning story. How 'bout you?"

"Things are moving faster than either one of us thought."

"Oh? How so?"

"While you were in the air between Georgia and California, our bosses in New York went to federal court in Washington to force the unsealing of Rose Gannon's autopsy report."

"I didn't see anything about it on the wire."

"We're not reporting it yet."

"Why not?"

"We don't want to make it into a federal case."

I laughed.

"I know. Bad joke. But seriously, yes, it's a federal case, but at this point we don't really know if it's a story, or not."

"Has the judge ruled?"

"Not yet. He's taking the arguments of both sides under advisement."

"What's the government's argument?"

"That the report needs to remain sealed for – quote – 'national security reasons.'"

"How can the death of a first lady threaten the nation's security?"

"Good question."

"Which I'm sure was asked in court."

"Yes. But it wasn't answered – at least not out in the open. There was then an off-the-record session with the judge in his chambers, but only the lawyers know what was said and they're gagged by the judge."

I thought for a moment. "I'm thinking out loud, here, Scotty: if Rose Gannon was murdered, and if her murder is a national security matter, then to me that means that a foreign power might have been behind her death."

"Agreed. Our argument is that by not publishing innuendo and conjecture, we're demonstrating our ability to be responsible and restrained in the investigation of the story."

I finished his thought. "And that investigating the story doesn't mean that we would report the story if it, indeed, threatened national security."

"Yeah. That's pretty much it."

"I'm trying to get a one-on-one with the prez."

"Good luck with that," he snorted.

"I hear your lack of confidence."

He laughed. "But on the off chance that you get some time with him, what's your game plan?"

"Hmmmmm. Not sure. I'll probably wing it. Speaking of which, we're taxiing now, so I'm about to lose our connection. Next stop Hawaii. I'll call you from there."

"Ah, no you won't."

"Why not?"

"Because it'll be two in the morning here in D.C."

"Oh."

"Call me from Beijing."

"Okay."

"Safe travels, Lark."

"Bye, Scotty."

Air Force One roared down the runway and into the air, then banked west. I sat back, put in my ear buds, cranked up my music (Beyoncé), and watched the plane's shadow scurry off the beach and out to sea, the late afternoon sun glistening like diamonds off the surface of the Pacific.

I must have been dozing again when a light tap on the shoulder jolted me awake. I turned to see Ron McClain standing in the aisle looking down at me. He crooked his finger in a silent come-hither signal.

I pulled the ear buds from my ears, unbuckled, and scrambled out of my seat.

"Come with me," McClain whispered in my ear.

"What's up?"

"The president would like to have a chat with you."

Instinctively, I checked my phone. I'd forgotten to recharge it and the dwindling battery power was below twenty-percent.

Shit.

CB ◆ BO

CHAPTER 26

I felt the eyes of every reporter on the plane burning into my back as Ron McClain led me toward the front of the plane and the presidential quarters on Air Force One. I could only imagine the deep-seated anger and jealousy a simple walk down the aisle could evoke in a highly competitive press corps.

My colleagues and I chafe at being in a bubble. We hate being spoon fed factoids that will make the administration – any administration – look perfect. I knew instinctively that after I left the presidential presence the other reporters on the trip would pummel me with questions about what the prez said. So, even before I talked with the president, I began praying that I could deflect their questions without lying.

Carpeting at the front of the plane is gray with a pattern of blue stars denoting that we're now in the president's personal space. A stern, burly Secret Service agent stood guard at the door to the president's cabin. The guy looked me up and down, but that was it.

McClain rapped sharply on the door twice, then opened it and entered when a muffled voice I couldn't decipher called out from inside.

As I followed Ron into the room, I shivered at the flashback from less than a week ago when I entered the flying bedroom of Francine Noyce aboard her private jet. But this time I wasn't alone. And I wasn't entering the president's bedroom.

President Gannon was sitting behind a brown desk, placed diagonally a few steps inside on the left. The desk was angled so that it partly faced the door and partly faced the rest of his office. The room could seat six comfortably including three on a brown leather sofa.

"Hi, Lark." Gannon stood and came around the right side of the desk and shook my hand. He wore a navy-blue windbreaker with the presidential seal emblazoned over his heart and *Will Gannon* stenciled in white cursive over his right breast.

"Good afternoon, Mr. President. Thank you for agreeing to meet with me."

Gannon looked at McClain. "Ron, would you mind leaving Lark and me alone for a few minutes?"

McClain looked surprised at being sidelined. His face reddened and he started to reply, stopped himself, then said simply, "Of course, sir."

Before turning to go, Ron gave me a laser stare that instantly made me realize he did not like being left out of the loop, and implying that I must have done an underhanded end run around him.

McClain left. Gannon and I were alone.

The president gestured at the leather sofa. "Please. Sit down."

I sat on the side closest to his desk by an end table with a lamp on it. Gannon chose to sit in a colossal easy chair in front of me that was to the left of his desk.

As I pulled out my iPhone and notebook, he waved them off. "Let's just talk informally," he said.

"Off the record?" I asked.

"Let's just talk." He sat back and crossed his legs. He was wearing jeans and those moccasins again.

"But you're the president. What you say is important. It makes news. News I'm supposed to report."

"But can't a president have a friend who also happens to be a reporter?"

"I'm not sure I know how it would or could work," I said.

The president answered his own question. "Seems to me JFK cultivated a pretty good personal relationship with Ben Bradlee of the *Washington Post*, even though the *Post* was still able to cover the president objectively. Later Bradlee wrote a book about it. *Conversations with Kennedy.* You should read it."

This was news to me. I made a mental note to ask Lionel about this. He'd known Bradlee, and certainly had strong feelings about the power of presidents to manipulate. Yet gregarious Lionel was still able to maintain cordial relations with some of the people he covered. But friendships? I'd have to ask.

I didn't have a ready comeback. I simply shrugged. *Why am I tongue-tied?* I asked myself. *Am I allowing my personal feelings, my visceral attraction to this man, undermine my usual clear-headedness?*

Before I could answer my own question, the president continued speaking. "Thank you again for the excellent questions you asked about grief. You made me think. I like that."

"Thank you, sir. And thank you for dinner. Your children are adorable – and I love hotdogs."

He laughed. "It was good to walk and talk with you. You're easy to talk with, Lark. I hope we can continue to talk from time to time. Rose adored you. Even though I enjoyed being a part of at least a few of your discussions with her, I must say I envied the way she was able to be so free with you."

"She was special. We had a great rapport. I miss that. I miss her."

"Yes."

"So, why did you agree to meet with me?"

"Just to talk. It's a long way to Hawaii, six hours. My head is crammed with facts from briefing books. I felt I could treat myself to a break to just sit with you and shoot the breeze."

I looked at him skeptically over the top of my glasses. "With all due respect, Mr. President. I'm not buying that. You know full well that I'm a reporter. And you, sir, are an effective communicator.   Let's cut the bullshit." I smiled, but I was dead serious. "You gave me your personal number and I used it to reach out to you. You know I want to talk. And you probably even know what I want to talk about."

He gave me his best hurt-puppy-dog expression, but I could tell he was kidding.

"Okay," he said, turning serious. "I'll cut the bullshit. Obviously, I know you're a reporter. A reporter who smells a story. But you're also a trusted friend."

"Believe me, Mr. President, under different circumstances, I'd love to be your friend. And maybe some day that will be possible when we're no longer wearing the hats we wear."

"But you were Rose's friend."

"Yes. I was. It was a relationship of trust. But I was still a reporter. And, as you may know, I've been taking some heat for keeping her secret."

"Do you regret going off the record with her?"

"No."

"Would you agree to have a similar arrangement with me?"

"What do you mean?"

"I, too, would like to be able to talk freely with you – in a relationship of trust – without having to fear that our private discussions will become public."

"I'd like that, too. But I can't promise you that."

"Why not?"

"The understanding I had with Rose was that one day our conversations could very well become public, but not until she was ready. Circumstances intervened, obviously, but I kept my word to her."

He bit his lower lip. "Yes. I see what you mean." He thought a moment, then went on. "I've heard it said somewhere that once you've cried with someone, it creates a special bond."

He looked at me to gauge my reaction.

I was a sphinx.

"We've cried together," he said simply.

"Yes. We have," I said softly. I had to stifle a sudden surge of emotion.

"I can't speak for you," he said, "but I feel we have a special bond."

"I won't argue with that, Mr. President, but – forgive me for being blunt – so what?"

He flinched. "Excuse me?"

"I don't mean to be rude, sir. Nor do I mean to minimize your grief – or mine. But I've got a few warning bells going off right now."

"Really? Why?" He seemed genuinely clueless.

I started to reply, but he uncrossed his legs, leaned forward, and touched my hand briefly to stop me.

"Actually," he said, "I think I do understand." He sat back. "Rose told me that one reason she liked you and felt she could confide in you was because she could tell you weren't the kind of woman who was susceptible to, um, presidential charms."

I smiled. "Yes. She told me that, too."

"So, I think I understand what you mean. Your so-called warning bells are suggesting to you that I'm trying to . . . " he paused, groping for the right word.

"You certainly wouldn't be the first powerful man who's tried – and failed – to seduce me. And I'm not suggesting that that's what you're doing." I gestured toward the empty room. "I'm only saying the circumstances are conducive to seduction, but I feel I need to make it clear that as attractive a man as you are, I'm still a professional journalist and a woman with enough dignity and self-respect to make it clear to you that if you had any of those motives of seduction – and if you acted on them – they would not be reciprocated."

"Okay. Good." He nodded resolutely. "I'm glad we're clear on that. Now, since you're the one who reached out to me, and it's not to shoot the breeze and get to know each other, what is it that you wanted to talk about?"

I got right to the point. "Are the reports true that Rose's autopsy report says she was poisoned?"

"Off the record?"

"No."

"Then I can't answer," he said, then pursed his lips.

We stared at each other. Glared is probably a better word.

He blinked first. "But I need your help."

"Help how?"

"To contain the story."

I shook my head. "My job is to report stories, not contain them."

"Even when national security is involved?"

"That depends. Right now all we know is there's an unsubstantiated report from a sketchy," I framed the next word in air quotes, "'news' organization that Rose was poisoned. The government is arguing in federal court that her autopsy report needs to remain sealed for national security reasons. That leads me to believe that a foreign power poisoned her."

He nodded curtly. "Yes. One could conclude that."

"Are you confirming that conclusion?"

"No." He drilled me with his eyes. "And let's not have any of that 'won't confirm, won't deny' bullshit. I'm not commenting. This is extremely delicate, Lark. I will have nothing to say on the matter," he paused for effect and his voice softened, "unless we can reach some form of agreement."

"Well, I can't agree to go off the record in the same way I did with Rose."

He scowled.

"But there is an alternative."

He leaned forward. "I'm listening."

"You could talk with me on deep background."

He nodded. "Go on. I think I know what you mean, but to avoid any misunderstandings, I want to know what you mean by the term."

"If you told me the story on deep background, it protects you as the source in the same way Woodward and Bernstein protected Deep Throat during Watergate. It doesn't preclude me from trying to confirm the story elsewhere. But if I do confirm it, it doesn't necessarily mean I'll write the story because I'd still have to discern the legitimacy of the national security claim."

He looked at me deeply, as if trying to see into my soul. Finally, he said, "I trust you, Lark. And I need your help. So, I will agree to tell you what's going on, but only if you agree that we're speaking on deep background according to your ground rules."

I swallowed hard. "I agree."

CS ◆ ℬ

CHAPTER 27

Just as I expected, as soon as I emerged from the president's private office aboard Air Force One and returned to the relative steerage of the press area at the rear of the plane, several members of the travel pool pounced on me. Leading the pack was Harriet, the correspondent from Reuters. Ron McClain stood stoically next to her, listening.

"What'd he have to say, Lark?" Harriet asked.

"We just shot the breeze."

The *New York Times* correspondent joined the fray. "For half an hour? Do you mean to tell me that during a half-hour of breeze shooting he didn't say anything newsworthy?"

"He said nothing that I'm able to report."

The CBS correspondent weighed in. "That's not the same as him not saying anything newsworthy."

"Guys. Guys. If he'd said something relevant to this China trip, trust me – I'd share it with you."

I could tell I was doing a piss-poor job of convincing them. Rather than getting into a tense back-and-forth haggle, I pushed past my (former?) comrades of the traveling press pool, lunged back into my seat and crammed the ear buds into my ears. This time I cranked up Grace Potter and the Nocturnals loud. Really loud.

Once again, I tried, unsuccessfully, to sleep. My head was spinning with the bomb the president dropped on me about Rose's death. I was sitting on a huge story, but was unable to report it unless I could confirm it elsewhere. But how? And when? I was hermitically sealed with no Wi-Fi inside the gigantic steel fuselage of Air Force One somewhere over the Pacific Ocean, hurtling at more than 500 miles an hour toward Hawaii and then on to China.

We touched down at Hickam Air Force Base in Honolulu, Hawaii five hours later at 9:30 in the evening, but it was already early Thursday morning in Washington. This stop was different and more substantive than the previous two.

Gannon went by motorcade from Hickam three miles to Pearl Harbor and the USS Arizona Memorial. Here's the story I banged out during the fifteen-minute drive back to Air Force One:

GANNON WARNS RUSSIA ABOUT NUKES

BY LARK CHADWICK

PEARL HARBOR (AP) – President Will Gannon today called upon Russian President Dimitri Yazkov to "choose peace."

Gannon, who is on his way to China for a summit with China's new leader Tong Ji Hui, stopped at Pearl Harbor, where a surprise attack by Japan plunged the U.S. into World War II.

The 1941 attack killed 2,400 Americans.

After his remarks, Gannon tossed flowers into the oily water above the sunken hulk of the USS Arizona as a tribute to the 1,177 sailors who died, most of whom are entombed there.

Six days ago, on April 5, Yazkov announced his intent to scrap all nuclear non-proliferation treaties and provide nuclear weapons to Iran.

Gannon used the Pearl Harbor backdrop to warn Russia of the U.S. resolve to "turn back tyranny."

But Gannon also used the symbolic setting to hold out an olive branch to the Russian leader.

In remarks to dignitaries, servicemen and women, and their families, Gannon spoke of a visit to the site in 2016 by President Barack Obama and Japanese Prime Minister Shinzo Abe.

Noting the power of reconciliation embodied in the Obama/Abe visit, Gannon said, "True strength comes when hated enemies become trusted allies."

Then, in a direct appeal to the Russian leader, Gannon said, "Peace is a choice, Dimitri. Choose peace."

Yazkov has not made any provocative comments since his April 5 announcement, and U.S. officials have said they have not seen hard evidence that Yazkov is following through on his threat.

I managed to file my piece just as we were taking off on the longest leg of the trip – a fourteen-hour flight to Beijing.

By this time, the trip was doing a number on my body clock. It still felt like I was operating on Eastern Time, which was three in the morning.

The long-haul to Beijing was a blissful break from email and the internet. I read, slept, schmoozed, and listened to music as I got acclimated to living life thirteen hours ahead of Washington.

But, for a reporter, being off the grid and out of touch with everything else that's going on in the world, is also panic-inducing.

As soon as we landed, I called Scotty.

"Hey," he said. "How was Hawaii?"

"It was dark. California's brighter – and me without any shades."

"Did you call to talk about the weather?"

"Yes. What time is it back in the swamp? I just reset my watch for the third time. It's now 5:30 Saturday morning here in Beijing."

"It's 4:30 Friday evening. Almost Miller time."

"What's the latest?"

"Not good. The judge ruled against us today. Rose Gannon's autopsy report will remain sealed."

"Shit."

"What about you? Did you meet with the prez?"

"I did."

"What did he say?"

I looked around, but I was still too close to the other reporters in the pool to risk giving them any hint of what Gannon and I discussed during our private, deep background session.

"I can't tell you," I said.

"Why not?"

"Deep background."

"I'm your editor, Lark."

"I know. But I'm not in a place where I can talk freely."

"Then I'll ask you yes/no questions."

"I'd rather you didn't because it's way more nuanced than that."

"Can you at least tell me if the government's national security argument is bogus?"

Harriet, the Reuters correspondent, had her head cocked my way, so I kept groping for ways to keep my answers devoid of content.

"There appears to be some merit to that," I said to Scotty, "but there are some leads I need to check out before I can confirm that – or anything else."

"Was Rose poisoned?"

"Or anything else," I repeated, my tone intense, my teeth clenched.

Scotty was quiet for a moment, then asked, "How long might it take for you to confirm what he told you?"

"It'll probably have to wait until I get back to D.C. I'll be in the bubble for the next few days."

"If you tell me what you know, we could track down those leads at this end."

"It's pretty delicate, Scotty. You need to trust me to work my sources first."

He sighed heavily. "Alright. I don't like it, but I understand. Gimme a hint – bigger than Watergate?"

"No comment," I said, but then added, "Yeah. Maybe."

CB ✦ EO

CHAPTER 28

One of the coolest things about covering the President of the United States is that you get to go to amazing places. One of the uncoolest things about covering the president is that once you get to those wonderful places, you don't get the time or the chance to really enjoy them. Such was my experience with China.

For President Will Gannon, the China trip was an opportunity to cement an already-solid friendship with Tong Ji Hui – a friendship that began when the two were law students twenty-five years earlier at Vanderbilt.

For me, the China trip consisted of smearing my nose grease onto the glass window of the press bus as it carried us to every presidential event.

The trip was a blur and a grind – an altogether draining experience. I was on constant deadline and had to be exceptionally diligent and vigilant, all while fighting morning sickness. I only had to hurl a couple times. For the most part, a steady diet of saltine crackers got me through the trip.

China is on the other side of the international dateline, so my body clock spun wildly on this trip. China is thirteen hours ahead of D.C., so it was disorienting to be on an entirely flip-flopped schedule from day-side folks back home like Scotty Barrington. But A.P. is a 24/7 operation, plus I'm used to being on a schedule in which "every minute is a deadline."

The trip was downright brutal for the network television crews. They still had to function on U.S. time to go live on prime time shows when they should have been able to sleep like normal people in China.

For much of the trip, the two leaders were behind closed doors – and the press office was mostly mum about what might be transpiring.

The rest of us were forced to speculate, but speculation isn't really news, so we mostly talked amongst ourselves, even as we tried to stay plugged in to the rest of the world.

One sobering development: As we were touching down in Beijing, we learned from news reports that Russian President Dimitri Yazkov had made a surprise trip to Tehran where he and the Iranian president were all buddy-buddy smiles. The Russian prez made a big deal about signing a "nuclear protection accord" with Iran. The accord made clear Russia's "intent" to supply nuclear arms to Iran.

The news sparked a spirited conversation between Harriet Wickham of Reuters and Drew Hill of the *New York Times* – two of the older and more experienced reporters on the press bus. Hill was in his late fifties and had covered the White House for the past quarter of a century. Wickham, mid-forties, had been on the beat a dozen years.

I sat next to a window on the bus, Harriet was next to me, and Drew was across the aisle from Harriet.

"This could all just be Yaz blustering," Hill said to Harriet as I listened while watching the scenery go by outside my window and munching a cracker.

"What do you mean?" Harriet asked.

Hill had a voice that could cut through sheet metal: "Yaz is a bully and a baby. Gannon's cozying up to China, so Yaz has to do something audacious to reclaim the spotlight."

I turned toward their conversation and joined in. "You mean he won't follow through with his intention to supply nukes to Iran?"

"Nah," Hill said dismissively. "In addition to being a bully and a baby, Yaz is also a liar. He'll say and do anything to be the center of attention."

"But why would he do something this audacious and dangerous?" Harriet asked Hill.

"Because he's also insecure. There's nothing like creating an existential threat to galvanize the world's attention so that you're relevant and taken seriously."

"But what if he's not bluffing?" I asked.

"Believe me. He is."

"But what if he's not?" I persisted.

"He's a narcissist," Hill shot back. "It's not in his self-interest to blow up the world."

"But isn't he a bit of a thug, too?" Harriet noted, seeming to side with me.

"Yeah," Hill conceded.

Harriet: "What if he really does supply nukes to Iran?"

"Then it's a whole new ball game," Hill mansplained. "Iran would love to annihilate Israel, and Iran's hardliners still consider the U.S. to be 'The Great Satan,' so we'd be in the crosshairs. And probably you Brits, too," he said to her.

"If you were Gannon, what would you do?" I asked Hill, thinking to myself, *This guy's an arrogant prick, but he's been around a hell of a lot longer than I have and probably knows what he's talking about.*

"I'd probably do what he's doing now," Hill said. "Keep a low profile and work behind the scenes to defuse this thing."

"What do you think, Lark?" Harriet asked.

I thought a moment, grateful that she believed my opinion mattered, but trying to find a way to balance what I knew from Gannon on deep background with what I could say to these two esteemed and experienced journalists who were my colleagues on the bus – but also my competitors.

I said, "I think it could very well be bluster, but the stakes are so high, that it would be foolish for Gannon to underestimate Yazkov and dismiss him as just an idiot noisemaker."

"Which he is," Hill assured me.

There's a saying in Washington: "Those who don't know, talk; those who know, don't talk." It's a phrase sometimes used by press secretaries to shoot down unauthorized leaks.

It's true that often leaks are trial balloons, tidbits put out intentionally to see which way the winds of public opinion are blowing – and who the blowhards really are. Other leaks are from disgruntled officials whose arguments are losing behind closed doors, so they're hoping to put public pressure into the mix as a way to add impetus to their dying ideas, or to inspire fear and outrage against a policy push that's prevailing. Still other leaks provide an accurate look at what's really going on behind the curtain.

But the Russia story, coming at the same time of the China summit, was not lending itself to leaks of any kind.

The absence of summit information for most of the two-day visit to China was maddening, too. As far as we in the traveling press pool were concerned – as well as the rest of the world – the China summit was one big photo op.

But it wasn't all ceremony and no substance.

The two leaders finished their talks late on Sunday afternoon, then stood side by side to deliver a joint address to a massive crowd of nearly a million people in Tiananmen Square, site of the massacre in 1989 in which the government snuffed out the nascent pro-democracy movement by killing as many as ten-thousand protestors.

The blockbuster lead coming out of the Gannon-Tong summit was that Tong agreed to hold "free and fair" elections in exactly two years. It would give him time to put into place a U.S.-style Constitution with the checks and balances of Legislative and Judicial branches of government to supplement his Executive Branch.

This was nothing short of revolutionary. And the pictures sent a strong and clear signal that the U.S. and China were now officially allies and should be seen by the rest of the world as being in political and philosophical sync – a historically big deal considering China's oppressive Communist past.

The impression Gannon and Tong projected to the world was one of a strong alliance between two gigantic nuclear powers. If the Teddy Roosevelt doctrine of "speak softly and carry a big stick" was still in play, then the message to Russia was, "We don't have to bluster because together we can kick your ass big time."

Traditionally, summits end with a joint news conference. This one didn't. After the joint Gannon-Tong address, the summit ended with a lavish banquet – great pix, but no Q and A.

"That's ironic," I noted to Harriet as we were walking back to the bus after the joint address.

"What is?"

"On a day when they announce the framework for democracy in China, which fundamentally means a free press and freedom of speech, they don't take questions."

"Right-o," Harriet agreed. "What do you make of that?"

I said, "Whatever is going on behind the scenes with Russia must be extremely delicate and fragile. So much so that even an off-hand remark could cause the nuclear crisis to unravel."

That's why it was so surprising when Will Gannon strolled to the press section in the back of Air Force One the next morning as we were about to head back to Washington.

We mobbed him.

I jumped to my feet, pulled out my iPhone and began recording. Fortunately, I was standing closest to the president as he stood just inside the doorway of the press section.

Behind me, reporters were also scrambling to get out notebooks, pens, and recording devices, and Jay McMichael, the CNN photog, got his camera in place. The still photographers contributed to the chaos with their *chik-oo, chik-oo* shutter clicks and the strobe flashes of their cameras.

The president had put on his blue windbreaker with the presidential seal. "I just wanted to come back here to thank you for all you did putting up with our crazy schedule." He had to raise his voice to be heard over the whine of the engines as the pilots readied the plane for takeoff.

"What's the most surprising thing that came out of your discussion with President Tong?" I asked, then held my iPhone so he could speak into it.

"I'm more pleased than surprised about my conversations with President Tong. He and I have always had a great rapport and it was wonderful to see my old friend again. We're as close as ever. And I'm thrilled at the prospects for democracy taking root in China."

"What about the Yazkov visit to Iran?" Drew Hill of the *New York Times* asked.

Gannon waved off Hill's question. "I just wanted to thank you all for your hard work." As he spoke, Gannon rested his hand gently and briefly on my shoulder and then backed toward the entrance to the press section. He waved at us when he got to the door. "Thanks, guys."

Then he was gone.

No news.

No memorable quote.

Only a strong visual impression of an upbeat and confident president. Message to Russia sent.

We just had enough time to file quotes, pictures, and audio before Air Force One was wheels up and streaking back to Washington.

The rest of the ride home was long (fourteen hours) and smooth. You would think this is the time when everyone would sleep. But no. Now that the pressure was off, job one – at least for some – was to blow off steam.

There was a lot of booze, someone cranked up some sixties rock, and there was dancing in the aisles. A few emotionally parched souls were making out in the seats. I've heard it's even more out of hand on the press charter that follows Air Force One carrying the rest of the press contingent. Presidential trips, I learned, are notorious for igniting whirlwind romances, some of which would later doom marriages.

But, as I've said, covering the president is not a normal experience. And covering him half a world away from home was downright upending. So, I was dead tired when Air Force One landed early Monday morning at Andrews Air Force Base.

As soon as we touched down, everyone made a dive for their phone now that we once again had service and could tap into the rest of the world.

As for my world? It was about to blow up.

The Media Bash website had a picture of a beaming Will Gannon standing in the aisle of Air Force One resting his hand familiarly on my shoulder. The banner headline read:

LARK CHADWICK PREGNANT WITH GANNON'S LOVE CHILD

The picture was cropped to look as though the president and I were sharing an intimate moment.

α ♦ ω

CHAPTER 29

Even as I stood stunned on the tarmac at Andrews trying to read the jaw-droppingly false story on my phone, it was blowing up in my hand with a bombardment of text and voicemail messages that had been accumulating while I was off the grid after our last filing in Beijing fourteen hours earlier.

Will Gannon must have seen the story by now, too, because when he deplaned, he bounded down the steps from the aircraft and lunged into the right rear of the presidential limo – affectionately named "The Beast" – his face grim, his jaw set, not bothering to even wave jovially at the bank of network cameras lined up to dutifully chronicle his arrival back in Washington.

Twitter was going nuts. I had to stop looking at messages because they were so vile. Several called me a "fucking slut" or a "whore" and more than a few referred to me as the c-word.

Harriet Wickham sidled up to me. "I hate to be the one to ask," she said apologetically, "but is the Media Bash story true?"

"No."

"I didn't think so. Hang in there, Lark."

"Thanks, Harriet. I know you're just doing your job."

I was fighting back tears as Paul and I clambered aboard the press bus for the ride back to the White House. It was after seven o'clock in the morning and the sun was just coming up.

After Paul filed a quick story chronicling the president's return to Washington following the China summit, he clasped my hand as I gazed numbly out the press bus window. He knew better than to say anything because he could obviously see how upset I was.

I squeezed his hand tightly. "Thanks," I whispered, then released it to listen to the voicemail I'd gotten from Scotty Barrington.

"Lark, come see me when you get back to town. Thanks."

In fewer than four seconds – the time it took to listen to his terse message – my blood went from fire to ice.

This can't be good, I thought.

I tried to sleep on the bus to the White House, and again during my Uber ride to the bureau, but was still physically dragging and emotionally numb when I got to Scotty's office.

Scotty, on the other hand, was alert, chipper, and was even wearing fresh-scented I-just-got-out-of-the-shower cologne. He met me at the door to his office.

"C'mon in," he turned and walked to his desk and sat behind it, adding "shut the door behind you, please."

I did as I was told and walked toward him.

Scotty remained seated and gestured at one of the two chairs in front of his desk.

"Have a seat," he said.

As I dragged myself over to the chair, I noticed a woman sitting in the chair next to it.

"This is Jane Glenwood from human resources," Scotty continued. "She'll be joining us."

Shit, I thought. "Hi," I said.

"Hi," Jane replied, her legs crossed primly.

"I'll get right to the point," Scotty said. "I'm suspending you – with pay – until our internal investigation into the Media Bash allegations is concluded." He nodded at Jane who, I presumed, would be heading up the internal investigation.

"Do I get a chance to explain?" I asked, now fully awake, my blood beginning to thaw, then slow-boil.

"Of course. During the investigation."

My insides were seething and roiling. I'd been sucker punched by a false story. Now I was being sidelined.

"For the record," I said, gritting my teeth. "I am NOT pregnant with the president's so-called love child."

"But are you pregnant?" Scotty asked softly.

"That, sir, is none of your fucking business." I looked at Jane, who was taking notes. "Nor is it H-R's."

I stood and stalked toward the door.

"Before you go, Lark, I need you to tell me what Gannon told you on deep background."

"Nope. Sorry." I said, reaching for the doorknob.

"I'm still your editor, Lark."

I turned to look at him. "Actually, Scotty, you're not. I quit."

I jerked open the door and slammed it when I left. It felt good.

൦ ◆ ൦

CHAPTER 30

After I left the bureau, I got on the Metro to Silver Spring, then lugged my luggage (now I know why it's called "luggage") to my apartment. I turned off my phone and slept until suppertime.

When I woke up, I was famished. I was about to order a thin crust vegetarian pizza, but decided if there was ever a time for a cheese-stuffed crust meat supreme, this was it.

I also opened a bottle of wine and spent the rest of the evening eating, drinking, and crying as I read as much as I could stomach about my imploding life. Then I cried some more because I remembered I really was pregnant and shouldn't be having alcohol any more.

Even though the mainstream media were not covering the *Gannon Love Child* story, I knew it would only be a matter of time before they'd have to because it was everywhere else. The picture of Gannon resting his hand on my shoulder for literally a nanosecond was now frozen in time, forever linking us romantically in the eyes of the world.

The story, obviously made up, contained enough kernels of truth to be unsettling. It's true that I'm pregnant, but only my doctor and Paul Stone know it. It's also true, as the Media Bash story alleged, that I was with the president at Camp David. But only Gannon, the Secret Service agent who trailed us, and my grief counselor Kris knew that I'd been alone with the president and had dined with him. The story neglected to mention that his children and housekeeper were also present. There was just enough there for an evil conspiracy theorist to make up new dots – and then connect them.

Ever since the Trump presidency, when he declared journalists "the enemy of the American people," there'd been an inexorable erosion of trust in journalism. He labeled stories that contained facts critical of him as "fake news," and he actively encouraged his followers to jeer reporters at his rallies.

Gannon, who as far as I could tell, was a man of integrity, had inherited an office and a government deeply distrusted by many, if not most, of the American people. For people on both the left and the right, facts that challenged their political and/or religious doctrines, were not to be trusted. The United States of America had become a polarized place where dogma trumps truth and facts.

By Tuesday morning, I couldn't wait to get to my counseling session with Kris. We had a lot to discuss.

CB ◆ BO

CHAPTER 31

I had mixed feelings as I "Metroed" to D.C. for my regular Tuesday grief counseling session with Kris. The Wendt Center is just a block away from a Metro stop. As I walked along Connecticut Avenue, the jobless part of me felt free, unlike all those other poor bastards I passed whose stern facial expressions masked their fears and concerns about the day ahead. At least for the moment, I was unshackled from the rat race. For the moment.

I arrived ten minutes early for my eleven o'clock session. We only had fifty minutes and I wanted every one of them to count. After signing in and paying my fee, I took a seat in the waiting room.

The latest edition of *Time* was at the top of a pile of magazines on the table in front of me. A picture of Gannon and Tong in Tiananmen Square graced the front cover. Just as I was reaching for it, Kris came into the waiting room to fetch me.

"Ready, Lark?" She smiled as I stood.

"Can't wait."

I'm about a head taller than she is. I followed her as she led me past a few other meeting rooms, their doors closed. She wore flats and a yellow print sleeveless dress.

I plunged into my favorite spot on the couch and built my comfortable fortress of pillows upon which I could rest my elbows. Kris sat in an easy chair across from me, pulled it a tad closer, then sat back and crossed her legs.

"How was your week?" she asked.

I took a deep breath, but just as I started to speak I burst out crying.

Kris handed me a box of tissues and waited me out.

"I don't even know where to start," I said as I dabbed at my eyes and blew my nose.

"Take your time, Lark."

"What do you remember from our last conversation?" I asked.

"You told me about being with the president at Camp David."

"Geez. That feels like so long ago."

"What's happened since then?"

"Lots."

"What's most important?"

"You mean what's the lead?"

She nodded. "Is that what you journalists call it?"

"Uh huh. But in this case, we have an umbrella lead."

Kris frowned, confused.

"An umbrella lead is when you've got several important things all under the umbrella of the same story."

"Okay. What's your umbrella lead?"

"Seriously? You don't know?"

"I don't." She frowned. "Should I?"

"It's all over the internet."

She shook her head. "I'm rarely online. For me, it's a waste of time. I haven't been on Facebook in a month and, other than the *Washington Post* and NPR, I don't follow the news. So, I guess you could say that, as far as your situation is concerned, I'm a clean slate."

"Geez. Okay. Lemme see. If Camp David is the last thing you remember, then I guess the umbrella lead is . . . " I held up a hand and began ticking off the points on my fingers. "Number one: I'm pregnant. Number two: an anti-media website with millions of followers alleges the baby daddy is Will Gannon, and, number three: I just quit my job." I continued holding up my hand and waggled my fingers. "There's more, but how's that for starters?"

Kris's eyes got bigger and bigger as I ticked off the three most important things going on in my life, but she's a professional, so her jaw didn't drop, and she remained relatively stoic.

"Yes," she said. "That's, shall we say, a substantive start. What do you want to talk about first?"

"Don't you want to know if the prez is the father?"

162

"Not if you don't want to begin with that. Our time is about you, Lark. Not prurient curiosity."

I grabbed two more tissues from the box because I felt a fresh build-up of emotion, but the tears stopped short of emerging, yet when I started to speak, my voice was unreliably wavery. I had to pause before trying again.

"I think that what's causing me the most pain is not that I'm pregnant, or that I'm conflicted about it, but that what I thought was private and personal is now spread all over the place. What makes it even worse is not only that it's a lie that Gannon is the dad, but that even my boss – my former boss – thought the allegation believable enough that he suspended me pending an investigation. So I quit."

"Uh huh."

"That's all you've got: 'uh huh'?"

"For now, yes." She opened her mouth, thought better of it, and let silence reign for a moment, then said, "You seem angry."

"Bingo, sister. You're goddamn right I'm angry," I nearly yelled.

"Are you able to put your anger into words?" Kris asked gently.

"This whole love child story thing is such bullshit." Spittle spewed onto the rug.

"Because?"

"Because there's such a double standard in this business." I gestured wildly. "No male reporter has to deal with this. My career is basically toast because of a false accusation that's being leveled at me purely because I'm a young, attractive woman."

"You mean it's not unique to you?"

"Hell no! So many women I know are accused of sleeping around for information with absolutely no proof other than they're young, attractive women who do good work. It's infuriating and it's something most guys in this business will never understand."

"So, you're upset because the situation is so unfair."

"Yes! Someone told a big lie about me, it's spreading literally around the world, and I can't do a fucking thing to counter it."

"Why not? You could deny it."

"It's not that easy."

"Why not?"

"It's complicated."

"In what way?"

"Because the more I say, the worse it gets."

"How so?"

"For one, if I say anything, it keeps the story alive. I just want it to go away."

"But that's not going to happen."

"Right, but even if I deny the story, it doesn't mean I'll be believed. People will think I'm lying. They'll think I'm being petulant and defensive. And that will simply reinforce their initial opinion that I'm a slut."

"Is that what people are saying?"

"That and worse."

"I see." She sat back, put the tips of her fingers to her lips and seemed to be pondering what I'd said so far.

We were silent for moment. It gave me a chance to collect my thoughts.

I continued. "And then there's the fact that I'm pregnant with no husband and no job."

"Uh huh."

"There you go again."

She smiled, but said nothing.

"Okay," I said, "I'll do your job for you: How do you feel about being pregnant, Lark?"

"Very good question. How do you feel about that, Lark?"

"I thought you'd never ask."

She nodded for me to go on.

"I don't know how I feel."

"Are you sure?"

"I guess I don't know how I'm supposed to feel."

"Who says you're supposed to feel anything?"

"Doesn't society revere motherhood, but abhor single-motherhood?"

"I suppose there are some people who feel those things, but for everyone who does, there are other women who don't want to be mothers, and some single mothers who'd rather be single than married to a jerk."

I nodded. "Okay. Good point."

"So, how do you – Lark Chadwick – feel about being pregnant?"

"I feel absolutely nothing."

"Really?"

"Yeah. Surprisingly."

"Why do you suppose you don't feel anything?"

"I think it's because so much other stuff has been going on that being pregnant seems more like an abstraction. Except for the pain-in-the-ass morning sickness, I don't feel any differently." I gestured toward my abdomen. "I definitely don't feel it inside me."

"It?"

"See what I mean? It. Yes 'it' is an abstraction, not a person. At least not to me."

"But on some level, you must also realize that unless you do something invasive, there will come a time when it – the fetus – will become less an abstraction and something more . . ." she paused, groping for the right word. "Something more real."

I nodded. "Yes."

I sat with that thought for a moment before plunging ahead.

"So, abstraction aside," I continued, "how do I feel about being pregnant?"

"Yes. Go on."

"I don't want to be a mom. And I definitely don't want to be a single mom."

"Why not?"

"Oh, Kris, let me count the reasons."

"Please do."

"First – I don't know how to be a mom. I never knew my mom, and the aunt who raised me had, um, issues. Annie was hardly a role model."

"Yes. We've talked about that. What are some of the other reasons?"

"I just never considered being a mom. Having a career was more important."

"Yes. But now you have no job."

"Right."

"Do you have more to say about being a mom, or should we set that aside for a bit and talk about the job situation?"

I thought a moment. "Let's stay with the mom thing for a bit more."

"Okay."

"In just a matter of weeks, I need to make a decision."

"About whether, or not, to be a mom?"

"Yeah."

"And what are your thoughts on that?"

"I've always been pro-choice."

"That's a political term. What does that mean to you personally?"

"It means I'm firmly convinced – firmly – that the woman should, *must* have the right to choose whether or not to be a mother. But . . . ."

When I didn't go on, Kris jumped in with a prompt, "But what?"

"But now things are different."

"In what way?"

"Now I'm pregnant, obviously." I looked at my tummy. "Well, not obviously, but you know."

She nodded.

"I still feel no one but me can dictate what I do with my body, but now I'm realizing no one is telling me what to do, so the decision really is entirely mine."

"And so what's your thinking?"

"I'm right on the cusp of figuring that out."

"Uh huh."

"And, believe it, or not, you're helping a lot."

"Thank you. That's my goal. It's your life. I'm just here to be a sounding board to help you clarify your thinking – and to help you help yourself understand your feelings. But this isn't about me. Back to you."

"So, the question is – the choice is – do I have an abortion, or do I become a single mom – a single mom without a job?"

"Is that the choice?"

"What do you mean?"

"It's true that your current status is soon-to-be jobless single mom, but joblessness and singleness are likely to change, whereas motherhood would be a constant. So isn't the more appropriate choice simply to be, or not to be, a mother?"

"I would agree that I probably won't remain unemployed indefinitely, but I might not ever marry."

Kris considered that, and nodded. "Yes. True. Good point."

"So, Kris, I think I have to make a decision based on the current reality: No job. No husband."

"Doesn't it depend?"

"On what?"

"What if you choose to have an abortion, but right after you have the procedure, you win the lottery and become a multi-gazillionaire?"

"I don't play the lottery."

She looked at me over her glasses and scowled. "You know what I mean."

I nodded. "I think what you're suggesting is that the answer to the motherhood question has to stand on its own, regardless of the other externals."

"Exactly. It seems to me the question has to be answered exclusively in terms of what's right or wrong for you personally."

"I see. But I don't think I agree."

"Why not?"

"Because I don't believe moral decisions can be made in a vacuum."

"You mean you don't believe in moral absolutes of right and wrong?" She seemed surprised.

I thought a moment. "I do. And I don't."

She smiled indulgently. "Uh huh."

"Look, I don't want to get into the philosophical weeds, but for example: I can believe it's absolutely wrong to kill – until a guy is coming at me with a gun."

"Fair enough. Let's not stray into the weeds when we're having so much fun in the current thicket."

I chuckled at her play on words.

She continued. "The question on the table: to be, or not to be, a mother. Go."

I laughed. This is why I like Kris. She makes me think. And she makes me laugh.

"To be, or not to be, a mother," I said, restating the topic. "I need to give it some more thought. I'm honestly conflicted."

She shifted in her chair. "Do you know why?"

"I think it's because I don't need to make a decision just yet. The more pressing one is my job. Or lack."

"Okay. We'll table the motherhood question for now and move on. But before we do, there's one other thing to consider."

"What's that?"

"Adoption."

I nodded. "I hadn't thought about that."

"Should we discuss that option now, or move on?"

"Let's move on."

"You quit your job. Tell me about that."

I told her, but left out the part about going on deep background with President Gannon on Air Force One. Deep background means deep background, plus I didn't think what Gannon told me was relevant to my time with Kris. Instead I told her about the incriminating photo of the president and me, the false story accompanying it, and my meeting with Scotty Barrington.

After I'd finished telling her the story, she leaned back and said, "So it seems there are two things going on here: What to do about the lies being told about you, and what your next career move should be."

"Right."

We both sat in silence for a moment.

"Any thoughts?" she asked, finally.

I shook my head. "Not sure. I think I'm toast as a journalist."

"Why do you think so?"

"I've become the story."

"That's nothing new for you. Why is this different?"

"Bigger stage – the world is watching. I'm alleged to be carrying the child of the President of the United States."

"But that story can go away with a simple paternity test."

"True. But we've been living a world where facts no longer matter. The new narrative is that Gannon was banging me while his wife was dying. In journalism, trust is the coin of the realm. If my integrity is torched, then no reputable news organization will hire me."

She frowned thoughtfully. "Yes. I see what you mean. So, what are you going to do?"

"I thought maybe you would tell me." I smiled.

She smiled, too. "Nope. But nice try."

"I've always been interested in psychology. And I think I can read people pretty well. I know how to ask questions that get the other person talking – and thinking. So, maybe I'll begin to think about heading in that direction."

"It can be a very rewarding field. I'll email you some links that you might find helpful."

"Thank you."

We looked at our watches at the same time.

"I know. Time's up, right?" I said.

"Sadly," she nodded. "I enjoy our talks, Lark."

There was actually a spring in my step as I walked out of the building and into the midday sunlight drenching Connecticut Avenue. I took a moment to sit on a concrete balustrade next to a small elm tree that was just beginning to bud, pulled out my iPhone, and made notes summarizing the highlights of our session.

As I entered the bullet points, I realized I now had a lot more clarity about what I should do going forward because I had a better sense of how to prioritize my problems. But I also realized that one of the biggest problems I faced I didn't bring up with Kris, and that brought a scowl to my face.

Even though I'm no longer the White House correspondent for the Associated Press, the President of the United States had just pointed me in the direction of a bombshell story, and burdened me with the responsibility of checking it out. But how? And what will I be able to do with it if I can confirm it?

I dialed Lionel's number.

CR ◆ ℧

CHAPTER 32

Lionel was out of breath when he picked up on the third ring.

"It's me," I said. "Is this a bad time?"

"If it's you, it's always a good time. What's up?"

"I quit my job."

"You get right to the point, don't you? Have you ever considered journalism?"

I laughed. "I did, but it wasn't a good fit."

"Jesus, Lark. What happened?"

"Got time to talk?"

"Always. Muriel and I are unpacking. C'mon over."

Ninety minutes later I was getting off the bus at the intersection of Utah and Quesada in Northwest D.C. While I'd been traveling with the president on his whirlwind summit trip to China, Lionel and Muriel were moving back to D.C. and were now setting up shop in their new place, a modest, two-story brick house on a leafy-quiet side street.

"The place was built in about 1942," Lionel told me as he gave me the quick tour. "The Federal style was popular back then."

"So were metal kitchen cabinets," Muriel chimed in. "Honey," she said to him with a hint of exasperation, "we really need to replace these atrocities." She opened and closed a cabinet door to demonstrate to me their ancient ancestry.

"Yeah. Yeah," Lionel said. He was flushed from carrying a box into the house from the PODS long-distance moving and storage container sitting at the curb in front of their house on Quesada.

The house was similar to their place in Pine Bluff, Wisconsin, but not yet as homey. The new place had a long, welcoming sidewalk leading from the curb to the front steps. Someone had fingered the name *Sven* into one of the sidewalk's cement slabs.

Just inside the front entrance, to the left, the living room had a hardwood floor and a fireplace. That room opened into a dining room with a low-hanging chandelier and a sunroom at the back of the house.

The kitchen, where we were standing, was cramped.

Lionel must have seen the horror in my face. "It obviously needs some work."

"Correction," Muriel said. "It needs a lot of work."

"Yes, dear," Lionel said dutifully.

There was a moment of uncomfortable silence as they glared at each other before Muriel said cheerily, "I'll make us some Arnold Palmers and we can talk."

Lionel and I drifted into the living room.

"Don't start without me," Muriel called after us.

Even though the house was cluttered with boxes, the living room had the basics – a sofa, a couple of easy chairs, and an oriental rug. Lionel and I chitchatted until Muriel entered the room and distributed three tall glasses filled with the yellow-brown mix of iced tea and lemonade.

I sat on the sofa facing Lionel who'd chosen a chair next to the fireplace. Muriel sat next to me at the end of the sofa closest to the dining room and kitchen.

"Okay," Muriel said to me, "Tell us what happened."

"You've probably already seen the Media Bash story," I began.

Muriel nodded.

"Yep," Lionel said. "It's brutal. What a crock of shit. The good news, I suppose, is it's only getting picked up by the lunatic fringe."

"But it's only a matter of time before it spreads. Soon the president will be asked about it. And as soon as he answers, it legitimizes the story."

"So, why'd you quit?" Lionel asked.

I told him about my aborted meeting with Scotty and the woman from human resources.

"Forgive me for saying this, Lark," Muriel chimed in, "but this sounds a little like the fight and flight tendencies you had when we first met you."

I looked at the floor and nodded. She'd put her finger on a sore spot. I was a mess when I met them in the office of the *Pine Bluff Standard*. I was still reeling from having found Annie, dead of carbon monoxide poisoning, and was looking for a newspaper clipping about the car accident that killed my parents when I was a baby. Muriel was the office manager and pointed me in Lionel's direction.

"Yes. Impulsiveness is still my biggest fault." I looked at her. "But it's also who I am."

"What are you going to do now?" Lionel asked.

"That's why I'm here," I said.

"You want your old job back, right? In case you hadn't noticed, I sold the paper. I'm retired," he beamed.

"So, what are you going to do now?" I asked.

"Oh, I've got a few irons in the fire."

"Such as?"

"My agent thinks she's found a publisher for my memoir."

"Oh? Have you finally finished it?"

"Not yet, but with non-fiction, it doesn't have to be. Plus, now that I'm back in D.C., CNN has signed me up to be a political consultant, so now I'll be a regular on their daily shout-fests. And, beginning with the fall semester, I'll be an adjunct professor in the Philip Merrill School of Journalism at the University of Maryland-College Park." He took an exaggerated deep breath to underline his busy importance.

"Excuse me," Muriel said to him, "maybe I missed something, but did I just hear you tell Lark that you're retired?"

"Um . . . yeah." There was an edgy defensiveness in his voice.

"Yeah. Right," she scowled.

Lionel turned to me. "What about you, Lark? What's next?"

"Two things," I said. "Thing one: I think I'm going to check out returning to grad school to get a masters in psychology."

They both nodded approvingly.

I continued. "Thing two: I think I know who poisoned Rose Gannon."

There was a stunned silence before Lionel broke it. "Need an editor?" He wiggled his eyebrows.

"I thought you'd never ask," I replied.

Muriel sighed heavily.

☙ ◆ ❧

CHAPTER 33

After we finished our Arnold Palmers, I asked Muriel, "Do you mind if I commandeer your husband to go for a walk? I need to talk with him confidentially about something."

"Sure. You two run along. I've got plenty to do in the kitchen, like admiring our metal cabinets." She laughed, but it was hollow.

"Do I detect a bit of friction between you two?" I asked Lionel when we were outside.

"Oh yeah. It comes and goes. Moving is stressful."

"Have you gotten to know your neighbors yet?" I asked as we made a right on Quesada and headed toward Utah.

"Yep," he said. "A retired Secret Service agent is on one side of us. A spokesman at the Smithsonian is on the other side – there." He pointed at the house to our right on the corner. "A couple of education think-tankers live across the street, and a retired U.S. ambassador lives behind our house across the back alley. So, it feels a lot like home."

We took a left onto Utah. It was then that I realized I'd been here before.

"This neighborhood feels all too familiar, Lionel."

"How come?"

"I'll show you."

At the end of the block we turned right onto 30th Street. "See that light pole up ahead?" I said.

"Uh huh. The one with the Neighborhood Watch sign?"

"Yeah. I see someone replaced the one I took down."

"Why'd you take it down?"

"It's where I found Doug's body."

"Jesus. I'm sorry, Lark." He put his hand gently in the middle of my back. "Do you want to turn around?"

"No. I'll be fine. I used to come here a lot." I walked quickly ahead to the light pole. "Ah. It's still here," I said.

"What is?" He pulled up next to me and followed my hand as I reached for the creosote-soaked pole.

"This bottle cap." I caressed it with my fingers.

"One hundred percent real," Lionel said, reading the words on the cap top.

"I nailed it here the week after Doug died," I explained. "Better that than some ostentatious shrine."

Lionel nodded soberly.

We stood in silence for a few moments. When we moved on, I realized I'd been resting my hand on my abdomen.

"Lionel, there's so much I need to talk with you about – and one thing in particular. But before I tell you about me, I want to better understand how you're doing."

He sighed. "Lots going on with me, too."

We walked slowly along 30th Street, no longer paying attention to the scenery. I studied the sidewalk as I waited for Lionel to say more.

"I'm really looking forward to getting back into the D.C. swing of things," he said, "but . . . "

"Muriel?"

He nodded. "I think she has mixed feelings – and expectations."

"She wanted to come back to D.C., didn't she?"

"Yeah. But I think she would have preferred a retirement community."

"Why didn't you go in that direction?"

"Got a great deal on the place on Quesada."

"But, let me guess: it needs work and Muriel feels that all of those responsibilities will fall onto her while you're out-and-about being the famous Pulitzer-Prize winning journalist Lionel Stone."

"Yeah. Pretty much. You make me sound like such a narcissist."

I poked him. "Takes one to know one." I laughed.

He didn't.

We walked in silence for a bit. Took a right on Tennyson, approaching Rock Creek Park. We crossed Oregon Avenue, entered the park and started down a trail.

"So, what about you, Lark? What did you want to talk about? You say you know who poisoned Rose Gannon?"

"I think I do, but before we go any further, I think we need to set some boundaries."

"Okay."

"You're my friend and mentor."

"Yes."

"You're my former boss."

"Right."

"But now you're retired, and I'm out of a job."

"Yet you're sitting on a huge story."

"Yes."

"And you feel you now have zero credibility and no way to tell the story even if you did."

"Uh huh. But first I have to confirm the story."

"So, all you've got is a lead?"

"Yes. But a solid one."

"How solid?"

"I can't tell you."

"Why not?"

"I got it on deep background."

He stopped and scowled at me when I turned to look at him.

"We've been here before, Lark. You know how I feel about off-the-record stuff."

"I do. And our big blow-up taught me the importance of getting independent confirmation. So, I learned from you."

"Then why can't you tell me about the lead you have and where you got it?"

"Because you're not my editor. Yet."

He resumed walking and I fell into step with him as we went deeper into the woods.

"But I could be your editor?" he asked after a prolonged silence. I could tell his mind was considering all the possibilities.

"Yes. But we'd need an outlet."

"I'm not going to run another weekly newspaper. I'm glad I'm out from under the *Standard*. It was getting to be a grind."

"What about *ProPublica*?" I asked.

Lionel nodded thoughtfully. "That's a very good idea, Lark. They're kick-ass investigative reporters, plus they've earned a bunch of Pulitzers in a short amount of time."

"Know anyone there?"

"Oh yeah. Lemme make some calls. But what should I tell them? Right now I've got nuthin' to pitch. Help me out here, Lark."

"Okay," I said after a very long pause. "But everything I tell you is on deep, very deep background. Are we clear on that?"

"Yes, ma'am."

"I'm serious about this, Lionel. This has geo-political implications."

Lionel turned sober. "Really? You mean this story is a bigger deal than simply big?"

I nodded.

"Who's your source?"

"Will Gannon."

"What'd he tell you?"

We came to a park bench. When I told him what the president told me, Lionel had to sit down.

03 ◆ 80

CHAPTER 34

Talking with Lionel always energizes and encourages me. After our walk-and-talk in Rock Creek Park, we returned to his new place on Quesada Street where he rejoined Muriel in their unpacking odyssey.

I retrieved my messenger bag, which contained my laptop. Lionel pointed me toward Connecticut Avenue and Chevy Chase Circle, and a great bakery where I could regroup and collect my thoughts. The day was breezy-balmy, so I sat outside on the bakery's shaded patio, ordered a latte and an almond croissant, and – out of habit – fired up my laptop.

Big mistake.

Social media was abuzz about Will Gannon and me. My Twitter feed was blowing up with nasty, personal attacks on me. One person – a woman, of all people – wrote that I should be raped and killed. Another person – a guy – said that if he ever runs into me, he'll shoot me.

The news organizations that I consider to be reputable members of the mainstream media had yet to run with the story, but that was cold comfort because websites with millions of followers – but no editorial oversight – were all over it. It seemed as though everyone had an opinion, never mind that their opinions were based on false information and speculation, not facts.

I take that back. One fact. I really am pregnant, but no one knows. I take that back, too. A few people know. But I trust them.

Should I?

I dug my journal out of my messenger bag and opened to a fresh page. I do my best thinking when I write in longhand, so I wrote, and wrote, and wrote, and wrote.

I lost track of all sense of time and space as I wrote frenziedly in my journal. I began with a just-the-facts recapitulation of the events of the last two days. That always leads me to do what I call "deep looking" into myself and my circumstances. The goal is to understand myself better, so I can see my way forward more clearly.

I concluded my journaling session this way:

1. Who poisoned Rose Gannon – and why? Lionel is checking with ProPublica to see if we have an outlet for the story if I can confirm it. But how do I go about doing that? Think, Lark, think!!

2. I need to get a job. Is now the time to go back to school to get a Masters in psychology, or social work? Kris sent me the names of some people to contact, and some links to check. DO IT!!!

3. How did my preggers condition become public? Who knows? My doctor, Kris . . . and Paul. Paul and I need to have a talk.

I put down my pen, sat back, and took a deep breath. That's when I saw him, sitting at the table next to me, an amused look on his face.

 C3 ◆ 80

CHAPTER 35

The guy at the table smirking at me looked to be about fifty and extremely fit – definitely my type. But I wasn't in the market. I was still reeling from Doug's death, was conflicted about Will Gannon, and had too many other more pressing issues to deal with.

"Are you a practitioner of automatic writing?" the guy asked, taking a sip from a glass of what looked like iced tea.

"Excuse me?"

"You were writing like a fiend, not even pausing to think."

"Oh. Yeah." I laughed. "I was writing in my journal. Trying to sort out some stuff that's going on in my life."

"You must be living one hell of a life."

"You could say that."

"The name's Jake." He reached over to shake my hand.

I gave his fingers a squeeze. "Nice to meet you, Jake."

"You live around here?"

"Nah. I was just in the area visiting a friend. You?"

"I live back over there." He nodded vaguely behind me.

As I paid my bill and packed up my stuff, I took stock of him. He wore a hunter green t-shirt – which he filled out nicely – khaki shorts, and sandals. No socks. His thick, salt-and-pepper hair was raffishly unkempt and curled at the ears and on the back of his neck. He was deeply tanned, except for a narrow strip of white skin on his ring finger.

"Well, it was nice meeting you, Jake."

"I didn't catch your name."

"I didn't throw it."

He laughed. "I like your sass. Lemme guess: it's Jennifer."

"Nope, but nice try."

"Seems like every hot chick I've been meeting lately is named Jennifer," he said.

"I suppose."

"You look vaguely familiar. Have we met?" he asked.

I shook my head. "I don't think so."

"I never forget a face, especially one as pretty as yours."

He probably thought he was racking up cool points with me, but Jake was striking out badly and didn't know it. I smiled perfunctorily and turned my attention to signing the check and stuffing my credit card and laptop back into my messenger bag.

Jake kept studying me, genuinely vexed that he couldn't place me. "Seems to me I've seen you on television. Are you famous?"

"More like infamous," I said without thinking.

"What do you do?" he pressed.

What do you do?" I've found that the best way to take the focus off myself is to shift the spotlight onto the other person. In my experience, people like to talk about themselves – and this guy was no exception.

"Mostly I work out and count my money," he laughed. "I highly recommend retirement."

"What'd you retire from?"

"The United States Marine Corps. Two tours in Afghanistan."

"Thank you for your service."

"You're entirely welcome." He dipped his head gallantly.

"And, at last count, how much money do you have?" It was a test question. Most normal people would be offended, but I suspected that Jake would relish the opportunity to brag.

He puffed out his chest. "At last count? A few mil, give or take." He scowled. "Seems like my ex is trying to do all the taking."

"Uh huh. You made your millions in the Marines?"

He shook his head. "Had my own company after I got out, then sold it for a nice chunk 'o change. Capitalism is the best."

"Well, Jake, it's been n—"

"I just figured it out!" he said, his face brightening.

"What's that?"

"You're what's-her-name, Gannon's girlfriend."

Now I was intrigued. "What gives you that impression?"

"It's all over the internet." He dug into his pocket, extracted his cell phone, and did some serious scrolling. "Here it is!" He thrust his phone toward me so I could see the Media Bash shot of Will Gannon with his hand on my shoulder. "You're Lark Chadwick. Miss Fake News herself," he said proudly.

"So glad to have made your day." I stood.

"Me, too. Say, is Gannon any good in bed?"

"I think we're through here, Jake."

"Hell, we're just getting started." His expression darkened and hardened. "Why do you liberal media types hate this country so much?"

"You don't even know me, Jake."

"Oh, I know your type. While I'm getting shot at in Afghanistan, you're banging the president – as his wife is dying, no less."

I should have walked away. Instead I took a deep breath, pulled my chair over to his wrought iron table, sat down, folded my arms on top of the table, and leaned toward him.

"A minute ago you're trying to pick me up," I said, "trying to impress me with how rich you are, trying to flatter me about how I look. Then, when you realize I'm a journalist, you judge me based on information that's not even true. But do you even c—"

He grabbed me by the forearm and squeezed so hard it hurt.

"Ow!"

He stuck his face in front of mine, lowered his voice, gritted his teeth, and hissed, "Listen to me, you stuck-up snowflake little bitch. In Afghanistan, I killed better people than you."

"Let go of me," I demanded, my stern, even tone matching his. We were eyeball to eyeball.

He tightened his grip. "You need to be taught a lesson." His eyes were wild, crazed.

I broke free, stood, lifted his glass of iced tea and carefully poured it into his lap.

"I'm leaving, Jake, but don't bother to stand. Everyone will think you peed your pants."

I snatched up my messenger bag, slung it over my shoulder, stormed onto Connecticut Avenue, flagged down a passing cab, and dove into the back seat. I looked back and caught a glimpse of Jake using a napkin to dab at the stain on his crotch.

As the cab pulled away from the curb, I noticed that an angry-purple bruise had begun to blossom on my forearm.

CB ✦ EO

CHAPTER 36

"Where to, lady?" the cabbie asked as I sagged against the back seat.

"Um . . . toward the White House, I guess."

I got out my iPhone and snapped a picture of my bruised arm, and a selfie holding the arm next to my pouting face. I have no idea why I did that or what I'd do with the images – if anything – but at least I'd have them if I needed them.

Then I speed-dialed Paul.

"Hey," he said. "It's too quiet here without you."

"You still in our cubicle?"

"Uh huh. They just declared a full lid, so I'm done for the day. Where are you?"

"In a cab heading your way."

"Got time for a drink? We should talk."

"Yes I do, and yes we should."

We agreed to meet at Shotzie's Pub at 17th and Connecticut.

"You look like your day was rougher than mine," he said, as we settled in at a table.

"I need to ask you something," I said.

"Sure. What?"

"Who did you tell that I'm pregnant?"

He looked stunned. "Um . . . . "

"Goddammit, Paul. You are the only person – other than my doctor and therapist – who knew. Now the whole fucking world knows. Who'd you tell?"

"Um . . . ." His face was flushed. He couldn't look me in the eye.

I thrust my bruised forearm under his nose. "Do you see this?"

He nodded.

"A media-hating asshole put it there. He said he's killed better people than me. He wanted to teach me a lesson for banging the president."

"I never said you did that."

"But you must've told someone about my . . . " I lowered my voice and looked around to make sure no one was listening, "my condition."

"Well . . ."

"Who'd you tell, Paul?"

Just then Alex came up to the table behind Paul, placed his hands on his shoulders and kissed the top of his head.

"Hi, Lark," Alex said to me brightly as he took a seat.

I ignored Alex and leaned over the table toward Paul's face. "Pillow talk, right?"

Paul nodded.

"Shit."

"I can talk to him about anything," Paul said. "We don't have any secrets."

"What am I missing?" Alex asked, looking back and forth between Paul and me.

"I'm sorry, Lark." Paul reached for my hand, but I pulled it away.

I turned my attention to Alex and gave him a laser stare and my best thunderstorm face.

"What?" Alex asked, genuinely confused.

"Who'd you tell, Alex?"

"Tell what?"

"You're not dumb. And neither am I."

"I'm not clairvoyant, either. What are you talking about?" He was still smiling, but it was forced.

"My condition."

"Yeah. I heard you quit your job. Sorry to hear that."

"I mean my other condition."

Alex turned to Paul, a questioning WTF look on his face.

"She knows that I told you," Paul said to Alex.

"Told me what?"

Paul lowered his voice. "That she's pregnant."

Alex's eyes widened. "No, you didn't."

Paul flinched and blinked.

Alex quickly added, "Or, if you did, I don't remember." He turned to me. "Um, congratulations?"

Now both Paul and I were looking at Alex, dumbfounded.

Alex said to Paul, "Honestly, hon, I don't remember you telling me that. I'm not saying you didn't, I just don't remember." He shook his head. "Maybe I'd dozed off, or something."

Paul turned to me. "Still, I'm sorry, Lark. He's the only one I told."

A waitress came to take our order, but Alex said, "Nothing for me. I just stopped by to say hi. I've got to work late." He stood. "I'll catch you later," he said to Paul, then looked down on me. "See ya, Lark."

Then, as suddenly as he'd appeared, Alex was gone.

"What the fuck just happened?" I said, more to myself than to Paul.

Paul looked dazed.

On impulse, I got up without saying a word and stalked after Alex. I rushed onto the street just in time to see him get into a cab. I tried to hail a cab of my own while keeping Alex's in sight. I imagined myself jumping into the back seat and shouting, "Follow that car!" But I never got the chance to use that cliché because every cab that went past was already full.

Sadly, I turned and walked back into the pub, slid back into my chair, and put my face in my hands.

"Are you okay?" Paul asked.

"Don't. Say. Anything."

"Lark, I a—"

"Don't!" I took my hands away from my face to glare at him, then retreated behind them again.

The place was beginning to get crowded and noisy. "You've Lost That Lovin' Feelin'" was playing on the jukebox.

"I'm so angry I could explode," I said, my hands still covering my face.

"Talk to me," Paul coaxed.

I slammed both my hands flat against the table. "I did! That's why I'm so pissed."

"Oh, c'mon."

"No." I stabbed a finger at him. "You c'mon. I can't trust anybody."

"That's not true."

"Really, Paul? Are you serious?"

"You can still trust me. That was a lapse with Alex. It won't happen again. I'm still your friend."

"Do you trust him? I sure don't."

"I'm having my doubts."

"Good. He's a stone-cold liar."

Paul pursed his lips. "He's been incredibly supportive of me while others probably consider me a self-mutilating traitor to my gender."

"Bullshit. He just tried to gaslight you."

"He did?"

"He did."

"Maybe he really did doze off and didn't hear me."

"I saw the way you looked at him. You knew you'd told him, and you knew he'd heard you, but when he boldly denied it, you began to doubt yourself. That's gaslighting."

"Gaslighting?"

"Yep. Classic psychological manipulation to make a person doubt what they know is true."

"Gaslight. Isn't that an old movie?"

I nodded. "And a play before that back in the forties."

"Never saw it."

"I saw it onstage at my high school a long time ago. I forget the plot twists, but it takes place in the 1800s before electric lights. The husband drives his wife insane by dimming the gaslights, but when she notices, he says she's nuts. And eventually she believes him, not reality. Big mistake, babe."

"Hmmmmm."

I shook my finger at Paul. "Don't you be like her."

He looked doubtful.

"Look, Paul. You know Alex better than I do, but I don't trust him. Do you?"

He nodded, but tentatively.

"Let's think this through. Assuming he really did hear you when you told him about me, who would he have told – and why?"

Paul shrugged.

"He's in finance, not journalism, right?" I asked.

"Uh huh."

"And you met at Brookings?"

"Right. A panel discussion."

"What was the topic?"

"Ethics in Journalism in the Post-truth Era."

"Weren't you on the panel?"

He nodded. "Along with your old pal, Francine Noyce."

"Oh, Jesus. Don't remind me. I'm still waiting for the other shoe to drop."

Paul laughed.

I didn't. "Did you see Alex talking with Noyce that night?"

Paul shook his head. "I only had eyes for him. And apparently it was mutual. What are you thinking?"

"I'm trying to figure out how the word leaked to Media Bash."

"Do you think it was Alex?"

"Maybe."

"But why?"

I began to bite the dry skin around my cuticles – a bad habit I employ when I'm trying to process my thoughts.

"What are you thinking?" Paul asked when I began gnawing on the fingers of my other hand.

I took a deep breath. "I'm trying to look at this thing objectively, rather than emotionally."

"Any luck?"

I nodded. "I'm seeing that the main reason I'm so fucking angry is that I feel like I'm being attacked. That it's all about me."

"Isn't it?"

"Not entirely."

"What do you mean?"

"It's really about the president."

Paul nodded slowly, thoughtfully.

"I've been off the grid for a couple hours," I said. "Has the White House commented yet on any of the Media Bash stories – the allegation that Rose was poisoned? The story about Gannon knocking me up?"

He shook his head. "Not yet. But the story about you and Gannon is now mainstream."

I looked at Paul in horror. "What do you mean?"

"INN broke the story an hour ago."

"Oh, shit."

I buried my face in my hands again.

಩ ✦ ಩

CHAPTER 37

It's bad enough when the haters and conspiracy theorists on the lunatic fringe begin to spread false stories about you on the internet. But it's downright terrifying when the mainstream news media begins to dig.

It began innocuously enough when INN broke the story. It was what broadcasters call a "reader" – a short, forty-five second anchor script delivered as an item during the network's evening newscast:

> I-N-N has learned that the House Judiciary Committee is quietly investigating allegations that President Will Gannon has fathered an illegitimate child.
>
> According to reports circulating on the internet, the alleged mother is former Associated Press White House Correspondent Lark Chadwick.
>
> Sources tell I-N-N Chadwick was fired yesterday when news of her alleged affair with the president surfaced.
>
> Gannon's ten-year marriage to his wife Rose ended two weeks ago when the First Lady died under what are now considered to be suspicious circumstances.
>
> The House committee is also said to be looking into that.
>
> So far, no official word from the committee, the president, or Chadwick.

A clip of the anchor reading the story, along with the transcript, were posted on the INN website. The story went viral. By ten that night, more than five million people had seen it – and that was just the version posted on Facebook.

I began getting phone calls early that evening from reporters trying to match the story and advance it. One of them was Harriet Wickham, the Reuters correspondent I worked alongside on the China trip. I like her and consider her a friend, so I picked up.

"Hi, Harriet."

"Hello, Lark," she said cheerily, her British accent a welcome bit of elegance in the midst of such a tawdry story. "Thanks for taking my call."

"Of course."

"By now you've seen the INN piece?"

"Uh huh."

"Do you have a response?"

"Off the record?"

"On, I'm afraid."

"The only comment I'll make is that the story is riddled with factual errors and flimsy sourcing."

"What are the factual errors?"

"Sorry, Harriet. That's as far as I'm prepared to go at this time."

"I've asked you this before, but I have to ask you again on the record: Are you pregnant, and is Will Gannon the father?"

I sighed heavily.

"You know I'm just doing my job, right, Lark?"

"Yes. I know. I wish I could say more, but I can't, so I won't, other than to say the story is riddled with errors and not one person is named as a source."

This time it was Harriet's turn to sigh. "Okay. Off the record? What kind of guidance can you give me?"

I chuckled. "You're covering this story exactly the way I would."

She laughed. "I consider that a high compliment. Thank you." She paused, then went on: "So, what can you tell me off the record?"

"The less I say, the better. You're a good reporter, Harriet. Just be fair, accurate, go for the facts, and go with your gut. That's what I'd do."

"I know this must be a tough time for you, Lark. You hang in there."

"Thanks, Harriet."

Lionel phoned as I was ending the call.

"Hey," I said.

"How you holdin' up?"

"Okay, I guess."

"You sound tired."

"I'm beyond angry. Now I'm weary – and it's just beginning. Francine Noyce's fingerprints are all over that INN story – I just can't prove it."

"Yeah. Probably," Lionel said, then changed the subject. "I talked with *ProPublica* today about the Rose Gannon possible poisoning story."

I perked up. "Really? What'd they say?"

"They're all for me working it, but they said – and this is a quote – 'Lark Chadwick is too hot to handle.'"

"I don't suppose they meant that in a sexual way."

"No," he laughed. "Hot, as in radioactive. So, they teamed me up with one of their investigative reporters. She actually worked for me back in the day at the *Times*, so that's cool."

"But I could still be a source for you, right?" I asked hopefully.

"Sure, but it'll have to be on the record. As your friend, I can tell you it's going to be getting very nasty for you, Lark."

"Going to be?"

"Yes. Believe me. You weren't around for the Monica Lewinsky thing."

"But this is different."

"Doesn't matter."

"Why not?"

"Times change. And journalism is changing with the times."

"What do you mean?"

"Well, journalism with a capital J hasn't changed. Facts and truth still matter. But now everyone with an iPhone and a Twitter account sees themselves as a journalist. But they have no editorial oversight, so they're free to spout opinion and speculation as if it's fact. It makes it harder for the mainstreamers because there aren't as many of us."

"And then there's cable television."

"Geez. Don't get me started. Now they all have partisan panelists shouting at each other and passing it off as news analysis."

"And you're about to become one of them."

"Yeah. I've been around the block a few times, so I've earned the right to be heard. Plus, it pays well."

"What's your advice to me?"

"The less you say publicly, the better."

"I just got off the phone with Reuters."

"Uh oh. What'd you say?" He sounded alarmed.

"No comment, other than to say the story is riddled with inaccuracies and flimsy sourcing."

He grunted. "That's fine. Did they ask any follow ups?"

"Sure. But that's all I'd say."

"Did you go off the record?"

"Tempting, but nope."

"Good. There might come a time when you have to say more. But for now, your denial is enough. Otherwise, you just add fuel to the fire."

"But the fire's gonna burn anyway, and I'll be the one getting singed."

"It's probably best if you try to ignore what's going on. Not easy, I know. Maybe now's the time to look into grad school. I sent you an email with some contacts."

"Thanks. On my to-do list."

"Have you given any more thought about how you're going to check out what Gannon told you on Air Force One?"

"Yeah. A little."

"Lemme know what you find out."

"Okay."

I sighed. My thoughts returned to the INN story about Gannon and me.

"Tell me this is all going to blow over, Lionel. Lie if you must."

"I wish I could. INN actually buried the lead – they went prurient and tabloid instead of substantive."

"What do you mean?"

"Mark my words, Lark. By tomorrow morning, the question the mainstream media will be asking is, 'Did President Will Gannon kill his wife?'"

Lionel wasn't kidding.

CS ◆ EO

CHAPTER 38

The next morning, Wednesday, when I was about to leave my apartment building in Silver Spring to get coffee at Starbucks, a growing gaggle of reporters and television cameras was staked out on the sidewalk in front of the entrance to the building.

I retreated to my seventh-floor apartment before they saw me. For a while, I fretted and paced like a caged lion. The idea of being a prisoner in my own place grated on me.

The more I thought about my predicament, the more I realized that I could probably give the reporters the slip by getting into my car parked in the building's underground garage. I looked out the windows and saw that some reporters were gathered by the garage entrance.

I weighed my options:

If I drove somewhere, I wouldn't have to answer questions, plus the only picture they'd get would be a blurry shot of me zooming out of the garage.

But they also might try to come after me. That would be dangerous – and futile if they caught up with me and thrust their mics in my face someplace else.

I decided instead to stay put and focus on researching my career options. I turned off my phone and fired up my laptop, making sure my social media apps like Facebook and Twitter were closed so I wouldn't be tempted to peek.

It was delightful.

I sent emails to the contacts Lionel gave me:

Hello, _____

My name is Lark Chadwick. You and I have never met, but my friend, mentor, and former boss Lionel Stone suggested I reach out to you about my current vexation: I'm thinking of switching careers – from journalism to psychology. (Or maybe staying in journalism, but writing about psychological issues. Or maybe going into law enforcement as a profiler. Or maybe . . . . ? Or maybe . . . . ? Or maybe . . . . . ?)

I'm 28 years old. I have a B.A. in English from the University of Wisconsin - Madison. I've been a journalist for the past three years – most recently as a White House correspondent for the Associated Press. But for a long time I've been thinking about diverting into psychology.

I think the main reason I'm considering a career switch is that I've come to recognize that I seem to possess a high amount of empathy gained from enduring many personal losses:

- *I was orphaned as an infant and raised by my aunt who died suddenly (I found her body).*

- *Two of my boyfriends met untimely deaths – one was murdered, the other died of a heroin overdose. (I found both their bodies, too).*

- *I've been sexually assaulted. (I testified at my attacker's trial and he is now in prison).*

- *I've also been held at gunpoint three times. In one instance, I talked my kidnapper into giving himself up.*

So, yes, I've been through a lot, but I think I'm a stronger person because of it. In addition, as a journalist, I believe I've learned to ask the kind of probing questions that can help a person articulate and understand their deep feelings.

Speaking of questions, I hope you don't mind if I bombard you with a few so that I can better discern my next steps. If you're too busy to reply, that's fine, but thought I'd ask.

Here goes:

1. *What's the best path to become a psychologist – and how arduous is the process?*

2. *Based on your experience, what are the highs/lows, strengths/weaknesses of your profession?*

3. *What do you wish someone had told you about being a psychologist when you were considering this path?*

4. *If you had it to do over again, what, if anything, would you do differently?*

Thank you for at least considering a response. If you're too busy to reply, I understand.

Sincerely,
~Lark Chadwick

I checked on the web and discovered that, probably unbeknownst to Lionel, one of his contacts specializes in transgender issues, so I added a post script to that person:

P.S. A good friend of mine, male, mid-thirties, recently surprised me by revealing he is bisexual, then shocked me when he told me he's considering a sex-change operation. I don't have a moral objection to any of these things, but my strong advice to him is that he seek counseling before he makes any final decisions. I understand transgender issues is one of your specialties. Did I give him the right advice? ~LC

As I was looking at the links that Kris had sent me, I got a quick – and daunting – reply from one of Lionel's former students, Kathryn Klett. Kathryn shared with me the joys and intricacies of studying for the Graduate Records Exams (GRE), the standardized test that's a prerequisite for getting into grad school.

She wrote that if she had it to do over again, "I would allow myself more time to focus exclusively on studying!"

Ugh. At least I've been warned.

Another of Lionel's contacts – Adrienne Kraft, a retired social worker – wrote that the most "prestigious" degree is a PhD in Clinical Psychology, but called that path "arduous" in that it could take six years.

Geez! No frigging way. I don't have that kind of patience. Or smarts.

She also mentioned an MSW – a Masters in Social Work – but that could take three years. Still not good.

But Ms. Kraft was very kind, writing: "You have been through more than any human being should have to endure." She praised my "resiliency" and desire "to use these experiences for the betterment of people and society."

She suggested other avenues I hadn't considered, including forensics and even the possibility of becoming "an expert witness" as a way to advocate for victims. But, given the current climate of scandal swirling around me, I could all too easily envision being eviscerated on the stand because of all the conspiracy theories circulating about me on the web.

Kraft also liked the idea of me becoming a "profiler," and wondered if any government agencies like the FBI or CIA would pay for my education. Now that idea sounded tantalizing.

Another email response came from Christine Talbott, a Licensed Clinical Professional Counselor (LCPC) living in Maine. Ms. Talbott wrote that the PhD route could cost me at least eighty thousand dollars.

Gulp.

Like Kraft, Talbott wrote that she doesn't like the bureaucracy of the job, especially dealing with insurance companies.

Talbott also gave me more ammunition in my conversations with Paul about his possible sex change:

> Your friend is required to have counseling for at least six months, and the counselor must attest that the surgery is appropriate using a specific criteria.
>
> If your friend is just bi-sexual, he is not a candidate for a sex change. One must be diagnosed as having "gender dysphoria."
>
> A really great book on this subject is "Becoming Nicole." It's about Nicole Maines, one of my clients. (I can give you her name because I'm identified as her therapist in this book.)
>
> It's a great read because the author alternates chapters on the research and Nicole's personal story (which includes her going to the state legislature and talking to every representative and senator in order to get an equal rights law in Maine, which did pass.) She's a hero to the transgendered folk here in Maine. Unique to Nicole is that she is one of a pair of identical twins and her brother is a heterosexual male.

I dashed off thank you emails to Klett, Kraft, and Talbott, then copied the transgender portion of Talbott's email and pasted it into an email I sent to Paul, topping it with a terse,

> "Hey.... I got this from a psychologist. Thought you might be interested. ~LC."

I blissfully lost all track of time and worked into the evening, barely taking time to raid the refrigerator and snack. But by seven p.m. I realized snacking wasn't enough – I needed protein. I ordered a pizza, then tipped my toe into social media.

It was as if I'd been gut-punched.

In the twenty-four hours I'd been off the grid, the story about Gannon and me had mushroomed. It was everywhere, not just on wacky fringe websites peddling conspiracy theories and anti-journalist hate.

The headline in the *New York Times* was sobering:

FBI LOOKING INTO ALLEGATIONS GANNON MURDERED WIFE. HOUSE JUDICIARY COMMITTEE WEIGHING IMPEACHMENT

By Drew Hill

I held my breath as I read the story.

What began just a few days ago as whispered conspiracy theories in the backwaters of the Internet has blossomed into a federal investigation that threatens to topple the nascent presidency of Will Gannon.

Several law enforcement sources confirm that the FBI has begun an investigation into allegations that President Gannon murdered his wife in order to pursue a romantic relationship with a former reporter he impregnated.

The FBI is neither confirming nor denying the existence of the investigation.

In the meantime, the House Judiciary Committee voted unanimously Wednesday to begin impeachment hearings on Monday.

"The allegations against the president are too grave to ignore," reads a joint, bipartisan statement issued by Judiciary Committee Chairman Rep. Harris Carmichael (R-Georgia) and ranking minority member Rep. Diane Shelby (D-Vermont).

Since INN broke the story on Tuesday, Gannon has not been seen in public, and the White House has had no comment.

The woman at the center of the story, Lark Chadwick, is a former White House correspondent for the Associated Press.

Chadwick has also dropped out of sight but told the Reuters news agency on Tuesday that the initial INN story is "riddled with factual errors and flimsy sourcing." She did not elaborate.

The *New York Times* piece, which I read online, contained the shot of Gannon resting his hand on my shoulder during his ever-so-brief aisle interview with the press travel pool on Sunday aboard Air Force One in Beijing just before we took off and returned to the states from China.

The rest of the *Times* story put events into context, repeating that Rose had died recently. On that matter, Drew Hill wrote:

> *Rose Gannon collapsed at the White House Correspondents' Association dinner February 19 as her husband was beginning his remarks.*
>
> *At the time, the White House said the first lady's collapse was caused by "exhaustion and dehydration."*
>
> *After the first lady's death, however, Chadwick reported that Ms. Gannon told her she was dying of pancreatic cancer but had asked Chadwick to keep the story secret.*
>
> *Ms. Chadwick was interviewing Ms. Gannon in the first family's private quarters in the White House two weeks ago when Rose Gannon suddenly lost consciousness just as the president entered the room.*
>
> *No other witnesses were present.*
>
> *The first lady was rushed to a hospital where she was pronounced dead.*
>
> *The Internet has been abuzz with unconfirmed allegations that Ms. Gannon was poisoned.*
>
> *The Associated Press, The New York Times, and other news organizations went to court last week to try to obtain Rose Gannon's autopsy report, but U.S. District Judge Brett O'Roarke ruled that the report should remain sealed due to unspecified "national security" concerns.*

I appreciated that Drew Hill's *Times* story was measured and accurate. What galled me is that it was a story not because the allegations were true, but because two powerful federal bodies – the Justice Department and Congress – were investigating.

Everything the *Times* reported was accurate, but the way the facts were assembled sure made it look like Gannon and I had a lot to hide.

And yet.

And yet Drew Hill wrote the story exactly the way I would have.

And yet.

And yet it sure feels awful when you're the reportee not the reporter.

But what to do about it?

I decided the time had come to act on the information Will Gannon told me on deep background aboard Air Force One, but it was after business hours, so I'd have to do that first thing Thursday morning.

Just then my phone buzzed, an A.P. bulletin:

GANNON TO ADDRESS NATION TONIGHT AT 8 E.T.

I checked my watch – 7:45. *Holy shit! Is he gonna resign?* I wondered.

Just then, my doorbell rang. I went to the intercom on the kitchen wall.

"Who is it?"

"Pizza for Chadwick?" The voice was male. Latino?

"Oh. Right. Thanks." I buzzed him up from the lobby entrance.

A few minutes later, there was a knock on my door.

Before opening it, I looked through the fish-eye lens. A dark-haired kid of about twenty stood patiently. He wore a blue polo shirt with the pizzeria's red, white, and blue logo over the left breast.

As I opened the door he smiled and removed the pizza carton from the large canvas container that had been keeping it warm.

"There's my dinner!" I said as I eagerly took the carton from him.

He placed a pen and the credit card receipt on top of the pizza carton for me to sign.

As I was adding a tip and scribbling my name, I heard a man say, "Lark Chadwick?"

I looked up. Another guy had walked up behind the pizza guy. He was cute. Mid-thirties. Reminded me of John Krasinski on "The Office."

"Lark Chadwick?" he repeated.

"Yeah."

He handed me an envelope. "You've been served."

"What!?"

"You've been served in more ways than one, apparently," the guy said cheerily as he walked away, chuckling.

I handed the pizza guy his pen and took the carton.

"He came in right behind me," the guy shrugged apologetically. "I thought he lived in the building."

"Yeah. Whatever."

I shut the door, bolted it, tore open the envelope, read the contents, and promptly lost my appetite.

C)3 ◆ ⑧

CHAPTER 39

As my pizza cooled and my blood turned to ice, I read,

"YOU ARE HEREBY COMMANDED TO APPEAR . . . ."

The document, a subpoena issued by the House Judiciary Committee, ordered me to testify before the committee at ten a.m. Monday.

I've never even gotten a speeding ticket, so to say I was intimidated was an understatement. Adding to that feeling were these words at the bottom: "Failing to appear could result in your being held in contempt of Congress."

I've always held Congress in a bit of contempt, but the prospect of facing criminal charges for it helped to rein in my surging emotions.

In addition to appearing in person to testify, the subpoena ordered me to submit to a pregnancy test, "and, if pregnant, provide the committee with a DNA sample of the fetus." The document even went so far as to order that if I've had an abortion or miscarriage within the past nine months that I should submit medical records certifying it.

Yes. I wanted nothing more than to prove that I wasn't pregnant with Will Gannon's baby, but I really resented the intrusive gall of the House Judiciary Committee. The Handmaid's Tale was no longer a dystopian novel written by Margaret Atwood, it was rapidly becoming the life and legacy of Lark Chadwick.

I grabbed my cell and dialed Lionel.

"Hey," he said, jauntily. "Did you call so we could watch Gannon's address to the nation together?"

"Shit," I said. "I forgot. Has he started speaking yet?"

"Any minute," he replied.

I fired up my TV. CNN was just finishing a panel of "experts" shouting at each other about something. The banner at the lower third of the screen screamed, "OVAL OFFICE MURDER MYSTERY!"

"There's something else I need to talk with you about," I said.

"Can it wait?"

"It's important. I just got subpoenaed to testify Monday before the House Judiciary Committee."

"Oh my God," Lionel exclaimed, sounding uncharacteristically like the Valley Girl he most certainly isn't.

The blue, white, and gold presidential seal filled the TV screen.

"Stay on the line," Lionel said. "We'll watch it together, then we'll sort out that subpoena bullshit."

"Okay," I said. "Thanks."

The presidential seal dissolved to a medium-wide shot of Will Gannon sitting behind the iconic Resolute Desk in the Oval Office.

"Good evening, My Fellow Americans." The camera slowly zoomed closer until only Gannon's face and shoulders filled the screen. He looked haggard.

"I speak to you tonight about a grave threat to world peace."

"So," Lionel chuckled, "I guess he's not going to confess to being your baby's daddy."

"Lionel!"

"Sorry."

"Jesus."

"Just twelve days ago," Gannon said, "at the very moment I was delivering the eulogy for my late wife Rose at her funeral, Russian President Dimitri Yazkov announced his intent to provide nuclear weapons to Iran. That dangerous and provocative statement set off a flurry of diplomatic attempts to defuse the crisis. So far, President Yazkov has been consistently intransigent to all peace overtures, both public and private.

"Within the past few days, intelligence agencies of the United States, as well as our allies, have found unmistakable evidence that Russia is now on the verge of shipping several suitcase-sized nuclear bombs to Iran."

"Holy shit!" both Lionel and I said in unison, followed by "Shhhhhh!" as we each shushed the other.

"As you know," Gannon continued, "for many years the regime in Iran has been belligerent to the United States and Israel. Possessing nuclear weapons, capable of destroying millions of innocent lives in the blink of an eye, would make Iran a clear and present danger to the United States and its allies.

"The United States and Russia have had a similarly fraught relationship: allies during World War II, adversaries during the Cold War, but then strategic partners in space exploration. Lately, however, with President Yazkov's dangerous and provocative actions, Russia and the United States of America are now in danger of becoming mortal enemies. It need not be this way."

"This reminds me of JFK's Cuban Missile Crisis address in 1962," Lionel said.

As if on cue, Gannon said, "On October 22nd, 1962, President John F. Kennedy sat at this very desk, in this very room – the Oval Office of the White House – to alert the world to a similar existential crisis. At that time, President Kennedy said this: 'Neither the United States of America nor the world community of nations can tolerate deliberate deception and offensive threats on the part of any nation, large or small. Nuclear weapons are so destructive that any substantially increased possibility of their use or any sudden change in their deployment may well be regarded as a definite threat to peace.'

"President Kennedy went on to say: 'The 1930s taught us a clear lesson: aggressive conduct, if allowed to go unchecked and unchallenged ultimately leads to war. This nation is opposed to war. Our policy has been one of patience and restraint, but now further action is required. We will not prematurely or unnecessarily risk the costs of worldwide nuclear war in which even the fruits of victory would be ashes in our mouth – but neither will we shrink from that risk at any time it must be faced.'"

"So, what's Gannon gonna do?" I asked, wishing I once again was a White House correspondent.

Gannon obliged and answered my question. "Accordingly, and in conjunction with our allies, the United States is leading an international coalition to confront and turn back this threat through all necessary means – diplomatic and military."

"He's talking about going to war," Lionel said.

Gannon then ticked off a series of actions.

He called for:

- An immediate emergency meeting of the United Nations to adopt a resolution demanding the prompt dismantling of the suitcase nukes under the supervision of U.N. observers.

- Stepped up surveillance of the nuclear suitcase bombs

- Putting Russia on notice that the U.S. "and its partners" would conduct swift "surgical strikes" to remove the nuclear threat if Russia attempts to ship the bombs to Iran "or to any entity outside Russia."

- Immediate economic sanctions on both Russia and Iran

Gannon ended his address on an ominous note:

"It shall be the policy of this Nation to regard any detonation of one of those tactical nuclear weapons now under the control of Russia against any U.S. ally as an attack by Russia on the United States, requiring a full retaliatory response upon *Russia.*"

"That's ripped almost word-for-word from Kennedy's speech," Lionel said.

Gannon said, "I call upon President Yazkov to halt and eliminate this clandestine, reckless and provocative threat to world peace and to work with me to stabilize relations between our two nations. I close with the words of President Kennedy: 'Our goal is not the victory of might, but the vindication of right. Not peace at the expense of freedom, but both peace and freedom. God willing, that goal will be achieved.' Thank you and good night."

The Oval Office feed faded to black, replaced by Wolf Blitzer flanked and outnumbered by a panel of more "experts."

"What do you think?" Lionel asked as I muted the television.

I looked at my uneaten, now cold, pizza. "I think I'm not hungry any more."

Just then I got a text from *POTUS.* Will Gannon's message to me was simple: "*NOW!*" Along with it, he sent a cell phone number.

I knew what he meant.

ଓ ✦ ଞ

CHAPTER 40

"Uh oh," I said, looking at my phone while, on my muted television, Wolf Blitzer rode herd on a studio full of international think tankers and foreign correspondents parsing every word of Gannon's we're-all-gonna-die address.

"'Uh oh' what?" Lionel asked, his voice tinny on the phone's speaker.

"I just got a text from Gannon."

"What's it say?"

"Now."

"Yes. Now. Tell me now."

"No, Lionel. 'Now' is what Gannon's text says."

"Oh. I knew that."

"Right. And Gannon texted me a phone number."

"So," Lionel said after a brief pause, "he's pulled the trigger on what you and I talked about the other day in Rock Creek Park?"

"Yep."

"You ready for the next step? The stakes just got decidedly higher."

"Yes, they did. And yes, I am . . . or as ready as I'll ever be."

"What's the plan?"

"I need to place the call."

"Okay. Call me back when the deed is done."

We hung up, I dialed the number Gannon sent me, and got the ball rolling, then I called Lionel back and we spent a few minutes gaming out the next steps. They involved bringing together what Gannon and I discussed privately aboard Air Force One, and the investigative piece about Rose Gannon's death I was working on with Lionel for *ProPublica.*

Once we finished discussing that, I shifted gears. "The next thing we need to talk about is the subpoena."

"What subpoena?" Lionel asked.

"How soon we forget. I've been ordered to testify before the House Judiciary Committee on Monday."

"Oh. That."

"Yes, 'oh that'."

"Read it to me."

I did.

"Christ," he said disgustedly when I'd finished.

"What do you think I should I do?"

"First, you need to lawyer up. Fortunately, I have someone in mind."

"Lionel, I'm unemployed. I can't afford a five-hundred-dollar-an-hour lawyer."

"I think they charge even more than that now," he said, unhelpfully.

I whimpered and felt my lower lip tremble and a weakness in my legs and the pit of my stomach.

"Let's set cost aside for now," he said.

"Easy for you to say."

"It's such a high-profile case that a lot of firms would take it *pro bono* for the publicity."

"I don't want one of those shrill ambulance chasing feminists who take delight in demonizing all men, especially this president."

"Whoa. This doesn't sound like the ardent feminist Lark Chadwick that I've come to know and love."

He was right. Was I unconsciously and instinctively trying to protect the president and abandoning my principles and cheapening the importance of the #MeToo movement?

I said, "Right now, there appears to be a growing appetite to take down powerful men – especially Gannon. This isn't a 'Me Too' case."

"So you say," he said, unconvinced. "Anyway, I've got the perfect guy in mind to represent you."

"But I don't want a guy to be my lawyer, either."

"Why not? He's great."

"Maybe so, but I'll feel better with a woman. A woman who'll understand the bind I'm in. Most of the guys I know don't get it."

"Thank you very much."

"You're different, Lionel, but sometimes even you can be a bit tone deaf."

"What?" He laughed at his joke.

I didn't. "I said tone deaf. Not deaf deaf."

"Oh."

"I rest my case."

"Okay, I'll think on it and come up with some names."

"I'll do some digging, too," I said. "This is as high a priority as the other thing we just talked about – assuming the world as we know it even exists on Monday."

Lionel grunted. "The Cuban Missile Crisis was one of the first big stories I covered for the *Times*. Those were scary days. Really scary days."

I'd told Lionel I was ready for "the next step." But honestly, I was scared, too.

CB ◆ BO

CHAPTER 41

To say Ruth Nicholas, the lawyer Lionel recruited to represent me, is classy and elegant is an understatement. She's about fifty with cheekbones so high she reminds me of Loretta Young, the glamorous actress of the 1930s, '40s, and '50s.

Ruth's perfectly coiffed white hair offset her navy-blue two-piece power suit accented with a red scarf and gold brooch. She sat across from me at my dining room table the next afternoon, Thursday, at one o'clock.

"Thank you for running the gauntlet of press staked out in front of my apartment," I said.

"Not a problem," she replied. "I think it might actually be thinning out."

"That's a relief. Not a surprise, either."

"Why?"

"There's nothing like the threat of a nuclear war to distract reporters from a sex scandal."

"Oh, but America loves a sex scandal," Ruth said. "It's much more fun and so much easier to understand – and judge – than geopolitics of any sort."

I frowned. "You're probably right. Sad, but true."

Ruth had accurately captured the essence of the political mood as it stood. Gannon's Oval Office address was dominating the current news cycle, but cynical pundits were suggesting the crisis was a "hoax" engineered to throw the spotlight off the murder investigation, the brewing impeachment hearings, and the sex scandal with me.

"Thank you for taking on my case," I said. "I'm unemployed and have very limited resources."

"Yes. That's what I understand. But I'm willing to waive my fee because I believe strongly in you. I've been a fan from afar for a long time."

"Thank you. That means a lot. Most of the country thinks I'm a gold-digging, power hungry slut."

"Which is why I'm grateful for the opportunity to prove them wrong."

Ruth opened her leather brief case, took out a yellow legal pad, and uncapped a fountain pen. "Let's get down to business, shall we? Do you have the subpoena?"

I slid it to her across the table.

She put on half-moon glasses and took a moment to read it. She tsk-ed a couple times, scowled a few more, and jotted some notes before taking off her glasses and looking up at me.

"They've got a lot of fucking nerve," she said.

That's when I fell in love with my lawyer.

"Yes," I agreed. "It's outrageous."

"So," she said. "First order of business is a pregnancy test."

"Wait. What?"

She nodded soberly. "I'm afraid so. You don't want to be in contempt of Congress."

"I'm so in contempt of Congress!"

"Me, too. But even though Congress has the power on its side, you have the truth on yours. Truth trumps power."

"But is what they're ordering legal? Why should I play their game?" I asked.

"Because you're not pregnant with Gannon's baby." She paused, then added warily, "Are you . . .?"

I shook my head. "No. But my pregnancy is none of Congress's business."

"I'm afraid it is."

"Why?"

"Because Gannon's the president and it's being suggested that he murdered his wife to carry on an affair with the mother of his illegitimate child. That easily qualifies as the Constitution's definition of 'high crimes and misdemeanors.'"

"But the allegation is being manufactured by his political enemies."

"Doesn't matter. We're now in an era of tribalism and hair triggers. Shoot first. Ask questions later. And, let's face it: a big chunk of the public considers you as the enemy of the people because you're a journalist. Plus you're an uppity woman. Let's prove them wrong."

"Doesn't submitting to an intrusive pregnancy test set a bad precedent?"

Ruth shrugged. "The alternative is to perpetuate a constitutional crisis by keeping a cloud of suspicion over the president at a time when he needs the moral authority to deal with a high-stakes international crisis."

I scowled.

"And stonewalling," she continued, "merely adds momentum to the belief that you have something to hide. The story just gets worse, like a blister."

"What do you suggest?"

She put the end of the pen against her lower lip and thought a minute. "Here's what I think we should do."

My eyes widened and I leaned in.

"I'll contact the chief counsel for the House Judiciary Committee and make arrangements for that person to join me in witnessing the pregnancy test."

"Holy shit. Are you kidding?"

"No. It's not some sort of gynecological exam with stirrups and probes. It's a simple blood test that will determine if you're pregnant. They can also take a blood sample from the fetus to do a DNA comparison with the president's DNA, which is already on file with the Secret Service, and probably a bunch of other spy agencies."

"But how will the committee know the test is legit?" I asked.

"The committee's chief counsel and I will witness the collection process and testing. That way the committee can't allege any hanky-panky because their representative witnessed the blood collection and testing."

"That should settle the matter, then, right?"

"It should, but this is Congress we're talking about, so there's only so far logic, reason, and good will can go."

"I'll also have to testify?"

"Yeah. Probably."

Just then my phone buzzed – an A.P. bulletin:

> *Former New York Times National Editor Lionel Stone is the latest high-powered man to be caught in the crosshairs of the #MeToo movement.*
>
> *The Pulitzer-Prize winning journalist is accused of making an unwanted sexual advance on a woman he supervised at the Times more than twenty years ago.*
>
> *The allegation appears in the latest edition of The Atlantic, which will be published later today. The Associated Press received an advance copy.*
>
> *According to the report, Stone's accuser is Francine Noyce, the CEO of Independent Network News (INN).*
>
> *"He pushed me against a wall and forcibly kissed me, shoving his tongue nearly down my throat," Noyce is quoted telling the Atlantic.*
>
> *Stone is also the former employer of ex-A.P. White House Correspondent Lark Chadwick, the woman at the center of the scandal threatening the presidency of Will Gannon.*

I slid the phone across the table for Ruth Nicholas to see.

"Oh, this isn't good," the lawyer said, scowling.

CB ◆ BO

CHAPTER 42

As soon as Ruth Nicholas left my apartment, I gave Lionel a call.

"Let's Skype," I said as soon as he picked up.

"I'm not near my computer. FaceTime?"

"Deal."

We hit the appropriate buttons on our phones and in no time, we were able to eyeball each other.

"How'd your sit-down go with Ruth?" he asked.

"Great. She's wonderful. Thank you for finding her."

"Not a problem. She and I go way back."

"You haven't seen the news, have you?"

"What news?"

"Oh, Lionel. I called because I thought you knew."

"Knew what?"

"I'm sorry to be the one to bring you the bad news."

"What bad news?" He was beginning to sound impatient.

"Do you have the A.P. app on your phone?"

"Of course."

"Apparently you missed their latest bulletin."

"I guess I did. Just a sec. Lemme check." His screen went blank while he went searching, but I could still hear him rustling and fumbling.

"Oh, Christ!" he exclaimed. "Christ!"

When the screen came to life again, one of his meaty hands covered his face. His breathing was labored, almost as if he was hyperventilating.

"Lionel. That A.P. story isn't you. I know you. This isn't the Lionel Stone I know."

He said nothing, but kept his hand against his face. He took a few deep breaths.

"Pure and simple," I continued, "this is Francine Noyce getting back at me by going after you."

"There's a problem," Lionel said, taking his hand away from his face. It was red and puffy.

"What's the problem?" I asked.

"What she's alleging might be true."

"What do you mean 'might'?"

"When she worked for me at the *Times*, I was a drunk, Lark. There are big chunks of time I can't account for. For all I know, I could have done what she alleges."

"But you don't know for sure, right?"

"That's not my point."

"Maybe it is. How would you describe your working relationship with her at the time?"

"It was fine. Professional. She was a kick-ass reporter and a solid writer. But that's not the point." He was getting angry. At me.

"Lionel, why are you trying to convince me to believe something awful about you?"

"I'm not. I'm just trying to explain that, as you well know, I'm not perfect. I've got a past, Lark. You're right: I'm different. But that's now, not then."

"Was there ever a time when you sensed that something was off between you and Noyce? Had she ever complained about your behavior? Gone to H.R. on you?"

"No."

"Well, okay, then."

"Not okay. I've read way too many of these 'Me Too' stories. Often women are too traumatized and afraid to file a complaint at the time. I get that. The absence of any contemporaneous corroboration proves nothing."

He had a point.

216

We were quiet a moment, each of us lost in our own thoughts, regrouping.

"What were you like back then, Lionel?" I asked softly.

He was quiet. His face was florid, his breathing still labored. "To be honest, I was an asshole, Lark."

"Do you mind if I ask you a few personal questions?"

"Hell, no. You're you. I can talk with you about anything. Plus, it's about time for the tables to be turned. I'm usually the one pummeling you with questions. Fire away. I need to talk, anyway."

"I've got a ton of questions, but let me ask this: what was your rock bottom? What prompted you to turn your life around?"

His voice cracked. "Muriel," he said. "She's the one who saved me."

"How? Why? What happened?"

"We met in Wisconsin when I was on a book tour promoting *Quagmire*."

"The book about Vietnam."

"Right. By this time, it had won me the Pulitzer, so I was feeling my oats. And sowing plenty of wild ones, too."

"Was Muriel one of them?"

He laughed, remembering. "I tried, but she was different."

"How so?"

"She had self-respect and standards."

I chuckled. "She wouldn't put out?"

"God knows I tried, but nope. She held the line."

"Were there sparks between you two?"

"Oh, hell yeah. But she'd only go so far, and it wasn't nearly as far as I wanted to go."

"Why didn't you just move on?"

"Because not only did she have standards, she had smarts. She was fun to be with. For a while, we had a long-distance relationship. She was finishing school in Wisconsin; I was covering the White House for the *Times*. So we talked long distance. A lot."

"Did she know you drank?"

"Yeah, but she didn't know how bad it was until much later."

"How much later?"

"Not until I became national editor of the *Times* and moved to New York. After she graduated, she got a job teaching English at a high school in Madison."

"If you guys were getting serious, why didn't she come out to New York and start her career there where she could be closer to you?"

"You'd have to ask her. That was certainly my preference, and I lobbied for it, but she held the line."

"I think I know why."

"Why?"

"By this time, you were a star. If she's anything like me, she knew instinctively that before she hitched her wagon to you, she needed to establish her own identity first. Otherwise, she'd always be living in your shadow."

"Yeah. Come to think of it, she probably did say something like that."

"So, what's the link between her and your decision to change?"

"As a teacher, she had summers off, so we spent more and more time together."

"In New York?"

He nodded. "Yeah. She visited a lot. We hung out. She did a lot of touristy stuff while I worked. When I could get time off, we traveled together a little."

"I've been told that traveling together is the true test of a relationship."

He nodded. "It is. It was for us."

"Obviously, you passed the test."

He smiled. "And so did she."

"What did traveling together teach you about each other?"

He chuckled, warming to the topic. "When you travel with someone, you see them at their worst – when they're tired, and when things go wrong. That's the test: you see them at their most authentic, when they have no emotional buffer."

"How was it you were able to pass?"

"Believe me, I'm as surprised as you are that I passed. Also . . . I have duly noted that you jumped to the conclusion that Muriel easily passed the test."

"You are correct, sir." I was amused and relieved that he still had the ability to banter with me even in the face of a ghastly accusation I firmly believed had nothing to do with truth and everything to do with Francine Noyce's revenge against me for thwarting her, then clobbering her.

"During our first trip together," Lionel continued, "Muriel said something that got my attention."

"What was that?"

"At the end of the weekend, she said, 'It's comfortable being with you. I don't feel like we've been in a power struggle.'"

"Wow. What do you think she meant?"

"I wasn't sure, so we talked about it. I came away realizing that even though I was a chauvinistic asshole—"

"Was?"

"Hush now."

"Yes, sir. Proceed."

"As I was saying," he ahem-ed, "even though I thought I was just being my jerk self – opinionated, assertive – I didn't mind when she offered opinions and suggestions of her own. I respected her, and apparently, she noticed."

"Okay." I paused and took a deep breath. "Now, do you mind if we fast-forward to your rock bottom?"

"Okay." He paused, scowled, and plunged ahead. "We were engaged. She'd left her teaching job in Wisconsin and moved to New York to be with me. We were at a party together. I got drunk and began getting amorous."

"And she was still holding the line?"

"No. By this time we were living together. I was getting amorous with someone else at the party. Or at least I was trying."

"And she became aware."

"Oh yeah."

"Not pretty, huh?"

"I don't know."

"What do you mean?"

"I don't remember."

"Really?"

"Uh huh."

"All I know is what she told me."

"What did she tell you?"

"She told me I began trying to make out with one of the chicks at the party."

"Chicks? Really?"

"Now I'm woke, Lark. Then I was a dope."

"So, what happened?"

"Somehow she got me to surrender the car keys to her. She drove us back home. The next day she gave me an ultimatum: it's either her, or the booze, but not both."

"Obviously, you chose her, but it must've been a struggle."

He nodded. "By the time I woke up the next day, she'd put together a list of A.A. meetings near where we lived – times and places. I chose one, and she took me to it."

"She went, too?"

"Yep. 'I'm in this, too,' she told me." His voice broke. It took him a moment to regain his composure. "And she's been with me ever since. We're partners. Companions. A good team."

"But wait. I've seen you drink."

"Look, I'm not the poster child of A.A. I don't follow the program religiously. Thankfully, I have an off switch – and usually it's off."

"Did the *Atlantic* reach out to you before they went to press?"

"Apparently, they did. Someone from there tried calling several times, but I've been too busy with the move to pay attention. Pretty dumb, huh?"

I ignored the question. "Now what are you going to do?"

"I don't know, Lark. I don't know."

"I know a good lawyer."

He laughed. "I just might give her a call. Thanks."

CB ◆ BO

CHAPTER 43

It was great to finally be outside again after being holed up in my apartment for two days while it seemed as though the entire Washington press corps was camped out on the doorstep of my apartment complex.

Their numbers had finally dwindled. I'd managed to give the few remaining die-hards the slip by wearing a ball cap, sunglasses, and leaving in Pearlie from the apartment's underground garage.

I found a place to park in the 2600 block of Wisconsin Avenue in D.C., a short walk from my destination – my mission.

It was a beautiful Friday in April, almost exactly a month after the official start of spring. For the first time in months, I could smell the loamy aroma of the earth.

Yellow daffodils were beginning to grow in the flowerbeds that fronted the buildings along the street. As the newest cycle of life and rebirth was once again taking root in D.C., I was struck with the realization of just how fragile and precious life is. I still couldn't feel the little life growing inside me, but I knew it was there – morning sickness is such a wonderful reminder.

I also realized that if my mission failed – a mission set into motion the night before by Will Gannon's text to me – there could very soon be a catastrophic nuclear war with Russia.

Lionel had told me just how frightening life was like during the Cuban Missile Crisis. His generation had lived under the fear of global nuclear annihilation, whereas my generation grew up in the shadow of the falling twin towers of 9/11, coupled with the terror that comes with the randomness of a crazed mass shooter. Both of our generations came of age with a vague sense of nihilism – or at least fatalism – and a sense of powerlessness.

My stride on this morning was purposeful. I wouldn't go so far as to say I was confident, but I was definitely determined.

As I walked, my mind returned to my private, "deep background" conversation with Will Gannon nine days earlier aboard Air Force One as we hurtled toward China – the conversation that laid the groundwork for my current path.

Here's how it played out that day with the president:

President Gannon took a deep breath and leaned back as if reassessing whether he would tell me what's going on even though I'd given him my word that we were now on "deep background," meaning anything he told me was not only off the record, but would have to be confirmed somewhere else. Basically, his role was now Authoritative Tipster, pointing me in the direction that will yield the answer to Rose's death – and the killer.

He leaned forward in the chair next to his desk until his face was just a few feet in front of mine where I sat at the end of the brown leather couch in the president's flying Air Force One office.

"Okay," he said, his mind made up. "Here's what we know and what we don't know."

"I'm listening."

"We know that Rose died of pancreatic cancer. Actually, it was a heart attack due to complications from her condition."

"Right. We already know that. So, why all the secrecy? Why seal her autopsy report?"

"Because the report reveals that Rose's pancreas had a lethally high concentration of a toxin that is heretofore unknown."

"Are you saying that she was, indeed, poisoned?"

He shook his head. "It's more complicated than that."

"What do you mean?"

"Whatever 'poison' was introduced into her bloodstream is unknown. Technically, yes, she was poisoned. But the 'poison' was in the form of an unknown toxin."

"What's the difference between a poison and a toxin?"

"For your purposes, it's probably a distinction without a difference."

"Oh, that's helpful. What do you mean?"

"I'm trained as a lawyer, not a doctor, so here's my best understanding of what happened to Rose and why it's so sensitive that I've imposed an information blackout."

"I'm listening."

"The CDC pathologist who conducted the autopsy told me he became suspicious because her pancreas contained something he hadn't seen before."

"Not a poison."

"Not exactly."

"I'm getting the impression that you and the CDC don't really know what you have."

He nodded. "We knew she was dying of rapidly advancing pancreatic cancer, but unlike most pancreatic cancers that don't have an easily identifiable cause, hers did."

"What was it?"

"The toxin. They're still doing tests on it to more accurately identify and understand it. They've never seen it before."

"Does it occur naturally or is it man-made?"

"The latter."

"How can they tell?"

"Beyond my pay grade."

"You're the president. We pay you a lot. The buck stops with you."

"Fair enough. Because what they found doesn't occur in nature, the assumption is that it's a man-made toxin specifically designed to target and embed itself in the pancreas."

"And it's already well known that pancreatic cancer is hard to detect and diagnose until it's far along and highly lethal."

"Yes."

"Which makes this toxin an excellent weapon."

"Yes."

"So, let me put two and two together: Rose's autopsy report is sealed for 'national security reasons.'" I used my fingers to air-quote. "Are you saying that the 'national security reason' for sealing the autopsy report is that you believe Rose was murdered by a foreign power?"

"Yes."

"Which one?"

"That's what we're trying to figure out. I don't want the murderer to know what we know, at least until we have a better idea of who it might be."

"Suspects?"

"A nation state with the means and ability to produce the toxin and the opportunity to deliver it."

"Let me guess: China?"

He scowled. "Possibly, but I don't think so."

"Why not?"

"It's true that before the recent China coup, they were pretty bellicose towards us, but Tong is my friend. This trip to China is to firm up our ties."

"And not to investigate?"

"Well, FBI agents and a team from the CDC are along for the ride on this trip, but I personally am not in investigation mode. I trust Tong and, unless confronted with evidence to the contrary, I'll continue to trust him."

"The trip is fence mending and bridge building?" I asked.

He nodded. "That and alliance building."

"How so?"

"As you know Russia is the real thorn in our side right now."

"Yes. Yazkov is becoming unpredictable and scary."

"Indeed. I want to firm up ties with China so that the Chinese can act as a counterweight against Russia."

"So, you think Russia ordered Rose killed?"

"Yes, but it's only a hunch."

"Means? Motive? Opportunity?" I asked.

"Means? The toxin."

"But you said you don't know for sure that Russia produced it."

"True."

"Motive?"

"We're not sure of that, either, but Russia is a prime suspect."

"Why?"

"Yaz is an insecure, infantile loose cannon. He'd been tight with China, but the coup neutralized a powerful alliance of his."

"Why is that a motive to kill Rose?"

"The working theory among my advisors is that Yaz had Rose killed knowing it would cause me to be grief-stricken and off balance."

I picked up the thread. "And that would then open the way for him to make an audacious and provocative move that would bolster and reassert his need to feel like a feared world power again?"

"Right. Hence his move to form a nuclear alliance with Iran."

"Yes. It throws off the balance of power."

"But it hasn't thrown me off balance."

"Why not?"

"I'm good at compartmentalizing. I have to stay emotionally steady. I can't afford to let Rose's death throw me. The stakes are too high."

As the president talked, I remembered something that might answer the last element of my means-motive-opportunity question. When I shared my hunch with him, he was quiet for several moments, subdued. Thinking. Then, he got up and paced to the door and back several times, hands jammed into his pockets.

I sat patiently, waiting, watching.

As Gannon paced, he bit his lower lip. His brow was furrowed. His face was contorted. It was as if he was having an inner debate with himself. Finally, he sat down across from me again. He planted both feet on the floor and leaned toward me.

"Do you know who John Scali is?" he asked.

I shook my head.

"He was a reporter for ABC News and he saved the world from nuclear war."

"Of course he did."

"No. Really. He was a back-channel link between the Soviet Union and JFK during the Cuban Missile Crisis. Would you be willing to me my back-channel link to Yazkov?"

I sat back, stunned and startled. "I-I don't know. Why me? How would it work? What would you want me to do?"

Over the next few minutes, Gannon explained his reasoning to me and I peppered him with questions. To be honest, I doubted I was the person for the job and tried to poke holes in his thinking.

It wasn't working.

"We've been using traditional diplomacy on the pending nuclear relationship between Russia and Iran," Gannon continued, "but I want to open a separate channel that the Russians will know is more personal."

"Why not just pick up the phone and call?"

"Because that raises the temperature too much too soon."

"What do you mean?"

"I'm trying to find a way not only to lower the temperature, but to turn off the stove. Diplomacy, whether traditional, or back-channel, gives both sides time to think, talk, and recalculate."

"What's the goal?"

"The ultimate goal is to work toward direct leader-to-leader talks rather than to risk having premature talks cause the house of cards to fall suddenly. If that happens, it makes it all the more difficult to re-establish peace and goodwill between the two leaders."

"I see."

"But will you be there for me?"

"With all due respect, sir, I'm still not convinced."

He put his elbows on his thighs and used his hands for emphasis. "Here's what I have in mind: if things get any worse between us and Russia, you'd be my ace in the hole."

"Geez. No pressure, Lark."

He laughed. "Who knows? Maybe I won't need you, but I want to know you're there if I do."

"Isn't it unethical for a journalist to be a president's personal emissary?"

Gannon shrugged. "I'm not aware that John Scali shared your concern. I think that in his mind saving the world trumped loyalty to journalistic ethics. Plus, remember: according to our deal, if you are able to confirm on your own what you and I have been discussing, then you've got a story free and clear."

I began to chew on a cuticle, thinking hard.

Gannon took advantage of my ethical plight and once again filled the silence. "It's not even a sure thing that I'll need your help. I'll only call upon you if it looks like you're my best hope."

"Last hope?"

"No pressure, but yeah. Probably."

"So, how will this work?"

Gannon explained that if things get dicey, he would alert his contact to expect a call from me requesting a face-to-face meeting. The president would then text me the person's cell phone number and accompany it with a text.

Gannon said, "My text to you will say 'now.' It will mean that the pump is primed for you to call, knowing that you represent me, but not the reason for the meeting. During the meeting it will be your job to convey what you know based on what you and I have just discussed about Rose's poisoning."

"Then what? Am I just a conduit?"

"Yes. Your job is to firmly convey what we know and to relay any response back to me."

"And you think this will work?"

"It could."

"Why do you think so?"

"Because it helped end the Cuban Missile Crisis. Formal diplomatic communication wasn't working."

"Why not?"

"Khrushchev, the Soviet premiere, had to appear strong for the hawks in his government who were keeping him in power. But he reached out privately to Kennedy through the KGB's D.C. station chief who contacted John Scali. It was Khrushchev's way to make a more personal appeal."

"And it worked?"

"Yes. Kennedy chose to ignore Khrushchev's bellicose rhetoric in favor of private, personal communication that was more peace-loving rather than belligerent and swaggering."

"But Khrushchev doesn't sound like Yazkov."

"True. Yaz is an unstable, narcissistic shit show. But maybe, when the rest of the world isn't his stage, and he's approached on a more personal level, he might be persuaded to set aside pretense."

"We shall see," I said.

"So, you'll help me?"

I closed my eyes, clenched my jaw and nodded. "Yes, but I have serious doubts."

CB ◆ ED

CHAPTER 44

I arrived at the front gate of the Embassy of the Russian Federation at 2650 Wisconsin Ave. a little before my ten-a.m. appointment. Gaining access through the front gate and onto the massive, sprawling, and heavily fortified compound was easy because I was expected.

An armed Russian soldier escorted me from the gatehouse up a brick driveway to the front door of the blocky, white, seven-story building.

As we walked, a sudden shudder shot through me.

I remembered what happened to *Washington Post* columnist and Saudi exile Jamal Khashoggi. He, too, was a journalist accused by an authoritarian regime of spreading "fake news." He was lured to the Saudi embassy in Turkey under the pretense of getting the proper papers so he could marry his fiancée. Instead, he was murdered, dismembered, and disappeared.

Those thoughts were racing through my mind as I realized I was now in the company of an armed guard inside the compound of the Russian embassy and approaching the front entrance.

Am I walking into a trap?

Just as the guard opened the door, a man hurrying out of the building bumped right into me.

"Excuse me," I said, instinctively.

"Sorry," he said.

For a moment, our eyes locked.

"Alex!" I exclaimed. "What are you doing here?"

He brushed past me without saying a word and scrambled down the steps.

"Alex!" I hollered.

He ignored me and dashed toward the street.

For a moment, I considered running after him. He'd gotten away with gaslighting Paul into believing he hadn't told him that I was pregnant. Now Alex was trying to pretend that he didn't know me.

"Do you know him?" I asked the guard who was my escort.

The guard shook his head and shrugged. "*Nyet.*"

"Yeah, Right. I'm down the rabbit hole now," I said more to myself.

I took out my cell phone and called Paul.

"Hey," he said brightly when he picked up on the first ring.

"Guess who I just saw leaving the Russian embassy?"

"I give up. Who?"

"Alex."

Stunned silence on the other end.

"Your boyfriend."

"I know who he is."

"He and I literally bumped into each other, but he pretended he didn't know me."

"What are you doing at the Russian embassy?"

"I'm here to do an interview."

"Who with?"

"Stop changing the subject. That's beside the point. Paul! You need to know that I don't think Alex is who he says he is. In fact, his real name probably isn't Alex. It's probably Comrade something. It's classic spy craft. He set a honey trap and you walked right into it."

More silence.

"Are you there, Paul? Did you hear what I just said?"

"Y-yeah. I heard." His voice was a weak whisper. "But why? Why me?"

"Good question. I think he's in cahoots with the Russians."

"How? Why?"

"He used you to get dirt on me. He's probably the one who told Francine Noyce I'm pregnant. Maybe she's in cahoots with the Russians, too. Maybe they're trying to create a fake crisis to destabilize Gannon."

The guard tugged my sleeve impatiently. "You. Come!"

"I've gotta go. But I wanted you to know. I'm sorry, Paul, but you've been had. We've been had."

I hung up.

The guard took me firmly by the arm to lead me into the building.

"Wait!" I said, digging in my heels. "I have to make one more call."

I dialed the number Gannon had given me. My plan was to change the meeting to neutral ground outside the embassy compound where I'd be safer than here.

The call went to voicemail.

"Shit!"

"You. Come. Now!" The armed guard's grip tightened. He pulled me into the building and slammed the door behind me.

⋯ ◆ ⋯

CHAPTER 45

Just before ten o'clock Monday morning, I approached room 2141 of the Rayburn House Office Building – the hearing room of the House Judiciary Committee. It was the same room where the Watergate hearings were held in 1973 during Richard Nixon's presidency and where, twenty-five years later, the committee voted to impeach Bill Clinton.

Ruth Nicholas, my lawyer, is a master of style. Instead of what I would have preferred wearing – jeans, sneakers, and a bulky sweater – Ruth outfitted me in an ensemble that consisted of a bright red power jacket with black trim, a white blouse that buttoned at the throat, accented by an understated gold chain that had been my mother's, a black pencil skirt, and black pumps. My hair had been styled by a professional Ruth paid for. My black-rimmed glasses completed the ensemble.

Frankly, I looked hot, but in a professional don't-fuck-with-me way.

Instead of a battered leather messenger bag slung over my shoulder, I carried an ebony Louis Vuitton clutch Ruth loaned me. It contained a packet of tissues, a ballpoint pen, a reporter's rectangular notebook, and my cell phone.

As I walked down the marble-tiled hallway toward the hearing room, burly U.S. Capitol Police officers surrounded me – a buffer to protect me from a score of protestors and counter-protestors who lined the hallway outside the hearing room.

On one side, anti-abortion protestors held placards showing grisly images of aborted fetuses. Why? Because that morning Media Bash reported that I'd had a secret abortion as a way to cover up that Will Gannon was the baby-daddy. No sources? No facts? No problem!

Several protestors chanted at me.

"Slut! Slut! Slut!" they hissed.

Their taunts echoed through the hallway.

On the other side of the corridor, a row of women stood silently, heads bowed. They wore blood-red robes and white-winged headgear, costumes worn by the handmaids in the dystopian TV show "The Handmaids Tale." It's about an oppressive patriarchal society in which fertile women are forced to produce children for the men of the governing elite.

I stared straight ahead. Ruth Nicholas walked alongside me.

The room was packed and brightly lit. Several television cameras were set up in various places in the room. The event was being carried live on all the major cable news outlets. Even the broadcast networks broke away from their extremely lucrative game shows, soaps, and celebrity gabfests to carry my testimony live.

I learned later more than forty million people were watching.

As I walked toward the witness table, an army of still photographers stood in the well between the table and the wood-paneled and elevated space where the committee members sat with members of their staff behind them.

A hush came over the room as I entered. The Capitol police officers escorted me to the table. The only noise I could hear were the shutter clicks of dozens of cameras. It sounded like a sudden hailstorm.

Lionel and Muriel sat in the front row, just behind where I'd be sitting. They both stood to greet me.

I hugged them.

"Go get 'em, kiddo," Lionel whispered in my ear.

"I'm praying for you, Lark," Muriel said, squeezing my hand.

Ruth and I took our seats at the table. The shiny-polished wood surface was empty except for a small microphone on a stand, a pitcher of water, and two glasses.

In videos of the event that I saw later, I look much more confident than I felt at the time. When I sat down, it was like being a grade-school kid who got moved from the kids' table to the grown-up table at Thanksgiving – I didn't belong and was in way over my head.

I put the clutch down on the table next to me and Ruth placed her briefcase in front of her, snapped it open and removed a sheaf of papers containing my prepared statement. She slid it in front of me, then poured a glass of water for each of us.

The committee had asked for an advance copy of my remarks, "as a courtesy," they'd said.

Ruth told them they'd already gotten blood from me; there'd be no advance text for their staffs to read and then think up questions for the elected officials to ask. The Representatives would have to listen and come up with their own follow-up questions based on what I said.

Also, I didn't want my remarks to leak. I intended to break some news.

Meanwhile, the photographers continued to jockey for position, shooting me from the left, right, and center. I tried to ignore them, but I knew a couple of them. An A.P. photog who'd worked with Doug and me caught my eye and gave me a wink and a discreet thumbs up. I almost burst into tears at that simple nod to human decency.

Congressman Harris Carmichael, the committee chairman, a distinguished octogenarian with a wavy white mane, banged the gavel and the photogs backed away. They took their last shots, then crouched or sat with their backs to the wood front piece of the committee's dais.

"This hearing will come to order!" Chairman Carmichael said with all the authority and seriousness he could muster.

I stood and raised my right hand.

"I appreciate your eagerness to speak, Miss Chadwick," Carmichael smiled indulgently, "but a couple of us up here have some speechifying of our own to do first."

"Oops. Sorry, Mr. Chairman." I sat down as fast as I could as a murmur of chuckling rippled through the room. My face felt as red as my jacket.

Chairman Carmichael and Vice Chairperson Diane Shelby did, indeed, pontificate for the next ten to fifteen minutes, intoning about the seriousness of the proceedings and the need for sober-minded "truth-seeking."

"Okay, Miss Chadwick," Carmichael finally said, turning to me. "Now we're ready to hear from you. Please stand and raise your right hand."

As soon as I stood, the photographic hailstorm erupted again. I hoped they wouldn't notice that the fingers of my upheld hand were quivering slightly.

"Do you solemnly swear to tell the truth, the whole truth, and nothing but the truth, so help you God?"

"I do," I said, my voice strong and resolute.

"Be seated. The floor is yours for as long as you'd like."

"Thank you, Mr. Chairman.

"Mr. Chairman, members of the committee. My name is Lark Chadwick. Until recently, I was a White House correspondent for the Associated Press.

"I'd thank you for the opportunity to speak to you today but, frankly, I'm here against my will. I've been ordered to testify, or face criminal charges. I've also been forced to submit to an invasive pregnancy test. Your so-called 'truth-seeking' comes at the expense of my right to privacy.

"That said, I do, indeed, intend to tell the truth, but I also intend to put my remarks in a broader context to better inform your deliberations.

"The reason we are here is to determine if President Will Gannon may have committed what the Constitution calls 'high crimes and misdemeanors.' Specifically, the committee is looking into whether or not he poisoned his wife so he could carry on an illicit relationship with me, who, it's claimed, he impregnated.

"How did we get to this point? And where do we go from here?

"We are now living in an age where salacious allegations trump truth. There is no longer a respect for facts.

"Ahhhh! Facts. Remember those? They're those little pieces of truth that, when put together, form a mosaic that reveals the Truth – Truth with a capital T.

"For the past several years there's been a systematic, partisan assault on the credibility of the institutions whose job it is to discern the Truth. Nowadays – and this is true of extremists on both the left and the right – if the facts don't support your particular political or religious doctrine, then the facts are called fake."

I was so nervous, I kept my head buried in my script, but paused to take furtive glances at the members of the committee. They were glowering at me. I moved my left thumb down the page as I spoke so I wouldn't lose my place.

"Mr. Chairman, I will assume, for the moment, that this committee really is interested in learning the truth. I hope and pray that this is so because my credibility as a reporter has been undermined, not just for partisan, political reasons, but for reasons of geopolitical power.

"Let me explain.

"This all began a few months ago when I was still a White House correspondent on the night Rose Gannon collapsed at the White House Correspondents' Dinner. It was also the night Doug Mitchell, my boyfriend and colleague, disappeared. He was later found dead of a heroin overdose.

"President and Mrs. Gannon reached out to extend their sympathy to me – a phone call that turned into an ongoing professional relationship with the first lady in which she disclosed to me her terminal illness. We began confidential conversations, interviews that would be part of her memoir as well as my biography of her.

"As is now well known, I was conducting one of those interviews with the first lady in the private quarters of the White House when she collapsed and later died. I covered that incident as part of my duties.

"What's not well known is what happened next.

"A few days later, I was invited to appear on an early-morning news program on I-N-N, Independent Network News. Moments after that appearance Media Bash, a website whose sole purpose is to castigate the role of reporters, published a piece critical of me and my work.

"At the same time, Francine Noyce, the president of I-N-N, came to the studio where I'd been interviewed and invited me to lunch the next day.

"Lunch turned out to be a flight aboard her private jet to Montreal where, during a meal at a swanky restaurant, she offered me a million-dollar contract to work for her. On the flight back to Washington, while I was still considering her offer, a steward named Cedric Boyd summoned me to Ms. Noyce's private cabin.

"While I was alone with Ms. Noyce in her cabin, I asked her for more time to consider her offer. In response, she sexually assaulted me."

Several people in the room gasped and the room began to buzz.

Bang!

Carmichael rapped his gavel. "Order!"

The room hushed.

"Continue, Miss Chadwick," Carmichael said, nodding at me.

"When I was attacked, I defended myself by slapping Ms. Noyce hard across the face. I ran out of her cabin and back to my seat aboard the jet. We were still 30-thousand feet in the sky on our way back to Washington.

"Mr. Chairman, I am submitting to this committee Mr. Boyd's signed affidavit, alleging – under oath – that he was an ear witness to the struggle between Ms. Noyce and myself. In his affidavit, Mr. Boyd also states that Ms. Noyce frequently brought people on her private jet to seduce them. When I didn't comply, she forced herself on me and I resisted.

"As soon as we landed at Reagan National Airport, I sent emails to my boss and a few close friends – two of whom are in this room – reporting the details of the assault. I'm submitting those emails to this committee, as well.

"In the weeks following the assault aboard the I-N-N jet, additional articles attacking me and my professionalism were posted on the Media Bash website. The stories contained a grain of truth that sprouted a forest's worth of speculative conspiracy theories.

"Those conspiracy theories eventually took root in more mainstream media outlets. Those news organizations weren't able to confirm the Media Bash stories, but repeated the false allegations when this committee and the FBI launched investigations.

"The bogus reports about me have resulted in frightening responses from some members of the public. I've been called vile names." My voice began to rise in indignation, despite my best attempt to remain calm. "One person said I should be raped and murdered. Protestors outside this room are calling me a slut. Total strangers on the street have menaced me. For the past several days I have been a prisoner in my apartment because of the round-the-clock media stakeout in front of the building where I live."

I paused and took a deep breath to calm myself.

"But I'm not here to complain. I'm here to explain.

"I'm here to explain what happened next and why I believe Will Gannon has not committed an impeachable offense.

"First: yes, I'm pregnant, but Will Gannon is not the father. I'm submitting to this committee the results of the DNA test of my fetus. The test was administered in the presence of my lawyer and the chief counsel of this committee. The DNA of the fetus was compared to President Gannon's, and also compared to the DNA of Doug Mitchell, my late boyfriend, acquired from him when he joined the Army after the 9/11 attacks. The report concludes that the father is Mr. Mitchell."

My voice caught. As I reached for the glass of water to buy myself a few seconds to compose myself, the photographers lounging on the floor in front of me came alive and the hailstones of their shutters began pinging again.

The moment reminded me of an old saying from my days as a reporter in Wisconsin: "If it moves, it's news" – a disparaging comment made by an aid to the governor, about the tendency of most journalists, especially broadcasters, to be easily distracted by shiny objects or, in this case, action – anything that moves.

"Next," I said when I had my emotions under control again, "as I speak, a representative of the law firm representing me is filing a defamation of character and libel lawsuit against Francine Noyce of I-N-N on behalf of myself and my former boss Lionel Stone, who's sitting behind me right now.

The lawsuit alleges reckless disregard for the truth in false stories Ms. Noyce planted about me, and for false claims of sexual assault she made about Mr. Stone. Her actions neutralized the ability of Mr. Stone and myself to investigate and report on the death of Rose Gannon.

"But there's a bigger question at play here, Mr. Chairman, and it goes way beyond the superficial tabloid scandal parlor game of trying to figure out who's the father of my child.

"The question is actually two questions: was Rose Gannon poisoned? And, if so, who poisoned her? For the answer to those questions, I need to call in reinforcements."

I reached into the clutch on the table next to me, took out my cell phone, opened it up to the text message app, typed the word "now" and hit *send*.

Seconds later, I heard a commotion behind me.

The chairman and everyone else on the committee looked toward the entrance doors, their eyes wide in surprise.

A collective gasp filled the room.

I turned to look.

Charging down the center aisle, flanked by a squadron of Secret Service agents, rushed a very determined President Will Gannon.

ଓ ✦ ଚ

CHAPTER 46

The mood of the room, which was already electric, became high voltage.

The photographers leapt to their feet, falling all over each other to get pictures of the oncoming president.

Everyone in the room began talking at once.

"Order!" Chairman Carmichael banged his gavel repeatedly. "There will be order, or I'll have the Sergeant at Arms clear the room. Order!"

Ruth and I stood out of respect when the president got to the witness table.

"Mr, Chairman," the president bellowed. "I demand that you swear me in. Immediately!"

The chairman who, moments before had been the master of pomposity, was now flushed and stammering incoherently.

"Th-this is, well, this . . . ."

"Mr. Chairman," Gannon continued, "the purpose of this committee is to determine if I should be impeached. I demand to be heard. And I demand that I be placed under oath."

The chairman struggled to retain his composure and to regain control of the hearing. "This is highly unusual, Mr. President." He looked pleadingly at his colleagues to his left and right. "Are there any objections?"

"No objection," several members of the committee from both parties said.

"Very well. Let's get a chair for the president," the chairman said.

There was some jostling on the dais as one of the staffers sitting at the far end gave up her chair. Someone carried it to the witness table and placed it next to me.

"Raise your right hand to be sworn, Mr. President," Carmichael said, standing.

The noisy shutters of at least thirty still cameras erupted as the photographers documented the historic moment.

"D-do you swear that your testimony will be the, the, the—" the chairman stumbled.

"The truth!" Gannon declared helpfully.

"Yes," Carmichael said, recovering. "Do you swear your testimony will be the truth, the whole truth, and nothing but the truth, so help you God?"

"I absolutely and unequivocally swear that the testimony I'm about to give is the truth."

"Be seated, sir."

Gannon sat.

So did Ruth and I.

The photographers returned to their crouching positions in front of the witness table. The rest of the room seemed to hold its collective breath.

"Thank you, Mr. Chairman," Gannon said.

Carmichael said, "Just before your dramatic entrance, Mr. President, Miss Chadwick asked the question was your wife poisoned, and if so, by whom?"

"I'll pick up the narrative from there, Mr. Chairman. The short answer is: yes, my wife was poisoned. She was murdered by the Russian government on orders from President Dimitri Yazkov.

The room erupted.

"Order!" The chairman rapped his gavel and the room immediately fell silent.

"Continue, Mr. President. I presume you have proof?"

"I do, Mr. Chairman. First, I'm ordering Rose's autopsy report unsealed and my office is submitting it to this committee.

"The reason I sealed the report in the first place is because a mysterious, man-made toxin was found in her pancreas. It suggested to the CDC pathologist, myself, and my advisors that a foreign power may have been behind her death. I wanted to give our government time to investigate and not create an international crisis.

"Meanwhile, Russia created an international crisis of its own – a direct reaction to the thaw in our relations with China. In order to reassert his influence on the world stage, President Yazkov scrapped the nuclear non-proliferation treaty and began cozying up to Iran in a way that threatened the United States and Israel with nuclear weapons. Meanwhile, false stories began spreading about Ms. Chadwick and me.

"Russia's motive was to kill Rose and create a sex scandal that would destabilize and incapacitate me. Ms. Chadwick played a direct and instrumental role in solving the mystery surrounding Rose's death, and defusing what has been a tense nuclear confrontation between the United States and Russia."

The president turned to me. "Lark, tell the committee – and the rest of the world – what happened next."

"Thank you, Mr. President. In the course of my investigation into the death of the first lady, I had a private conversation with President Gannon aboard Air Force One on the way to the summit in China. During that conversation, I remembered and told the president an anecdote the first lady was telling me just before she died.

"In her story, she told me she was sitting next to Russian Ambassador Rudolph Petrovsky at the White House Correspondents' Dinner just before she collapsed and was later diagnosed with cancer. She said the ambassador bragged about his country's tea, then produced a tea bag from his pocket. She drank the tea he made for her, but she said it was horrible."

Gannon picked up the story from there. "When Lark told me that story, everything fell into place for both of us. It became clear that the fatal toxin may have been given to Rose by Ambassador Petrovsky at the banquet.

"Meanwhile, the crisis with Russia was escalating and traditional diplomacy wasn't working. Lark agreed to be my back-channel contact with the Russian ambassador if all other efforts failed to resolve the crisis."

By this time Gannon and I were vamping without notes, like jazz musicians trading four-bar improvisational solos. He turned and handed off the narrative to me.

My solo: "The president laid the groundwork for me to meet one-on-one with the Russian ambassador, a meeting set in motion immediately following the president's Oval Office address last week."

As I was testifying to the members of the House Judiciary Committee, I remembered my meeting with Rudolph Petrovsky the previous Friday at the Russian embassy, and how nervous I was at the high stakes.

Aboard Air Force One I'd asked the president, "Do I try to browbeat him into making a confession?"

Gannon had replied, "A confession would be wonderful, but unlikely. This guy's obviously a stone-cold killer, so you probably won't be able to rattle him. Your job is to firmly convey to him what we know. He'll probably deny it and brush you off. But I know you well enough to know that it's not your style to take no."

"You're right about that," I'd told the president.

"No matter what he says," Gannon instructed me, "just make it clear that once he has conferred with his boss in the Kremlin, he is to use you as his direct link back to me, if that's the way they choose to respond."

Nine days later, as the armed soldier marched me deeper and deeper into the bewildering warren of offices of the Russian embassy, the president's words "stone-cold killer" echoed in my memory. So did thoughts of what it must have been like for dissident Saudi journalist Jamal Khashoggi in the brief moments before his murder and dismemberment at an embassy in Turkey.

Here's how that meeting with Petrovsky unfolded:

The guard brought me to Ambassador Petrovsky's cavernous, opulent office on the top floor of the embassy, then left us alone.

The last time I'd seen Petro was just two weeks earlier at Rose Gannon's funeral at National Cathedral, a ten-minute walk north of the Russian embassy. But the man who stood and came around to the front of his desk to greet me was a shell of his former self. Petro's complexion was pale and he looked emaciated.

"Hello, Miss Chadwick." He held out a boney hand to me. It was cold to the touch.

"Thank you for meeting with me, Mr. Ambassador."

"You're quite welcome." He pointed to a sofa and easy chairs off to the side. "Let's sit where it's more comfortable."

I took a seat at the end of the sofa adjacent to an easy chair where he sat.

"Could I interest you in some tea?" he asked.

He's got to be kidding, I said in my head. To him I said out loud, "No, thank you. I'm fine."

Lionel and I had gamed out how I should handle this moment. Even though I was wearing two hats – reporter and presidential emissary – the stakes were so high that we agreed that my primary goal was to do what I could to defuse the current nuclear showdown with Russia. Whatever happened here would be my word against his.

Although Petro was gracious and affable, his demeanor was stiff. So was his smile. It occurred to me that he might be as nervous as I was.

I was about to say something, but he held up his forefinger to silence me. Then he reached over to what looked like an air freshener on the coffee table between us. He flipped a switch and a white-noise hiss began to emanate from the machine.

"There," he said. "Now our conversation is private."

I relaxed a little. But I was still out of my element. Normally, in an interview situation, I'm a take-charge person, confident in being able to guide the conversation. But this felt different. Actually, it was different.

My comfort zone was asking questions, so that's where I began.

"Tell me, sir, what's your understanding about why we're meeting?"

"Your president, who apparently is a close friend of yours," his eyebrows danced suggestively, "has dispatched you to talk with me. That's all I know. I, of course, presume it is about the current tensions between our two countries."

"Yes," I said. I paused, not sure how blunt I should be.

Petro used the silence to turn the tables on me. "What's your understanding of the purpose of our meeting, Miss Chadwick?"

"It's similar to yours, sir. My intent is to convey to you information that's not widely known that President Gannon hopes you will find credible and compelling. He wants you to use this compelling information to persuade your president to step back from actions that could unleash events neither of our countries will be able to control."

Petro nodded gravely and waited for me to say more. So I did.

"As you may know, I was with President Gannon's wife Rose when she died earlier this month."

"Yes. Very sad," he said.

"I was interviewing her about her life for books we were both planning to write. While we were talking, your name came up."

His eyebrows went up slightly in surprise, but he said nothing and waited for more.

"She told me an amusing story," I continued.

The hint of a smile played on his lips. "Involving me?"

"Yes, sir."

He gestured invitingly. "Please. Continue."

"She was telling me about the evening the two of you sat together at the head table at the White House Correspondents' dinner."

The half-smile froze on his face.

"She told me a story that involved you and tea."

He remained impassive.

"Do you remember?"

"I might."

"Do you remember telling Mrs. Gannon how wonderful Russian tea is?"

"I tell everyone how wonderful our tea is."

"Do you routinely carry tea bags around with you?"

"I'm not sure I follow your line of questioning."

"It's a simple question, sir. Do you usually carry tea bags?"

"Rarely, but sometimes."

"Did you pull a tea bag out of your pocket that night and offer to make tea with it for Rose Gannon?"

He hesitated.

"You'll remember, Mr. Ambassador, that the room was full of reporters and the event was televised."

I had no idea if there was video of him producing the tea bag for Rose, but he didn't know that, either.

"Did you make her tea with one of your tea bags?" I pressed.

He looked at me, a sickened expression on his face. "You said this was an amusing story," he smiled stiffly.

"Rose thought it was."

The ambassador stared at me sphinxlike.

"Do you want to know why she thought it was amusing?"

He nodded dumbly, reflexively. What he really seemed to want was to disappear. And, in a few more weeks, if his dissipation continued, he might simply waste away.

"Rose Gannon laughed as she told me the story," I continued. "She said you told her that the tea was so wonderful that you insisted that she try some. Do you know why she was laughing?"

He shook his head.

"Because she said it tasted terrible."

The ambassador swallowed hard. His eyes moistened.

"You know why it tasted so bad, don't you, sir?"

He nodded almost imperceptibly.

"Why did it taste so bad, sir?" I whispered.

His lips moved, but no words came out.

"Do you know?"

He sighed and looked down.

"President Gannon knows."

The ambassador looked up at me, slightly surprised and inquisitive.

"He sent me to tell you that he knows that you murdered his wife." My voice was steely-soft. I drilled him with my eyes. "You murdered Rose Gannon, didn't you, Mr. Ambassador?"

He nodded slightly and, as he did, his body seemed to relax, as if a great weight had lifted from his shoulders.

"That's why I'm here, Mr. Ambassador."

"Why?" he asked.

"Because the president, in spite of the enormity of his personal loss, is willing to—"

The ambassador held up a hand to stop me from speaking, then he turned a dial on the white noise machine. The hissing got louder.

"I have a message for your president, Miss Chadwick."

"Okay." I reached into the pocket of my jeans. "May I record your message, Mr. Ambassador, so that there's no misunderstanding?"

He paused and thought a moment, weighing my request. Finally, he nodded. "Yes," he said quietly. "I have nothing more to lose."

I whipped out my phone, opened the audio app, hit *record*, and held the device between us, close enough so that the white-noise hissing wouldn't overpower him.

"Go on," I prompted.

On the following Monday, my testimony before the House Judiciary Committee continued:

"During my conversation with Russian Ambassador Rudolph Petrovsky," I told the committee, "he confessed to using the poisoned tea bag to kill the first lady. He then gave me permission to tape record this message to President Gannon."

I picked up my cell phone, opened the voice memo app, and adjusted the microphone on the witness table so that the mic was pointing directly at the phone. When I hit play, the voice of the Russian ambassador filled the room:

> AMBASSADOR PETROVSKY: I would like you to tell your president that justice has already been done.

> ME: What do you mean?

> AMBASSADOR PETROVSKY: I mishandled the tea bag that evening with the first lady. I, too, am sick with the same cancer. It is justice for my deed.

> ME: Oh my.

> AMBASSADOR PETROVSKY: Also, please tell this to your president: there are many in my government, myself included, who feel that our leader is unnecessarily pushing the world closer to war. I want your president to know that I will personally, *personally* do what I can to prevail upon President Yazkov and turn him away from his reckless path.

> ME: What do you plan to do?

> AMBASSADOR PETROVSKY: That is not important. I am leaving tonight to go back to my homeland. I, too, am going to die. But I want your President Gannon to know that he has my solemn word that I personally will right this wrong. It's the least I can do.

I stopped the recording and the president picked up his solo: "When Lark arrived at the Russian embassy, she ran into a friend of hers who pretended not to know her. She knew this person as Alex, but the FBI has identified Alex as Vasili Kuznetsov, a Russian intelligence officer tasked with penetrating U.S. news organizations. Relationships he developed with Francine Noyce and with a friend and colleague of Ms. Chadwick's led to the planting and creation of the fake stories that prompted your investigation, Mr. Chairman.

"The FBI arrested Mr. Kuznetsov last night and he will be charged with espionage.

"Finally, Mr. Chairman. Just before I entered this hearing room, the director of national intelligence informed me of a shooting in the

Kremlin. Ambassador Petrovsky assassinated President Yazkov today and then took his own life."

Many people in the room gasped – including me.

Gannon continued, "Shortly afterward, the Russian defense minister informed my secretary of defense that the suitcase nuclear bombs destined for Iran are being deactivated, will be destroyed, and the terms of the nuclear nonproliferation treaty will be reinstated."

Gannon looked at me, smiled, wiggled his eyebrows, then turned back to face the committee. "Mr. Chairman, Ms. Chadwick and I are now ready to take your questions."

The room erupted in loud and sustained applause.

03 ◆ 80

EPILOGUE

Following our appearance, the House Judiciary Committee voted to drop its impeachment investigation.

Before they voted, committee members, wanting to take advantage of the vast television audience, asked questions of both Gannon and me to clarify some of the details. Many from both parties fell all over themselves to praise the president for defusing the crisis. Others voiced their sympathy over the murder of his wife. A few thanked and praised me for the role I played.

Vasili Kuznetsov (a.k.a. "Alex") was an official covert agent of Russia and, therefore, had diplomatic immunity. He was declared *persona non grata* and expelled from the United States.

Francine Noyce, however, has had a tougher time of it. During the discovery phase of the defamation of character lawsuit Lionel and I brought against her, we learned that while studying abroad thirty years earlier in Scotland, she'd been recruited by Russian intelligence to be a sleeper spy in the U.S. She was activated by President Yazkov and ordered to work with Vasili/Alex to taint the reputations of Lionel and me. In an effort to avoid prison, she has been cooperating with the CIA in their counterintelligence efforts. I've heard Hollywood is considering making a biopic of her life.

Paul Stone has begun seeing a therapist who specializes in transgender issues.

Lionel's #MeToo scare was the catalyst he needed to resume attending Alcoholics Anonymous meetings regularly. He and Muriel are also seeing a marriage counselor again.

President Will Gannon, still in the early days of his presidency, now enjoys a ninety-two percent approval rating, a few notches higher than George H. W. Bush's numbers at the end of the first Gulf War in 1991.

For the first time in recent memory, there's a feeling of hope and optimism in this country.

As for me, I have a lot on my mind. A lot.

It felt great to be exonerated and have my reputation reinstated on such a large stage, but I have yet to determine my next steps. It was a topic of discussion a few hours after President Gannon and I testified before the House Judiciary Committee.

The president and I sat alone in the upstairs private residence of the First Family. We were in the West Sitting Room near the Lincoln Bedroom going over the details of our dramatic appearance.

As we were talking, Octavia, the nanny for the two Gannon children, brought Grace and Thomas into the room to say goodnight.

"Hello, Grace," I said. "Are you reading any good books lately?"

Grace came and sat next to me on the loveseat. "Oh, yes, Miss Lark. I've decided to reread all of the Harry Potter books."

Thomas crawled into my lap. "Are you going to be our new Mommy?"

I blanched.

"Thomas," Gannon said, sternly. "Lark is my friend. Our friend." He stood and scooped Thomas from my lap. "C'mon, guys. Time for bed. I'll tell you a story."

"Yay!" Thomas said.

"Goodnight, Miss Lark," Grace said. "I hope you'll come again and have hotdogs with us. Maybe we can watch a movie together and have popcorn."

"Do you like popcorn?" I asked.

"It's ambrosia," she gushed.

I laughed and marveled at her grown-up vocabulary.

"Do you mind waiting, Lark, while I put them to bed?" Gannon asked.

"Not at all."

"Thanks. Save my place," he quipped.

While he was gone, I had a chance to reflect on the events of the day, and ruminate about my future.

I got up and walked to the window. It looked out over the West Wing of the White House and toward the Eisenhower Executive Office Building. From my vantage point, I could see "Pebble Beach," the area along the driveway from the press room to the Northwest Gate where network cameras are set up so reporters can do their live shots and stand-ups with the White House as their backdrop.

Today had been a huge news day. I watched as the NBC correspondent flipped through the pages of her notebook as she got ready for her live shot. She wore a bright yellow overcoat. A field producer sprayed hairspray onto her blonde hair. The camera lights accentuated the cloud of vapors rising and dissipating into the air.

Several reporters walked briskly along the driveway, heading toward the briefing room. They talked and gestured animatedly among themselves as they walked.

It felt strange not to be among them. But did I miss it? Did I long to be back in the fray with them? I realized I was still somewhat shell-shocked and needed to sort out my future. Would I stay in journalism? Would I continue to pursue psychology?

And, holy shit! I'm pregnant.

Would I have an abortion? Give the child up for adoption? Be a single mom?

My life was about to change in a big way – but in what way?

I wasn't aware that Gannon had re-entered the room until he was standing right next to me at the window.

"What are you thinking?" He was standing so close to me I could feel the heat radiating from his body, but he didn't touch me.

"I'm thinking about how busy they are." I nodded toward Pebble Beach.

"Do you miss it?"

"I was just asking myself the same question."

"Did you get an answer?"

I shrugged. "Too soon to know. I still have the muscle memory of the old job."

"Meaning?"

I reached instinctively for the back of my neck. "Meaning I still have tension all along here." With my finger, I traced a line back and forth behind my neck between my shoulders.

As soon as I did it, I regretted it. Would he think I'm coming on to him? Worse: would he be eager to assume I'm coming on to him and take the bait?

He grunted and stuffed his hands deeply into his pockets.

The bond between us was powerful, magnetic, but I was relieved he didn't make a move. I had no idea how or what he was feeling. All I knew about myself is that I felt entirely comfortable with this man. I was grateful for just the present moment. I wanted to savor it without having to make any decisions or judgments.

Does he feel the same way? I couldn't be sure.

We stood silently for a while looking out the window. The sun had set, but its afterglow cast a peach tinge across the sky.

"I should let you get back to running the world," I said.

"Stay for a while. We need to talk." He moved away from me. "Let's sit down. Do you want something to drink?"

I turned away from the window to look at him. "Will you join me?"

"In a heartbeat."

He walked to a wet bar against the south wall. "Let me see." He opened a cupboard and rummaged around. "Hmmmmm." He pulled out a bottle and pretended to read the label. "October. A good month." He looked at me enthusiastically. "Do you like Ripple?"

I laughed. Actually, it was an unladylike guffaw.

"How about a Malbec?" He retrieved a corkscrew from a drawer, but before he could *foop* the cork, I stopped him.

"No! Wait!"

"What?"

"I can't. I'm pregnant."

"Of course. How stupid of me. My apologies." He rummaged around some more. "How do you feel about Ginger Ale?"

"Not as good as wine, but it'll do. It'll more than do. Thank you."

He popped the tabs on two cans and began to pour. "I'll fill two wine glasses. We can at least pretend it's wine."

As he handed me one of the glasses, I said, "And it's a generous pour. Thank you."

He held up his glass. "To your health."

"And to yours."

We clinked, then sat. I returned to my place on the loveseat. He chose the easy chair at my end.

"You said that we should talk," I said. "About what?"

To my surprise, he sighed. A heavy one.

"What's wrong?" I asked.

"I don't know if anything's wrong, but there's something we need to at least begin to talk about, and maybe now is as good a time as any."

I put my glass down on the coffee table and sat up straight. "Well, you've certainly got my attention."

He reached to the breast pocket inside his suit coat and retrieved a sealed envelope, embossed with the words THE WHITE HOUSE in the upper left.

The letter was sealed with my name written in neat cursive on the front.

"It's from Rose," he said. "She wrote to both of us. I presume mine is identical to yours."

I looked at him. His expression was hard to read, but definitely serious.

"From Rose?"

He nodded.

"What . . .? When . . .?"

"Just read it. Then we'll talk – if you want to."

I opened it. It was handwritten and dated the day before she died. I began to read:

The White House
Washington

Sunday, March 31st

My Dearest Will and My Dear Friend Lark:
I know I don't have much time, so I feel a special sense of urgency to tell you both what I've been thinking about a lot since my diagnosis: that you should at least consider a life together after I'm gone.

I know it's presumptuous for me to even suggest it, but hear me out – and then decide for yourselves.

Will – You have been a wonderful friend, companion, and lover on our journey together. Being your personal First Lady (as well as the nation's), and the mother of our two wonderful children, has been a blessing, a joy, and a delight – the highlight of my life.

Lark – Your friendship and companionship in my final days has been a comfort. Thank you. As you know, I have tremendous admiration for your bravery, spunk, and emotional level-headedness.

As you both know, I'm a realist. I know I'm dying. I also know that the presidency is an enormous burden – even more so when carrying the grief that comes from the loss of a spouse. I'm well aware that both of you, for a myriad of reasons, will initially recoil from my suggestion. I understand. All I ask is that you consider my words.

Will, you've told me how much you admire Lark.

Lark, as much as I respect that you yourself are still grieving the loss of your Doug, you remind me of, well, me. That means that it's only natural that you would be attracted to someone like Will, and that he, too, would have a natural rapport with you, much like he's had with me.

I can already hear your objections: "I'm a journalist!" "What about the 20-year difference in our ages?" "What will people think?"

I say, "To hell with all of that!"

All I'm asking is that you seriously consider pursuing what I see as an obvious connection between you that could strengthen Will's presidency and bring much-denied joy to Lark.

I'm also realistic enough to know that the human heart is fickle. I accept that you will either reject these sentiments as the ravings of a dying woman. Or that you will simply both decide to go your separate ways.

Fine.

But, if indeed there is an attraction between you two that, until now, you've been denying, or resisting, please consider these final words of mine to be my blessing.

Much love and Godspeed to you both,
~Rose

I was crying by the time I got to the end.

"What do you think?" Will asked. From the worried expression on his face, I could tell it was not an idle question.

"I don't know what to think. I don't know how I should I feel."

He pursed his lips and furrowed his brow. "When it comes to feelings, I don't think there are any shoulds. Feelings just are."

"Do you know yours?" I asked, tears still welling in my eyes.

He nodded curtly. "I do."

When he didn't say more, I asked, "Well? What are they?"

"I still miss Rose. You know that. The loss and emptiness and pain are still fresh."

I nodded – and noticed he was still wearing his wedding ring. "Same here with Doug," I said.

"But . . . . " he began, then stopped.

"But?"

"I feel something for you, Lark."

I nodded, but didn't dare say any more.

"I feel we have a special connection, but maybe that's just me being delusional."

"No," I said. "I know what you mean. There's something there. But . . . . "

"But what?"

I shook my head. "I don't know." I began to cry, but didn't know exactly why. It was a frightening feeling because I almost always know my heart so well, but this time I was on emotional glare ice, feeling like I was in an out-of-control skid with no hope of traction any time soon. "There's just so much we need to sort out," I said when I could finally speak.

"I know."

"Let's go slow, Will. Let's take this one step at a time, okay?"

He nodded resolutely. "I think that's wise."

We sat quietly for a moment then he said, "I have a suggestion."

"Okay," I said.

"Right now you're officially not a journalist, correct?"

"You are correct, sir."

"How are you coming with that biography you're writing about Rose?"

I scowled. "It's stalled. I've been kind of busy."

"Do you have a publisher? An agent?"

"Hadn't gotten that far in the process."

"Publishers have been contacting the press office for the past week trying to get me to write about Rose."

"That's a great idea."

"I agree. But I've been kind of busy, too."

"I have an idea!" I said excitedly. "Are you thinking what I'm thinking?"

"I am! I'll write Rose's biography, but you'll be the as-told-to ghostwriter. That means you'll have a paying gig that won't be a conflict of interest."

"Yes!" I said eagerly.

"And," he added, "it will give me a chance to let the grief process run its course. I'm not ready to let go of Rose." His voice caught.

I swallowed hard.

"Lark?"

"Yes."

"Would you consider accepting the official title of First Friend?"

I laughed. "Yes. It would be an honor."

He held out his hand, knuckles forward. We sealed the deal with a fist-bump.

೦೩ ✦ ೱ

ACKNOWLEDGMENTS

I am indebted to a great many people who helped me guide *Fake* to its publication, especially Ron Chepesiuk, the publisher of Strategic Media Books, and Barbara Casey, my agent for the past fifteen years. Thanks, Ron and Barbara, for continuing to believe in me – and Lark.

Investigative broadcast journalist Jenna Bourne was my canary in the mine throughout the creative process. As I wrote the first draft, I'd regularly send her chapters as the story painstakingly unspooled from my imagination onto the page. Thankfully, she staved off suffocation by sending me suggestions for mid-course corrections just in time. Every writer should have a smart, astute friend like Jenna.

Beta readers are those enthusiastic people who are willing to take early drafts of the manuscript for a test drive, then give honest feedback on what's not working well. For the creation of *Fake*, I was blessed to have these people in my life: Judy Colbert, Lois Cooksey, James DeDakis, Jillian Harding, Carolyn Presutti of VOA, Lisa Strickland (who also happens to be my amazing publicist), and Treva Thrush.

Others weighed in at various points along the way to provide insights based on their personal or professional expertise:

- Retired U.S. Army pathologist Brad Harper, MD, a fabulous writer himself (*A Knife in the Fog* – Seventh Street Books), provided helpful guidance on poisons and toxins. (During the holidays, he's Santa at Busch Gardens in Virginia).

- The Rev. Benjamin Straley, former Organist of Washington National Cathedral, read the chapter on the service for Rose Gannon. His comments helped her funeral come alive (so to speak).

- Anna Stockamore and Wright Smith were two millennial students in a "From Novice to Novelist" writing workshop I lead at The Writer's Center in Bethesda, Maryland. They helped me come up with the right way to describe post-summit canoodling aboard Air Force One.

- Speaking of Air Force One, friends of mine who have flown on that magnificent aircraft provided me with their insights: ABC News White House Correspondent Tara Palmeri; Former CNN White House Correspondent Kathleen Koch, and CNN Photographer Jay McMichael.

- I needed help coming up with just the right international crisis to vex President Gannon. I'm grateful to the following people who were helpful sounding boards: International business consultant Enrique Rueda-Sabater; Leila Piran, a former policy fellow at George Mason University in Washington; and David Cariens, a former CIA officer who attended one of my writing workshops at the Hampton Roads Writers' Conference. He is the director of the Writers Guild of Virginia and invited me to be the keynote speaker at their 2018 Author Expo in Kilmarnock, Virginia. He's also written extensively on gun violence.

- Lark needed music for the long trip to and from China for the summit, so who better to turn to than my long-time friend Jillian Harding, formerly of CNN, CNBC, CBS, and now a producer at Yahoo! Finance. Thanks, Jill, for sharing with me your "Power Girl" music playlist (not to mention your many insights on what it's like to be a young, attractive, female journalist in a #MeToo era).

- As Lark thinks through her possible career change, I'm deeply indebted to the following people: Kathryn Klett was one of my stand-out students when I was a journalism adjunct at the University of Maryland-College Park; Adrienne Kraft was my grief counselor at the Wendt Center for Loss and Healing in Washington. She helped me navigate through the awful time when my youngest son Stephen died in 2011; Christine Talbott is a psychotherapist in Bangor, Maine. Chris is my wife Cindy's best friend and sang at our wedding.

Speaking of wives, Cindy has been my loving companion for more than forty years. Will Gannon's eulogy for Rose could just as easily apply to Cindy. Her insights were especially helpful as I brought the final draft of *Fake* in for a landing.

And finally, to my alter ego Lark Chadwick: You inspire me. Thank you for making it so much fun to write. To be continued!!

John DeDakis
Baltimore, Maryland
May 2019

Also by John DeDakis:

Fast Track
Bluff
Troubled Water
Bullet in the Chamber

Praise for Previous Books

Praise for **BULLET IN THE CHAMBER**:

"John DeDakis gets inside the head of a modern-day White House journalist who has no idea what's in store for her when she begins this rollercoaster of a ride."

~*Josh Lederman, Former Associated Press White House Reporter*

"John DeDakis combines the heart-stopping and heartbreaking in a story of drugs, drones, corruption and politics. Lark's latest adventure is entertaining and harrowing. And always riveting."

~*Henry Schuster, CBS News "60 Minutes" Producer*

Praise for **TROUBLED WATER**:

"As a young female journalist, I spent most of this novel wondering how John DeDakis got into my head. *Troubled Water* is sharp, suspenseful and—most importantly—utterly believable."

~*Jenna Bourne; Investigative Reporter, WTSP-TV (10 News, CBS), Tampa-St. Petersburg, Florida*

Praise for **BLUFF**:

"DeDakis can so accurately write from a woman's point of view – with all the intrinsic curiosity, emotion and passion – [that it's] nothing short of astounding."

~*Diane Dimond; Author and Investigative Journalist*

Praise for **FAST TRACK**:

"*Fast Track* is one of those rare novels that you simply can't put down. I was hooked on page one and it was non-stop until the very end – an emotional roller coaster."

~*Wolf Blitzer; Anchor, CNN's "The Situation Room with Wolf Blitzer"*